A FALLING FOR FABLES NOVEL

FORGED BY MAGIC

FORGED BY MAGIC

JENNA WOLFHART

Cover Illustration by Deandra Scicluna

Cover Typography by The Book Brander

Map by Cartography Bird

Chapter Art by Zaeyos

Dragon Logo by Lily Droeven

Editing by Noah Sky Editing

For anyone in search of a fun, escapist adventure with lots of romance and a happily ever after

AUTHOR'S NOTE

Dear reader,

Grab a blanket, a mug of tea, and say goodbye to brutal kings and hello to grumpy village blacksmiths. This tale *is* one for the faint of heart and those in search of a feel-good palate cleanser with only a pinch of danger.

However, I would be remiss not to mention a few potential triggers: captivity, harassment, fire, brief violence and mentions of blood, and sexually explicit scenes. This book has a cozy vibe, but it isn't strictly a cozy fantasy since it *does* have spice in it and a bit of danger.

And dragons. Don't forget the dragons.

So curl up on the sofa, settle in with that blanket and tea, and get swept away into the whimsical world of Falling for Fables.

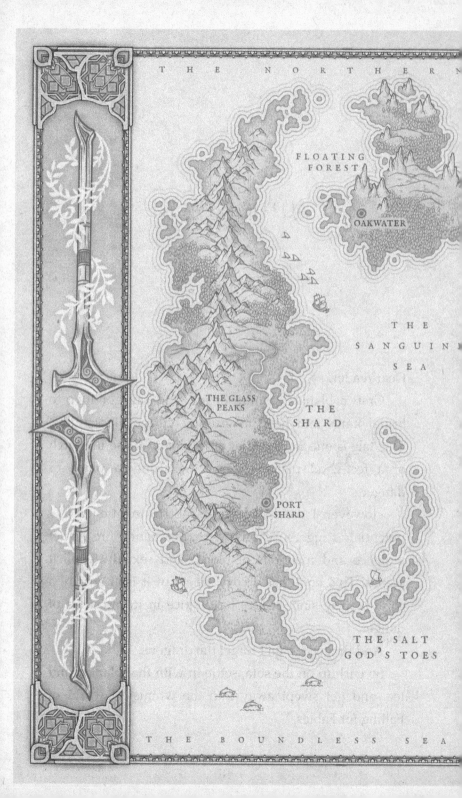

THE ISLES OF
FABLE

OCEAN

RIVERWOLD

CASTLE
RUINS

SUNLIT
RIDGE

MILFORD

WHISPERING
WOODS

ASHBORN
FOREST

MOUNT
FORGE

WYNDALE

HEARTHAVEN

I

DAELLA

The outward door's locks tumbled for the first time in a year. I stood from my perch on the tower's window seat and schooled my features into an expression of contentment, even as my heart thudded against my ribs. There could only be one reason the guards were unlocking that door instead of the inner one the maidservants used. The emperor had called for me.

It's about bloody time.

The door swung wide, creaking on unused hinges. Two armored guards strode into my circular room, both unfamiliar. They were human, judging by the smooth curves of their ears and the curiosity in their eyes. They'd probably never seen an orc before, not even a half-orc like me.

The taller of the two flicked his eyes up and down my body, likely taking in the deep green tint of my skin and the sharp points of my ears. Unlike true orcs, I lacked tusks. It was one of the reasons Emperor Isveig had let me live. He seemed to think it made me less threatening.

And, as much as I hated to admit it, I supposed that was true. I was his prisoner, after all, even if he kept me locked in a luxurious tower instead of a dungeon cell.

"Emperor Isveig wants to see you," the taller one said after a tense moment. "He has a job."

The shard of ice embedded in my hip pulsed. That old thing annoyed me almost as much as the emperor did.

Almost.

"How lovely," I said with the fake smile that everyone believed.

The shorter of the two, a stocky boy who couldn't be more than seventeen, smirked. "Lovely?"

"Of course. I'm always happy to help the emperor." *Lies.*

The shorter one narrowed his eyes. "Right. Well, come on then. Just remember what will happen if you try something."

The ice shard pulsed again, but I showed no reaction.

The two guards led me out of my tower room and into the castle beyond. As soon as I stepped into the corridor, the humidity thickened, no longer broken by the breeze from the windows I kept open all summer long. Even in the winter, it was difficult to find relief inside Keystone Keep. An ever-present cloud lurked over the buildings, caught on the tallest tower. It had hung there for seventeen long years. When a heavy rain wasn't drumming the tiled roof, sprays of saltwater dew misted down from the pregnant cloud. It had not stopped once in all these years. No one understood why, not even the Magisters.

So of course the emperor blamed fire magic, no matter that saltwater rain had nothing to do with Fildur —the power of flames.

After winding down the dark and silent stairwell, I followed the guards into the Great Hall, fondly called the Great Hel by Emperor Isveig's servants, slaves, and prisoners—of which there were many. At the end of a narrow strip of carpet, the ruler of the Grundstoff Empire sat upon a throne crafted from cooling granite only found in the North, where he'd been born. Shame he hadn't stayed there.

I walked the length of the carpet, flanked by the guards, and stared into the face of the ice giant who had conquered my home. Tall with ghostly blue skin, he was a towering mass of long, sleek muscle. He smiled as I approached, twirling one of the dozen rings that decorated ears that were as long as any dagger. Even though he'd rarely seen a battle himself, he covered his shoulders, forearms, and hips with gold plates, though his long legs were bare. Golden horns grew from the top of his head, sharp and deadly.

When I reached the foot of the dais, I stopped and waited, still beaming like a fool. In front of the emperor I always wore my smile. It was a lesson I'd learned a long time ago. *Never show true emotion.*

"Daella," he said in a voice that crackled like ice. His

3

eyes glimmered, pale blue like his skin. "You're looking well. I forgot how much your smile lights up this gloomy place."

"It's been a long time."

His smile faltered. "That's your own fault."

I bit the inside of my cheek.

"Don't look at me like that," he continued. "If you hadn't tried to escape, you'd have more freedom, just like you used to before last year."

Freedom. That was rich. I'd had no more freedom than the horses forced to drag the emperor's carriage on the long, muddy road up North every time he got sick of the heat—which happened at least three times a year. The lovely beasts might get out of the cramped city and breathe in the fresh air, but they could not let loose their manes and gallop across the fields. The exhilarating thrill of freedom would never be more than a dream for them.

Or for me.

I was one of the few orcs to have survived Isveig's conquest, and there had only been a few hundred of us before then. I'd been but a child at the time, and Isveig had believed it might be useful to keep a few of us around to do his dirty work. And so I had, always smiling. For sixteen long years. Until last summer when I'd tried to escape.

"What is it you'd like me to do, Isveig?"

He nodded to the tall human guard who stood beside me. I followed his gaze, stiffening when he pulled a dagger from his belt. My breath hissed through my clenched teeth, despite myself. I would never fail to recognize that curved blade, hilt engraved with the ancient orcish words *Ris upp ur oskunni,* meaning *Rise from the Ashes*—no matter if five thousand years passed before I set eyes on it again.

It had been my mother's.

I turned back to the emperor, my hands clenching. "I told you I don't want to kill for you anymore."

"Not even purveyors of dragon magic?" he asked, arching a brow.

I held my breath. Dragon magic was lethal and toxic, but... "All the dragons are dead. You made certain of that."

Isveig leaned back in his throne and drummed his fingers on the granite armrest. "There's a rumor that some survived. In the Isles of Fable, somewhere near the Glass Peaks."

"You still believe those islands exist? No one has ever been able to prove they're real."

Years ago, Emperor Isveig had sailed the Boundless Sea, hunting for these legendary isles. Several dwarves had appeared on the mainland not long after his conquest, bringing tales of magical islands hidden deep in the waters west of the empire. Isveig, as always, had decided he wanted to conquer those lands. He'd hunted for them ever since.

"Those dwarves didn't come from nowhere." He leaned forward and draped an arm across his knee. "Take the dagger. Sail with a score of my best warriors to find these islands, then root out the dragons and their bonded masters, the Draugr. Can you do that for me?"

He expected a smile, so I gave him one. But I still had to ask, "Root them out? Or kill them?"

"Don't pretend you don't enjoy handling a sword. I've seen the look on your face when you train."

"There is a very big difference between dancing with a sword and taking a life with one."

"You may hate me, Daella, but I know you hate the Draugr just as much—if not more. They're dangerous. Their blood is poisoned by madness. I did conquer your kingdom, but only because someone had to do it before the Draugr burned it all down instead."

I ground my teeth and glanced away, hating that he'd torn away my mask so easily this time. "Please. Anything but this."

"I'll free you."

I whipped my head back around so fast, I felt dizzy. "What?"

"You heard me. Do this, and I'll free you."

The pounding of my heart echoed in my ears. I had been his prized prisoner for seventeen years. He'd told me time and time again he would never let me go. As one of the few remaining half-orcs in the world, I was too valuable. There were still so many ways he could use me.

To dangle this carrot in front of me, he must be desperate.

"Explain," I said, blinking back the tears that threatened to fill my eyes. I refused to give him the satisfaction of seeing exactly how much hope ballooned in my heart.

I could be free, I could be free, I could be free.

"I just need you to do this one last thing for me, and I

know you need more motivation than the ice shard in your hip. So here it is: I will free you if you do this. Rid the world of the Draugr once and for all."

Rid the world of anything and anyone who could ever stand against him.

Because everyone else had given up.

For a moment, I couldn't bring myself to speak. I'd abandoned hope a long time ago, accepting the reality of my future—the fact I would never have one. Eventually, Isveig would use the shard he'd embedded in my hip to transform me into an ice sculpture he would proudly display to the rest of his empire.

The last of the orcs, he would say. *Look at how I conquered them.*

But that hope—it was a seed budding in my hollowed-out heart that I could not ignore. I wanted to say no to him, but I couldn't. I would do anything to gain freedom, and he knew it.

"Fine. I will search for the Draugr, but I won't raise a weapon against them if I do locate where they're hiding," I said. He opened his mouth to argue, but I cut him off before he could. "You have dungeons. Lock them up, but don't kill them. This is your chance to prove the rumors wrong and show that you aren't scared of the flames."

"Me, scared? What a ridiculous notion."

I shrugged. "That's what people are saying. And if I heard these rumors while being locked away in the tower, I can only imagine the words that pass through the streets."

"You have no negotiating power here, Daella."

"All right, then." I turned to go. "No deal."

He let me walk halfway across the Great Hall before he cleared his throat. "Wait."

Got you. Smiling, I faced him once more.

He stood from his throne and ran his fingers through his thick head of pale blue hair, and for a moment he looked like the youthful boy of sixteen who had passed me sweets from the dinner table when his royal family had come to visit. I'd been a serving girl then, barely six years old. But he'd been kind to me.

And then three years later, he'd invaded with his army after his entire family, save his sister, was killed in a Draugr attack.

"All right, then." He nodded. "I'll lock the Draugr in my dungeons if you agree to find them. And then you'll go free. But I'm only giving you two months. If you don't return before then, I'll assume you ran off, and I'll be forced to use the shard."

Which would mean certain death, as he could control it from afar. And still, I could not say no to this.

"Swear it," I said, my heart pounding. Emperor Isveig was a lot of things, but an oath-breaker was not one of them. "If I do this, you won't kill them, and you'll let me go free."

"I swear it." He folded his arms. "So do we have a deal?"

Freedom. My heart clenched. "We do."

Only a few hours later, I stood on a ship with my mother's dagger strapped to my side, watching the city of Fafnir vanish on the distant horizon. The ancient city was nestled in the lush hills along the coast, the stone-baked roofs reflecting the summer sun. Centuries ago, it had been built by orcish tools and orcish hands. You could see the remnants of our people in the architecture: towers that cut toward the sky in the shape of tusks, stone skulls decorating each corner of the battlements, and a portcullis made of bones. But now, only humans and giants roamed the winding streets.

It turned out Emperor Isveig had about as little patience as he had battle experience—he had done little of the fighting himself during his conquest. We'd set off as soon as I'd dressed in my gear—thick leathers with Isveig's wolf sigil stamped on my shoulder—and packed a satchel of clothes and dried meat.

"I bet you're glad to be out of your tower." Isveig's only living sister, Thuri, swaggered across the deck, the harsh wind tugging at her long, blue braid. She stepped beside me and closed her eyes, coming alive beneath the saltwater spray.

I smiled despite the unease threading through me. Yes, my blood sang in response to the elements of the Galdur—*magic*—that wound through the very essence of the outside world. And yes, my heart pounded with that desperate hope for freedom. But a haze of gray wrapped around me, drowning that hope in darkness. We sailed for the Isles of Fable, which no one had ever been able to find. We were just as likely to get swept into the Elding, the near-constant storm that churned through the rough waters of the Boundless Sea. It was one of the many reasons the Isles of Fable had never been found. It was too dangerous.

As if the ancient Old God of Thunder heard my thoughts, lightning spiked through the distant, dark skies.

Thuri frowned. "We'll have to sail south if we want to avoid the Elding."

"The long way around, then," I said in a chirpy voice. "Just warn me if we're going to get rain, so I can get below deck in time."

She gave me a look. "I don't understand how you can be so happy about this."

"It's like you said. I'm glad to be out of my tower."

"He's sent us to our deaths, and you know it." Her face clouded over as she gripped the wooden railing. "Better ships than this have been lost to the Boundless Sea, and the Elding."

Surprised, I took in her dark expression. "Why would he want to get rid of you? You're his heir."

Thuri frowned, glanced over her shoulder at the warriors—a collection of giants and humans—stationed around the deck, then shook her head. "In case we survive, I cannot say."

For the first time in a long while, I looked at Thuri —*really* looked at her. And I recalled laughing with her in the kitchen when she'd wanted an extra dessert, back when we'd both been no more than six and eight. I thought of all those letters we'd exchanged before her brother had invaded. We'd written each other in a secret language that only we understood, gossiping about meaningless court romances. I remembered her bright smile that I rarely saw anymore. Even her eyes carried sadness now. The recent rumors were about more than Isveig's fear of flames. They also told a tall tale about Thuri and how all those years ago she'd tried to stop her brother from killing every dragon and every orc he could find.

"You'd make a better ruler," I told her. "And I'm not the only one who thinks so."

She tensed, cutting her eyes toward the nearest human warrior, then dropped her voice to a whisper. "Stop. You can't say things like that out loud. You could get us both killed."

"Except, like you said, Isveig already sent us on a doomed mission." I cracked a smile, nudging her shoulder.

I'd meant what I'd said. Unlike Isveig, Thuri had never threatened me, she'd never locked me in my tower room, and she'd never raised her sword against the people of Fafnir. I truly believed she'd tried to hold Isveig back during the conquest. Once, I'd even spotted her scurrying through the alleys handing out bread and coin to the poor. For weeks after, Isveig had complained about a thief in the castle, but he'd never suspected his own dear sister worked against him.

11

Thuri sighed. "Speaking of this doomed mission, do you smell any Draugr yet?"

I took a sniff of the saltwater air, even though I already knew the answer. "No. We're not close enough."

Suddenly, she reached out and clutched my hand. Lowering her voice, she whispered. "Do you truly believe I could do it?"

"I do, Thuri. I really do."

Lightning flashed; thunder boomed. A monstrous wave suddenly came from nowhere and slammed into the side of the ship. I didn't even have time to gasp for air as I was tossed from the deck.

Angry waves pushed me onto the shore, and my lungs burned as I coughed up seawater. I dug my fingers into the coarse sand and dragged my aching body away from the spray. I tried to think around the overwhelming sense of *wet* that clung to every inch of me. At least it was salt water. It was the only kind my skin could endure.

What had happened? The last thing I could remember, I'd been standing on the deck of one of the emperor's grandest ships, and now I was here, clawing at the beach like a drowned cat. I glanced behind me at the churning skies.

Where was Thuri? Had anyone else survived?

Boots thumped beside my head. I lifted my eyes to spy a six-foot-five elven man with brilliant silver hair, staring down at me and scowling. His soft blue linen tunic clung to a muscular chest, draping down to a perfect V where it tucked into his brown trousers. He pointed the tip of his sword, as sharp as the curves of his ears, at where my mother's dagger had washed up beside me. Before I could stop him, he leaned down and plucked the blade from the sand.

"Now what do we have here?" he asked in a deep, melodic voice. "Hello, little murk."

I'd always hated that term. It was short for mercenary. Someone who would do anything for a bit of coin. That wasn't me.

Coughing, I peered up at him. "I almost died. Do you really need to hurl insults right now?"

"I suppose not. I'll just hurl something else instead." And with that, he hauled back his arm and tossed my mother's dagger into the sea.

2

DAELLA

M y chest burned as I fought the urge to cry out. That was the only thing of my mother I had left. And this...this *bastard* had thrown it away like it was nothing more than a piece of rubbish.

"How dare you?" I asked, shakily pushing up from the beach. "That was mine. It meant something to me."

His face remained impassive. "We don't allow weapons to be brought into Hearthaven, especially by one of the emperor's murks."

Hearthaven? I'd never heard of a Hearthaven before. That must mean...we'd made it to the Isles of Fable. Or at least, *I'd* made it. The Elding had come from nowhere and bashed the side of the ship. We'd been miles from any land. How had I even gotten here?

"This is one of the Isles, isn't it?" I said to the elf. "How close are we to the Glass Peaks?"

He held on to his stony expression, but I didn't miss

the brief flash in his eyes—a hint of wariness. "Not close. You washed up on the wrong island."

And then he turned to go.

Moonlight bathed his muscular form in silver. Tall and powerful, he looked like he could handle that sword well. It had been a long time since I'd seen an elf, and while they were known to be attractive, I didn't remember them being quite this striking. It was unfortunate he didn't have the personality or manners to match his looks.

With his back turned to me, I took the opportunity to sniff the air. No hint of dragon magic. Just smoke and leather and steel. And he was about to leave me stuck on this beach. I patted my waist where my small pouch had been. It was gone, along with all my coin, plus the satchel with my food, my clothes, my salt, and my protective tent. I wouldn't get very far like this.

"That was my mother's dagger," I called after him.

I didn't expect him to stop, but he did. Tensing, he glanced over his shoulder, his face hidden in shadows. "Your emperor can give her a new one to replace it."

Pain pulsed in my hip.

The elf started walking away from me again. Narrowing my eyes, I jogged to keep up with him, my wet boots squishing with every step. "Look, I know you think I'm some kind of mercenary—"

"Aren't you?" he cut in as he continued forward, not even casting a glance my way. "Or do you just wear the monster's wolf sigil for a laugh?"

I bit the insides of my cheeks, noting his outright

hostility. Truth be told, Isveig wasn't particularly popular due to his conquest, even among the ice giants who'd remained in the North. But something in the tone of this elf's voice prickled the back of my neck. He could be hiding something—the very thing I'd sailed here to find. Yes, I'd landed on the wrong island, but what if the dwarves were mistaken? What if the Draugr were in Hearthaven, and I'd already found my first one?

And so I chose my words carefully. "I'm not a mercenary. He makes everyone in Fafnir wear one of these."

"A half-orc from Fafnir?" He stopped and arched a silver brow. "Then that must make you Daella Sigursdottir, the infamous tracer who roots out dragon magic. If that doesn't make you a murk, then I don't know what does."

My cheeks flamed with heat. "At least you've heard of me. I can't say the same for you."

"Good." He continued up the sloping beach, heading toward a copse of trees that backed up against the bank. I kept pace with him as we drew closer, and a thin dirt path cut through the looming woods. It occurred to me that I was about to follow a hostile elf who believed the worst of me, right into a dark forest. I was unarmed. He wasn't.

But what else could I do? I had no coin, no shelter, no food.

And by the look of the pregnant clouds, rain could slash down from the sky at any moment. I didn't want to be caught outside without my tent and my salt when it did.

"Well, you know my name. What's yours?" I asked him in my much-practiced chirpy voice. As much as it pained me to lose my mother's dagger, I couldn't focus on those emotions right now. I had to bottle them up, like I always did.

To my surprise, the elf actually answered. "Rivelin." He stopped at the edge of the path and narrowed his eyes. "Stop following me."

"I'm not staying out here on the beach. It looks like it's about to rain."

"So?"

I fought to hold on to my smile. "I'm half-orc. My skin can't tolerate fresh water, and I doubt it rains salt here like it does in Fafnir. Most places in the world don't."

"Perhaps you should have thought of that before sailing into the Elding so you could hunt down Draugr for your ice giant emperor."

"Keep talking like that, and I'll think you're a Draugr yourself," I quipped.

A low rumble sounded from his throat. "Fine. Follow me back to the village, but don't expect any help. They'll all feel the same as I do."

"Why, because they're Draugr, too?"

"Watch it," he said, curling back his lips into a snarl. "This is a peaceful island, and we do not raise our weapons at each other—or at strangers, most of the time —but I will not hesitate to protect my people from your emperor *and you*. That doesn't make us dragon magic users. It makes us free folk who do not bow to any crown."

And with that, he took off into the trees. My heart pounding, I quickly followed him, breathlessness taking command of my lungs. It had been a long time since I'd heard someone speak so boldly against the emperor. Even the other Draugr I'd helped track down had rebelled in silent secrecy. They hid their truths behind closed lips and in dank, dark tunnels carved through the earth.

"If you're dealing in dragon magic, then you're far more dangerous than me," I said, picking up my pace to slide in front of him. I spun on my heels and jogged back, watching his expression for any sign of a reaction.

But his face betrayed none of his thoughts. He stopped in the middle of the path, and his fisted hands hung heavily by his sides. With a snarl, he stalked toward me and came so close that barely a breath of air stood between us. Keeping his eyes locked on mine, he leaned in and exposed his neck to me. His tanned skin glistened from the dense humidity of this place.

"Go on, then. I know you half-orcs can smell Draugr."

Swallowing, I sniffed his skin. Just as before, he was all leather and smoke, but nothing more. A twang went through my belly when he pulled back and smirked.

"See?" he said. "Nothing."

He took a step closer to where I stood in the way, between the beach and wherever he was heading—his village, he'd said. A light wind blew across my face, rolling in from the angry sea just beyond the trees, rustling the leaves against the ground. I took him in with a lifted chin and refused to look away, even if he'd won this small battle. I didn't trust him, and I didn't believe for one moment that he wasn't hiding something. Everything he'd said and done so far *screamed* rebellion.

And if I could prove it, I could spend the rest of my life free from Emperor Isveig. I could find an empty expanse of land, surrounded by woods and birdsong, and I could build a cabin there. Somewhere far, far away from Isveig, the ice giants, and that cramped tower so high above the earth and the soothing essence of the elemental Galdur magic.

I would be free.

I pasted on a smile. "Nothing. So all I need is somewhere to stay for the night, and then I'll be on my way back to Fafnir. The emperor will be happy to know the Isles of Fable are free of dangerous criminals."

He grunted. "The Isles of Fable?"

"That's what the people of the Grundstoff Empire call this place. Does it have another name?" If I got him talking, perhaps he'd let something important slip.

"No, we just call them the Isles." He made a move to step around me, but I followed this dance with a step of my own. "And as for you returning to Fafnir...unfortunately for everyone, you're stuck for a while. It's not safe to sail until the Elding passes on, so no ships will dock in our harbors for another six weeks—the day of Midsummer."

My heart jerked. "Six weeks?"

My hip ached in sudden pain. The shard didn't like the sound of that. It was cutting things too close. I had two months to return to Fafnir, although it was likely less by now. I didn't know how long I'd been gone. And if I didn't arrive in time, Isveig would release his control over the shard and allow it to freeze all the breath in my lungs.

"Trust me," Rivelin said with a frown. "I'm no happier about this than you are. Playing host to one of Isveig's murks is the last thing any of us here want."

He took a step around me, and this time, I let him pass. My mind tried to make sense of this new information. If the Elding attacked the waters around this island for six long weeks, what did that mean for the fate of the others who had been on that ship? Where was Thuri?

As an ice giant, she'd have a far better time of it out there than me, but I'd been the only one to wash up on the shore of this island. There was no sign of her or the rest of Isveig's warriors. Could she somehow have survived? If so, where was she?

We reached the end of the path only moments later. The woods fell away to reveal a bustling village, even with the storm brewing in the nighttime sky. Clusters of homes dotted lush, rolling fields blooming with a kaleidoscope of colorful flowers. The sweet scent of them drifted toward me on the wind, along with the lilting voice of a bard and his lute. Every window was bathed in light. Every front door was wreathed in vines and flowers. And every burst of laughter sounded genuine and full of life.

My chest felt hollow. That was how Fafnir Castle had sounded all those years ago.

"That's the inn." Rivelin led me toward a cheery timber building at the edge of the village. The bard's upbeat song grew louder as we approached, as did the laughter and the cheers. The window boxes were over-flowing with jasmines and tulips, and vines of wisteria crept up the side of the building toward the roof. I cocked my head. That was curious. Wisteria normally didn't grow on hot, humid islands like this one.

Hinges creaked as the overhead sign swayed in the wind, stronger now than it had been only moments ago. I glanced up as it rattled. *The Dreaming Dragon Inn.*

I arched a brow. "Curious name."

"Don't get any wild ideas. It's just a name."

He turned just as the wind gusted my wet hair into my face. I swiped it aside and called after him, "Where are you going?"

"Home." He nodded at the door. "You said you needed shelter. There you go."

"I don't have any coin."

A slight smile curved his lips. "Not my problem. Good luck, murk."

3

DAELLA

I frowned at Rivelin's back. He waltzed off like he didn't have a care in the world. The bastard. When he vanished around the corner, I turned to face the inn's door, steeling myself and schooling my features back into a pleasant, agreeable expression. I wouldn't talk my way into a free room if I stormed in there scowling at everyone.

The storm gusted against my back, and a haze of mist sprayed onto my skin. Pain licked across my bare arms. I hissed through my teeth. If I didn't find shelter soon, I'd be in a world of hurt when those heavy clouds dumped their rain.

I grabbed the door handle and pushed inside. A cacophony of sound consumed me, snapping my attention away from the lingering pain. Despite being within a tiny village that couldn't be home to more than three hundred folk, if that, the inn was packed.

23

Lanterns spilled soft, cozy light across the oak tables that filled the center of the floor, angled toward a small stage along the far wall. A small, floppy-eared bard with a long ginger beard stood on top of a stool, thumping his foot in time with the tune he played on his lute.

Grinning wildly, he spun on the stool. His booming voice went sharp when his gaze landed on my face. Suddenly, the music stopped, and every single eye in the room turned my way.

I beamed at them all, swallowing down the hitch in my throat. I was used to the scrutiny. Every time I left my tower, people whispered and stared.

There goes the emperor's pet orc.

Truth be told, that was probably what everyone here was thinking too. If Rivelin knew who I was, there was no doubt the others in this village would as well. Even if my reputation didn't precede me, it was difficult for us orcs to blend in these days. There were far too few of us left, and the entire known world knew it.

I lifted my hand in a little wave. "Hello. Which one of you is the owner?"

"That'd be me." A shadow demon called out from behind the bar as she folded her arms on top of a wooden keg. Horns curved from the top of her head, much like Isveig's, though hers were a deep, impenetrable black. A soft darkness gathered against her pale skin, pulsing with every beat of her heart. Unease whispered down my spine. Well, this was certainly unexpected. Isveig *hated* demons. Theirs was the only

24

kingdom left in the land of the folk that he had not conquered, though he'd tried.

I walked over to the bar, my boots still squishing from the salt water logged inside the leather. The whole room remained silent, and the weight of everyone's gaze was enough to make me shudder.

"I'm just passing through," I said to her as quietly as I could. "I'd like a room for the night."

"Is that so?" Her midnight eyes flicked to the emperor's sigil on my shoulder. "Got any gold, or do you only have that fancy ice coin of Isveig's? I'd also take a bag of Galdur sand, if you have any. We don't get much of that around here."

A few murmurs rose and fell like waves. I fought the urge to glance over my shoulder. Galdur sand was more prized than gold, due to its rarity. It could be one of four kinds: Fildur for fire, Vatnor for water, Vindur for air, or Jordur for earth. Anyone could use the sand to harness the elemental magic of the world, but you had to find some first. Not even Isveig had much of it.

"I'm afraid I have none of those things," I said. "Everything I had got lost in the Elding. My ship was destroyed, and I washed up on shore here, and—"

"No coin, no room."

My heart sank, but her response had been expected. "You can put me to work. I'll wash dishes or serve ale or sweep up crumbs. Anything you need, I'll do. I have nowhere else to go. My ship—"

She gave me a wicked smile, leaned forward, and shot a strand of shadow toward me. "No coin, no room."

I nodded. "All right. That's fair, I suppose."

Hiding my disappointment, I turned back toward the rest of the room. Everyone instantly sprang into action, returning to their conversations and their ale. The dwarf plucked his lute and dragged his gaze from my face before breaking out into a tune about the trolls in the distant mountains. I wandered over to the nearest table. There was an open spot at the end of the bench, next to a group of elves.

The shadow demon owner appeared beside me the moment I sat.

"You've got to be a paying customer to take up space at this table." She motioned at the rest of the bustling room. "It's a busy time of year for the village of Wyndale, and we've got a lot of visitors who want drink, food, and seats. *Paying* visitors."

I blew out a breath of frustration. "Please. It's about to storm, and I have nowhere else to go."

"No coin, no table."

"Fine." I shoved up from the bench. Now that she was no longer leaning against a keg, the shadow demon towered over me, and darkness seemed to stretch toward me. A tremor went down my spine at the dangerous look in her eye. "I'll just wait out the storm in the corner, and then I'll leave."

She smiled. "No coin, no corner."

I swallowed. No matter what I said, she wasn't going to let me stay inside this inn. Even if I had coin, I doubted she would have given me food and a room. Everyone in this place saw me for what I was: a servant of their enemy. And so I did the only thing I could. I held my head high and walked toward the door, where the brewing storm was waiting.

I didn't blame her. Not even a little. They *shouldn't* trust me, especially if my suspicions were true. Because I would not hesitate to turn every last one of them over to Emperor Isveig. My freedom for theirs.

As I shoved through the door, I blinked back the tears that threatened to spill down my cheeks. There was no reason for me to feel ashamed of it—no reason for that guilt clawing at my heart. Dragon magic was a volatile, wicked thing. It was too dangerous. I'd seen the ramifications of its power. I knew exactly what horrors it wrought.

Draugr had killed my mother and father. And so I would help Isveig stop them from killing anyone else.

4

RIVELIN

"We knew Isveig would send someone eventually," Haldor said from where he leaned against the door with crossed arms. He looked far too at ease about this whole thing. The little murk could ruin everything. But he hadn't seen her, not like I had. She'd looked like a drowned rat, gasping for air, but even then, I hadn't missed the strength and confidence in the way she carried herself. Daella Sigursdottir couldn't have survived in this world by being anything short of spectacular.

And she needed to get the fuck out of my village.

Odel, a bubbly pixie with deep brown skin, black curly hair, and fluttering pink wings, pranced over to Haldor and shoved a finger into his chest. "You seem to be forgetting something. The opening ceremony for the Midsummer Games is tomorrow. We can't have one of Isveig's pets here for that."

"It's fine," he drawled, arching a bushy brow the color of flames, much like his hair and skin. As a fire demon, everything about him ran hot, except his temper. I'd never before met a fire demon, or anyone else for that matter, who could remain unruffled in the face of anything the world could throw at him.

It was one of the reasons the people of Wyndale had chosen him to be a part of the Village Council, along with me, for my unmatched skill with the blade, and Odel, for her cleverness. Together, we'd kept this village thriving for fourteen good years. And I was not about to let our people lose out on a fifteenth one because of a pesky murk.

"How is it fine?" I frowned, bracing my fists on the small meeting table set up in the back of the Wyndale Village Hall. Several lanterns illuminated the carvings on the wall—relics left behind by the humans who had called this village home centuries before. They'd abandoned it now. "She'll return to Fafnir and tell her emperor about the Games, and then he'll send a fleet of ships here to conquer us. As soon as he learns what this island can do, he'll want a piece of it."

"No, not a piece," Odel corrected. "He'll want the whole damn thing."

"Because if Isveig is anything," I continued, "it's a conqueror."

Haldor held up his hands. "All right. Let's just think this through. What, exactly, did she say to you when you found her on that beach?"

I thought back to the moment I'd set eyes on her,

when she'd been coughing and sputtering and clawing at the sand. At first, my instincts had propelled me forward to help. The Elding must have attacked her ship, and she'd somehow survived when few did. Orcs weren't known to be good swimmers, not when fresh water welted their skin. But she was there. And she'd needed help.

That was when I'd spotted the dagger in the sand and the emperor's sigil on her shoulder.

"She asked about the Glass Peaks," I told them. "She didn't seem to know anything about Hearthaven."

"See? She's hunting for Draugr over on the mountain island where the dwarves live. She's got no business here," Haldor said.

"And yet she *is* here," I countered. "We won't be able to get rid of her for six bloody weeks because of the Elding. That will take us through the whole of the Midsummer Games. She'll see everything."

Odel tapped a finger against her chin. "We could send her up to Milford, or even Riverwold."

"Bad idea. She'll just come back when she finds out half their residents are *here* for the Games," Haldor said.

"He has a point." Odel frowned and turned back to me. "We're going to have to convince her we're not dealing in outlawed dragon magic and charm her enough that she won't want to tell the emperor about our island. We need to show her we're just a small village of peaceful people who don't want any trouble. If she believes that, she won't tell Isveig a damn thing."

I grunted and folded my arms. "If you'd spent any

time around Isveig's murks, you wouldn't believe that any more than I do."

Haldor crossed the room to gaze out the open window, where the sounds of celebration poured into the Village Hall. Soon, it would die down as the Elding's rains swept across the village, signalling the beginning of our annual Midsummer Games. We had so many visitors this year, so many hopefuls who wanted to throw their hat into the ring or cheer for the spectacle. It had brought a riotous atmosphere to our quaint village, and the streets were practically buzzing from the excitement.

Not me. All I could think was that so many people lessened my odds.

"Uh oh," Haldor said as he moved back from the window. "Elma's chucked the orc out of the inn. She's walking this way now, probably looking for shelter."

"Of course Elma did. No one's going to help a half-orc from Fafnir," Odel said. "Everyone knows who she is."

Both of them folded their arms and stared at me.

I frowned. "What do you expect me to do about it?"

Odel sighed. "Orcs are allergic to rain, right? So we're not going to endear her to us if she's banished outside on her first night here, after what I'm assuming was quite the ordeal with the whole shipwreck and all. She needs some food, a dry room, and a cozy bed."

Haldor nodded enthusiastically.

I barked out a laugh. "No, absolutely not. If you want to play savior to Isveig's pet orc, then be my guest, but

I'll have no part in it. His murks have done enough to ruin my life. I won't let one near my house."

"Think about it, Rivelin." Haldor sidled up to me with a wicked grin. "We can't leave her outside for six weeks, braving the elements. That will only make her hate us. She'll poke around. She'll find reasons to tell Isveig about us. Someone needs to keep an eye on her and make her sweet."

"Then *you* do it," I said through clenched teeth. I couldn't believe we were having this conversation.

"I'm married," he said with a shrug. "You're not."

"You must be joking."

"He has a good point," Odel said in a singsong voice. "Lucien would not be thrilled if Haldor brought home a beautiful orc, mercenary or not. You know how jealous he gets."

I heaved a sigh and pinned both of them with a flat stare. "He wouldn't be 'taking her home' and neither would I. You said you want to keep her from poking around? Fine. But I don't see how that has anything to do with Lucien's jealousy. It's not as if you're going to romance her."

"I mean, it's not a bad idea," Odel said. "It'll keep her distracted."

"So then *you* do it."

Her cheeks reddened. "I know nothing about romancing a woman, unfortunately. You, on the other hand, are handsome, unmarried, and women love you. You could charm anyone."

I scowled. "I am not a charmer, and you know it. I haven't courted anyone since I moved here."

Haldor clapped a hand on my shoulder. "Well, you might be a grumpy recluse, Rivelin, but the women still love you with your annoying elvish looks."

"I hate mercenaries and the emperor."

"Too bad." Haldor grinned.

"This is for the good of the village, which you've said time and time again is all you care about," Odel added, edging a step closer. They'd boxed me in now, two against one. And I knew whatever I said now, they'd never let this go. "All you have to do is give her somewhere to stay for six weeks. Keep her happy, make her love this place. Then when we send her off to the Glass Peaks, she won't want to tell the emperor anything about *us*. And the dwarves are smart enough to figure out what to do with her when she gets there."

"Won't it seem suspicious? I've just dropped her off at the inn and basically told her to fuck herself."

"Perhaps." Odel pursed her pink lips, bright against her skin, and glanced at Haldor. "Any ideas?"

For a moment, he stared off into the distance, and I thought I might get out of this meeting without being saddled with Isveig's half-orc murk for the summer. But then Odel snapped her fingers as a look of glee brightened her pixie face.

"I've got it," she said in an eager whisper. "Get her involved with Midsummer. Make her some kind of deal. You won't just give her a free room. She'll have to work with you at your blacksmith shop, either helping out during the festivities or helping *you* win the Games if your name gets chosen. Of course, we'll need to get her some clothes. Tilda's about her size, and she has plenty."

My hands fisted. The last thing I wanted was for my enemy to help me win the Midsummer Games and everything that came with it. But there was a strange sense of irony, I had to admit. Because if I won, I knew how I'd use my winnings. I would make certain this island and its people would never again be threatened by the crown, which included *her*.

Plus, I did need an assistant, and I hadn't known who to ask. Everyone else had already paired up. I was a strong contender, but Haldor was right. I was known as the village's recluse.

"What about Gregor?" I asked. "The murk's a new woman on the island. He'll probably try to claim the island sent her to him."

Odel scowled, an expression I rarely saw from her. "I wouldn't wish Gregor on my worst enemy, and Daella might very well be that. We're not sending her to him. And if he tries anything, we'll just remind him that his request was outside the boundaries of the island's rules."

With that, I agreed. "Still, he might be a problem."

"Unfortunately for him, you're the best damn fighter on this island," Haldor said with a chuckle. "And knowing how Isveig trains his murks, I'm sure the half-orc is more than capable of standing up for herself."

I couldn't believe I was agreeing to this. Only hours ago, I'd been hopeful for the summer. My name had never been drawn for the Midsummer Games, and I felt my time had come. I would finally take part, and I would win. It would mean Isveig would never find this place. *His people* would never find this place.

But it seemed fate had another plan in mind.

If I were to take part this year, it would be with my enemy by my side. At least, at the end of it all, I would be able to protect this place from *her*, too. She would likely never even make it back to the mainland.

Thunder boomed in the distance. The rains would be here soon. With a heavy sigh, I resigned myself to six weeks of living Hel.

"Fine," I said. "Six weeks. Then we send her off on the first ship we can. But you two have to play a part in this, too. Make her believe this place is paradise and that it's worth protecting. Shouldn't be hard, because it's the truth."

5

DAELLA

I wandered through the village as the strong winds whipped up leaves and dirt. The place was bigger than I'd first assumed—closer to a town than a tiny hamlet home to only a few families. Cottages and shops crawled along the hills, all engulfed in vines and blossoming flowers. The scent of it was almost staggering—so sweet, so *earthen*. Back in Fafnir, most of the greenery had been replaced with stone and steel.

The sky cracked with thunder, and I flinched. I couldn't bring myself to start knocking on strangers' doors and begging for a place to stay. I already knew what they'd say when they caught sight of me. To the people of this village, I was the enemy.

I spotted stables at the corner of the dirt road, so I headed that way. Animals were often better company than people, anyway. When I reached the door I tried the handle, but it wouldn't budge. I should have expected as much. Sighing, I looked up at the small overhang just over the door. It wasn't particularly wide, but it might keep away some of the rain.

I settled onto the dirt and pulled my knees up to my chest. My clothes were still soaked through, and my feet felt like mush. The wind was whipping faster now, chilling my clothes. Most of the time, I ran hot, but even I wasn't immune to the cold. Shivering, I dropped my chin onto my knees and tried to focus on the positives.

At least I was alive. Deep down, I knew Thuri and the others might not have survived. The Elding had taken out dozens of ships over the years, and most of the time, no one ever came back. Their bodies were lost to the Boundless Sea forever. I was lucky to even be here.

I was cold and wet and soon I would be in terrible pain, but I was no longer trapped inside that damn tower. I was out in the elements now, where I belonged. The dirt beneath me felt grounding, comforting. Orcs had never been meant to spend their lives indoors.

The sound of footsteps snapped my attention away from my thoughts. The thudding grew closer, and I steeled myself. Perhaps the owner of the stables had seen me squatting out here, and they'd come to chase me away. I'd have to find somewhere else to wait out the storm. Perhaps I'd be better off returning to the woods, where the trees would provide a little shelter.

A tall, muscular elf strode into view, and my stomach dropped. For fuck's sake. It was that damn Rivelin again.

He swept his gaze across me, his expression hard.

Was fate working against me somehow? If these stables were his, I hoped the ground would swallow me whole.

"You look cold," he said, coming to a stop only a few feet away.

"What an excellent observation."

"Why are you here?"

"I told you. I lost all my coin in the sea. Seems free room and board isn't a thing here."

"And so you decided to sit outside the stables."

"I didn't see any other inns, so unless they're invisible it seems I'm out of luck."

"Another inn wouldn't offer you a room, either. That's *if* we had one, which we don't. Wyndale is a small, peaceful village. We don't get many visitors when it's not Midsummer, let alone murks."

"Fantastic information. Thank you for telling me. I think I'd like to get back to my nap."

His lips curved. "Nap? It looked more like glowering to me."

"I don't glower," I insisted, reminding myself that I did, in fact, need to stick to my motto despite how dreadful I might feel at the moment—with my puffy eyes, my clammy skin, and the headache throbbing at my temple. These people would only stop seeing me as the enemy if I didn't act like the grumpy bastard who stood before me. So, I wiped away the frown. "I'm just tired, that's all."

He shifted on his feet, suddenly looking a little uncertain. "You can't sleep out here."

"Let me guess. You don't want the *murk* anywhere near your horses."

"No, I mean..." He closed his eyes and spoke his next sentence through gritted teeth. "No one should have to sleep on the ground. I have a room. You can stay with me. For one night."

For a moment, all my words and thoughts left me. Surely I hadn't heard him right. Out of everyone in this village, *he* was the one offering me a bed? Had the storm already started, and I had gotten delirious from the rain? Or had I fallen asleep, and this was nothing more than a dream?

"I thought you hated anyone associated with the crown," I finally said.

"I do." He opened his eyes, and the gleaming yellow of them speared me. "But I won't have you roaming around Wyndale hungry and cold. So get up and follow me." Rivelin barked the words like an order, and I bristled.

Ah, I understood now.

Did he think I was a fool? He didn't want me roaming around Wyndale because he and the others were hiding something. If he hadn't already made it clear what he thought of me, I might have fallen for it, but I'd spent most of my life in Fafnir Castle. I knew what scheming looked like. He wanted to keep me close so that I wouldn't find anything.

"Nice try," I said with a smile. "But I think I'll be far more comfortable out here in the rain than in your house."

The scowl was there and gone in a blink of an eye, but I caught it. "Fine. Suit yourself."

He turned and walked off without another word. Now that he was gone, I dropped my smile, and then settled against the stables once more. But try as I might, I couldn't pull my eyes away from him. I watched him walk to the end of the road and then climb a short flight of stairs to a two-story timber house with white and red beams, the many window boxes vacant of flowers. The ground floor had wide doors and a metal sign in the shape of an anvil that read, *Rivelin's Forge*.

That explained a lot. No wonder he smelled like smoke and steel.

When he vanished inside, I blew out a tense breath. He was going to be difficult to deal with, I could already tell. Suspicion practically swam in his yellow eyes when he looked at me. The fact he'd invited me into his home meant he would try to do his damndest to keep me from finding out the village's secrets.

I'd just have to be smarter than him. Shouldn't be hard.

A peal of thunder shook through the skies, and the clouds opened up. Buckets of rain fell in sheets. I scrabbled back, pressing my body as close to the stable wall as I could, but it was no use.

The wind sprayed the water over me like a thousand shards of glass. Pain consumed my body, stealing my breath away. I fisted my hands and gritted my teeth, flinching with every blast of water against my skin. Unwanted tears burned my eyes, and I twisted my face to the side, if only to give one cheek a brief respite from the blinding pain.

It had been five years since I'd felt freshwater rain on my skin. I'd done so well these past years avoiding it, always carrying a tent and salt with me everywhere. And in Fafnir, it only rained salt water.

Moments passed in excruciating torment. My blood roared in my ears as the rain lashed and lashed at my skin. Shuddering, I peeled open my eyes and risked a glance at the sky. An inky black consumed the world overhead, only occasionally shot through with bursts of lightning that revealed the heavy clouds. They'd barely moved an inch. This storm wouldn't end for a good long while.

I was soaked through now, and rivulets of water ran down my back, driving a wedge between my leather armor and my skin. My entire body burned. I choked out a cry. It was too much. As strong as I was, I couldn't handle this.

Rivelin's words echoed in my ears. He'd offered me a place to stay, at least for the night. Everything within me flinched away from the thought, but I couldn't stay out here like this. The rain might not kill me, but it could weaken me, leaving behind angry red welts that wouldn't heal for weeks. And if I was too ill to hunt down the Draugr, then I'd have no hope of escaping my gilded cage.

And so I pushed up onto my trembling legs and half-ran, half-stumbled down the road. The village was silent now, the windows dark. Everyone had gone home to their warm and dry beds to wait out the storm, though I spotted movement behind the curtains in a few buildings I passed. Nevertheless, I made it to the blacksmith shop and I crawled up the steps, my mind nearly numb from the pain.

I raised my fist to knock, but the door swung open before my knuckles made contact. Rivelin leaned against the doorframe, folded his arms, and smirked.

"Fancy seeing you here," he said. "Have you come to peddle your murk services? If so, I'm afraid I'm not interested."

Another gust of wind hurtled the rain against my back. I stumbled forward a step, hissing in pain.

"Please don't make me beg," I managed, my voice barely above a whisper. "I'll take the bed. Just for one night. I need to get out of this rain."

His eyes flashed with something resembling concern, but that was likely my delirium. He opened the door wider. "It's yours. Come inside."

I stumbled into the elf's home, and that was when the scent of dragons struck me.

6

DAELLA

I'd know that smell anywhere. It had dogged my every step as a child. It had followed me into my dreams—and my worst nightmares. It was sulphur and spice, dust and cooked meat, salt water and leather. A unique combination of scents that only dragons and Draugr carried with them—or had, once, when they'd been alive. Emperor Isveig called my sensitivity to that smell my special power, though most orcs could scent a dragon from miles away. To us, it was more than a scent. It was a feeling—a thudding in our hearts.

The smell had always called to me, though I hated it.

I tried not to react, which was fairly easy when the pain of the rainfall still consumed every inch of me. The water had soaked through my clothes now, and all the salt water from the ocean had been washed away, leaving nothing but the blaze.

Rivelin glanced at my hands. My skin was growing

redder by the moment. Without another word, he handed me a towel and a dry pair of nightclothes: soft linen trousers in an emerald green with a matching tunic. By the look of them, they were clearly women's garments.

"Why do you have this?" I said with a shudder, my jaw still clenched from the unyielding pain.

"Don't worry about that now. Just go get changed." He motioned to a closed door at the end of a short hallway. I stumbled forward, barely taking in the rest of the home. All I could focus on was my feet—on one step in front of the other. Shaking, I shoved inside the room.

The scent of dragons grew stronger, but I barely paid it any attention. I tossed the fresh trousers on the bed, wriggled out of my wet clothes, and breathed in a ragged breath of relief. My hands shook as I toweled off the rain. With every brush of the fabric against my skin, the pain faded until it was nothing more than a dull ache. My skin was still red, but no welts had formed yet. I'd likely feel fine in the morning.

Thanks to the elf.

I pulled on the soft nightclothes and then took a moment to look around the room. It reeked of sulphur, so strongly that there was no doubt in my mind Rivelin had been in contact with a dragon or a Draugr not that long ago. A day at most. Maybe two.

Curious, since all the dragons were dead.

The room itself was sparsely decorated. A small bed took up most of the space, covered in periwinkle sheets and a patchwork quilt faded by sun and time. Beside it sat a single nightstand that held a glowing lantern and a leather-bound book. A storage chest at the foot of the bed was the only other piece of furniture.

A knock sounded on the door, startling me. I pressed down the front of the nightclothes and tried to look nonchalant, though I wasn't the one hiding something.

"Everything all right?" Rivelin called out through the door.

I cleared my throat. "Yes, I'm dressed now. You can come in."

The door swung wide, and Rivelin stepped into the bedroom. His eyes glowed as they trailed across me, and a strange heat filled my cheeks. I folded my arms, suddenly all too aware the shirt was pale and thin. I'd pulled off my undergarments along with everything else. Could he see through the material?

"Grab your wet clothes and follow me," he said in a gruff voice.

I frowned at his tone but used the towel to gather my clothes from where I'd piled them on the floor, then followed him back down the hallway. We came to a large living space I'd only seen a glimpse of on my way inside. Unlike the bedroom, furniture and knickknacks filled the room, along with a cozy sofa, a ruggedly constructed desk, an armchair, and a woven rug. A fire blazed in the hearth, spilling heat across my chilled body.

Rivelin took my clothes from my arms and went over to a rack beside the hearth. He hung them without a word, carefully arranging them like he'd done this very thing a hundred times before. Everything about this moment struck me as odd, especially his gentle actions and this cheery room, so unlike the man he'd shown himself to be—so far, anyway.

"Why are you being so nice to me?" I asked, finally cutting through the silent tension.

"I'm not being nice." He turned to face me. The orange flames splashed light onto one side of his face, leaving the other half hidden in shadow. "I just didn't want your clothes dripping water all over my floor. It'll warp the wood."

Of course. "Such a gentleman."

"This is the living space," he said, ignoring my quip. He pointed at an archway leading to the rear side of the building. "Through there is the kitchen and the pantry, though I'm not much of a cook. You've seen the bedroom already."

"And the spare room where I'm staying? Where's that?"

He folded his arms. "You'll be staying in the room I already showed you."

"Where's your bedroom, then?"

"Don't get any wild ideas in your head."

I snorted, though I couldn't stop my cheeks from heating. "In your bloody dreams."

"More like my worst nightmare." He grinned, though there was nothing cheerful about his expression, especially since it resulted in flashing his sharp canines. They glinted like the deadly look in his eyes.

"You don't actually have a guest room, do you?" I eyed him and then searched the room for something I could use as a weapon. "Why did you really bring me here? Is this your demented way of getting rid of the emperor's murk? You lured me into your home so you could kill me?"

"Like I told you on the beach, we don't do violence here. Unless you do something to provoke it."

"So then what do you want with me?" I folded my arms. "You were eager to get rid of me before, and I know how you feel about who I am and what I've done for the emperor. You're not just offering me your bed out of the goodness of your heart. You want something."

"You're right," he said with a nod before motioning to the sofa. "I'll be sleeping there. You can have the bed. In return, I want you to help me win the Midsummer Games. You'll be my assistant, my teammate."

"The Midsummer Games? I've never heard of it."

"Of course you haven't. No one in Hearthaven wants Emperor Isveig to find out and decide he wants to take part in the Games himself."

"All right, I'll admit I'm intrigued." I perched on the arm of the sofa and waited for him to continue.

"Every year, Wyndale hosts the Midsummer Games. They take place in the summer—"

"Yes, I got that. Can you skip to the good part?"

"Perhaps if you didn't interrupt me, I'd get there sooner."

I just gave him a brilliant smile.

He scowled. "People from all around the Isles come to take part or spectate. That's why there are so many visitors here right now, and why the inn was so packed.

Everyone looks forward to it every year. Some say it's the best part about living on Hearthaven."

"All right, so what do you do? How do you win? And what do you get? It must be good if you're willing to stoop so low as to team up with me."

"There are seven participants every year, drawn at random. They go on to compete in a series of four challenges. Each one corresponds to one of the elements. After each challenge, spectators vote on the winner. Whoever has the most votes at the end wins the Midsummer Games."

Four challenges, each representing one of the elements. It made sense. Our world revolved around the elements, just as most magic did.

"And the winnings?"

Rivelin gave me a long, hard stare, as if he were trying to decide whether he'd tell me the truth. It was something big, then. Something to do with dragons, perhaps?

"Not coin, if that's what you're thinking. This island is special. All these islands are. How do you think they've stayed hidden for so long?" he finally said. "It holds power of its own, one it likes to gift its residents. There are rules, though, made a very long time ago by the island itself. We get one gift per year. Otherwise, we'll use up the magic too quickly."

"I've never heard of *an island* having magic," I said slowly.

"Is it really so surprising?" he asked. "With Galdur sand,

we can bend the elements to our will to create magic. Those elements can harm as well as heal." He gave my bare arms a meaningful look. They weren't as red as they'd been before, but they were clearly still irritated. Irritated by water—one of the four elements. And the heat from the hearth soothed some of that pain. Fire always did make me feel better.

"So you take part in four challenges and win a gift from the island?" I asked.

"You can ask for anything you want," he said in a low voice that was almost drowned out by the crackle of the flames. "*Almost* anything. It will not directly harm anyone or anything. And you can't ask for it to change something on the mainland, unfortunately. It will only alter things that are here."

Well, this was far, far more interesting than I ever could have dreamed.

"If you want to win so badly, you must have something in mind?" I cocked my head. "What are you going to ask the island to give you?"

"I'm going to ask it to protect the folk of this place from Emperor Isveig. Others have tried in the past, but they always get the wording wrong, since the island sometimes translates in unexpected ways. But I know what to say to make it right."

My heart thumped against my ribs at the sudden passion in his voice. I'd hated Isveig ever since he'd brought his invading army into Fafnir, but I may have just met someone who hated him even more. Someone whose home reeked of dragon. Someone who was the ticket to my freedom...in more ways than one, potentially.

My hip ached from the icy sting of the shard, an ever-present reminder of who owned me, at least for a little while longer.

"Any idea what these challenges are?" I asked. "How dangerous are they? What kind of weapon will we need? You know, I'd be a much better help if you hadn't tossed my mother's dagger into the sea."

"I should have known your first instinct would be violence. I told you, we don't do that here," he said with narrowed eyes. "No one is killing anyone for a little bit of magic."

It was all I could do not to gape at him. "How long have you lived here?"

"On Hearthaven?" he asked, a suspicious tone to his voice. "Fourteen years. Why?"

"Then you've forgotten what it's like out there," I said, vaguely gesturing at the world beyond the storm-tossed sea. "Back in the Grundstoff Empire, people do kill others for magic. Mostly Isveig's warriors. The ice giants are terrified of anything they can't control, and that's most magic. If it's not ice, it has to die."

Rivelin stared at me. His eyes roamed across my face, down my body, and then back up again. A shiver went through me. There was something so feral in that look, like he was peeling me apart, inch by inch.

At long last, he spoke. "You're not made of ice and you're still alive."

"No," I said slowly. "I'm not ice. And Isveig keeps me on a tight leash because of it."

My answer seemed to satisfy him—for now—because he nodded. "Well, you're no longer in the Grundstoff Empire, Daella. The Midsummer Games are a celebration of our freedom and of this island's power. Now, do we have a deal?"

I didn't even have to think about it. "We have a deal. I'll help you win your Games. And you'll give me some-where to stay until I can board a ship and leave this place."

"Fine."

"Good."

The fire crackled in the awkward silence. I shifted on my feet, cleared my throat, and Rivelin cast his gaze around the room as if he were trying to look at anything and everything other than me. This was probably a terrible idea. I didn't know this elf, and he had a massive grudge against me. But I'd handled Isveig for a very long time. I could handle a grumpy blacksmith.

"Well, I'm tired," I finally said, making a move for the hallway. "I noticed the bedroom door doesn't have a lock. If you try anything…"

He grunted. "I would rather swim out to sea and let the Elding take me. Sorry to disappoint."

I arched a brow and sidled up to him, not entirely sure why. I should just retire to the bedroom and get some sleep, and yet…I dropped my arms to my side, no longer trying to hide anything the elf might be able to see through the tunic. And there it was. His eyes briefly flicked down—quick as a snake, but I caught it.

"You're a rude blacksmith who lives alone and had to make a deal with a stranger you hate, just so you could have someone help you win a competition." I winked as I backed away. "I don't think I'm the one who's going to end up disappointed."

"Oh, is that a challenge?"

"Absolutely not. You keep your hands to yourself."

"Scared that I'd win, are we?"

My foot snagged on a table leg, and I went stumbling sideways into the wall. I caught myself just before my knees buckled beneath me. Furious flames licked my cheeks when I glanced up and found Rivelin smirking at me.

"Feeling flustered?" he asked.

I glowered at him. "Oh, fate take you."

And then I spun on my feet and started down the hall.

But he called after me. "I know I should take that as an insult, but at least you stopped wearing that fake smile of yours."

This time, I didn't give him the satisfaction of a reply. If the bastard wanted to get a rise out of me, he'd have to try a lot harder than that.

7

DAELLA

Back in "my" bedroom, I took a moment to steady my breathing. I didn't know what I was so worked up about. It had just been an irritating conversation, and the elf had only been trying to get a reaction. We had a partnership of sorts, but that didn't mean he held anything but disdain toward me. And the feeling was mutual. At the end of the day, he was only using me the same way Isveig always had.

The only difference was, I was using him, too.

Our conversation echoed in my ears as I pulled back the patchwork quilt and climbed into bed. Rivelin wanted me to help him win four challenges so he could ask for the island's blessing. One gift. Endless possibility, as long as it did not cause harm.

Heart thumping, I slid a hand down to my hip and pressed my fingers against the shard. It had been years since Isveig had branded me with the ice, and the skin had mostly healed over it now. But the rough, pink scar was still there as a raised bump, and the shard beneath throbbed and whistled like steam, as if it were calling to its master from across the Boundless Sea.

The damn ice was the only thing that kept me tethered to Isveig, and even then I'd tried to run away a year ago, despite knowing what could happen. I'd reached my breaking point. I would have done anything just for a moment outside with the sun on my face, free to follow my desires.

Even when I knew that moment might be my last. It had been the darkest point in my life.

Sighing, I closed my eyes and sagged against the pillows. When I'd tried to escape, his guards had caught me. And now here I was, in a strange land, in an even stranger man's bed.

But maybe, just maybe, there was another way to be free of it all. A backup in case I failed to fulfill my quest. If I helped Rivelin win the Midsummer Games, perhaps I could beat him to the punch and ask the island give *me* the gift. The only thing I'd ever wanted: freedom.

I would never have to look into Isveig's face again. When the ships came, I could just sail to wherever I dreamed. My life would be mine and no one else's.

The thought tasted like berries on a warm summer's day. And with that hope in my heart, sleep called me away.

A hammer beat the walls. Disoriented, I jerked up from the bed, my eyes swimming as I stared at the unfamiliar room. My rich, silken sheets from my tower bed were gone. The plush settee where I spent hours flipping through bakery books was nowhere to be found. Even the drab light from the ever-present cloud had been replaced by a beaming sun pouring in through the window just beside the bed.

I blinked again, taking in the flowers creeping in through the windowpane and the brilliant birdsong and the soft quilt that covered me. This was not my tower.

The knocking sounded again, and memories poured through me. Thuri's face, troubled on the ship, followed by the storm that blasted us all apart. Me, sputtering as I crawled up the shore. Rivelin, tossing my mother's dagger into the sea. The bastard.

"Daella?" the elf called out through the door.

"Yes, yes, I'm awake." I rolled my eyes at the ceiling. "No one would be able to sleep through all your noise."

"Are you dressed?"

"Do you truly believe I'd risk getting naked anywhere near you?"

A pause. "I'm going to take that as a yes."

The door swung wide and Rivelin stepped into the bedroom. I was immediately struck by how different he looked in the light, how inexplicably...*better*. His silver hair seemed to glisten, the damp strands curly around his sharply pointed ears. And his eyes, they seemed to glow as bright as the sun itself. Even his tanned skin evoked the hazy feel of summer.

I glanced away before my eyes wandered further south to his broad chest. His light brown tunic was tight enough to highlight his biceps, which were...not small.

"Oh. You're still in bed," he said, his voice a bit rough. He was clearly caught off guard, even though *he'd* been the one to storm in on *me*.

And I couldn't help but wonder what he saw now when he looked at me? Did I look better in the light, like him? Or worse? My hair was a wreck from the storm.

Not that it mattered.

"Is there something you want?" I asked.

He held up a bundle of linens. "I brought you a towel and some fresh clothes. There's a bath through the door across the hallway."

"Oh." I sighed. "I can't take a—"

"I've put a bag of salt in the bathing chambers. I think it should be enough," he said gruffly.

I lifted a brow, wondering if I was still asleep and dreaming. "You got me some salt?"

"Don't get excited. I already had some stocked in my cupboards." He held up the towel and the clothes. "Now do you want to stop babbling and get clean, or what?"

I gave him my trademark smile. "You, Rivelin the Blacksmith, are a lot softer than you want everyone to believe."

"If you start thinking that, you're going to be sorely disappointed." He strode across the room, dumped the clothes on the bed, and walked straight out the door without another word.

The bathing chambers were far more luxurious than I'd expected. In fact, I'd assumed I'd find nothing but an old, beat-up tin tub full of cold water. Rivelin might have scrounged up some salt for me, but it was unlikely he'd have taken the time to light a fire, heat up the water, and lug it all the way in here. It would take several trips, at least.

And I was right. He hadn't done any of that. Because he hadn't needed to.

Holding the towel around my chest, I twisted a metal valve and marvelled at the deluge of warm water that spilled through a spout, filling the stone tub in only moments. I'd never seen anything quite like it before. How could a tiny island village have something like this when Fafnir didn't?

It boggled the mind.

After pouring some of the salt into the water, I settled into the soothing heat and sighed.

I might have fallen back asleep like that, for a time. One blink later, the steam from the blazing bath had vanished, and the water had cooled. My body ached from my fight against the sea, the pain settling into my muscles now that I'd had a bit of rest. I could have happily spent the next day and night sleeping, but I had things to do and elves to spy on—and help win some challenges. I probably needed to do both to ensure I got my shot at freedom.

After rinsing off the soap and the flecks of sand still stuck to my skin, I toweled off and changed into the clothes Rivelin had given me. Shockingly, the deep brown trousers fit me like a second skin, and the leather belt was a perfect fit. I pulled a dark green tunic over my head but frowned at how it clung to my stomach and arms. The humid air of the island would soon make this shirt more than a little uncomfortable.

Nevertheless, it was all I had, and beggars can't be choosers.

Back in the bedroom, I combed through my hair with my fingers and pulled the wet strands up into a high ponytail, wishing I had a mirror. I needed Rivelin to see me as pleasantly unthreatening so I could convince him to share his deepest, darkest secrets with me—and the prize from the Games, if we managed to secure the win. If I looked a mess, it'd take a lot longer to get on his good side.

I smoothed down the top of my hair and sighed. This was the best I could manage with what little I had to work with. Time to put on my best smile and do what I came here to do.

8

RIVELIN

"**H**ere, boy." I plucked a slice of bacon from where I'd been cooling it beside the fire, and I tossed it toward Skoll. He caught it midair, his teeth crunching into the crispy meat. He wagged his tail and looked at me expectantly. With a chuckle, I ruffled his fur and turned back to the fire.

The hallway floorboards creaked, and I stiffened. Daella had taken a long damn time in the bath, but now she was coming. Skoll let out a low growl as he sniffed the air. I couldn't remember the last time I had a visitor who wasn't my sister.

Daella walked into the room with a brilliant, though obviously fake, smile on her face but froze when she caught sight of Skoll. His lips curled back to reveal his sharp canines. I expected to see a hint of fear, even if she tried to hide it. Her throat would bob as she swallowed

61

or her hand would shake. Much to my surprise, her eyes brightened. This time, it seemed real.

She knelt and held out a hand toward Skoll. "You have a wolf?"

"A fenrir. His name is Skoll." I kept a close eye on his fangs as he took a sniff of her hand. And then he wagged his tail and licked her fingers. "Huh. He likes you. I'd take that as a compliment. He can be pretty grumpy with strangers."

I knew what was coming the second the words left my mouth. I'd walked right into what she'd say next.

She snorted. "It sounds like you two have a lot in common."

I lifted a brow. "Did you just snort?"

Ignoring me, she turned back to Skoll, ruffling his gray fur. "He's very cute and fluffy. So maybe you don't have that much in common, after all. Where was he last night?"

"Out hunting. He likes to roam the nearby forest at dark."

She stood, and it took me a moment to remember what I'd been doing. I hadn't noticed when she'd first walked in, too focused on what Skoll's reaction to her might be. Then she'd been crouching, so I hadn't seen but...fate be damned, those trousers hugged the curves of her long legs, and that tunic accentuated a pair of perky breasts I hadn't noticed in the shadowy night. And now that her hair was no longer plastered to her long, slender neck...

I frowned at myself. None of those things mattered.

She was *not unattractive*, but she was Isveig's murk, and appreciating even a hint of her felt like a betrayal to everyone I'd once loved.

I turned back to the bacon sizzling on the skillet above the fire. "You hungry?"

"Famished," she admitted.

Feeding the enemy also felt like a betrayal. I hoped my parents weren't rolling in their graves back in our homeland, the Kingdom of Edda.

Still, I couldn't very well starve the girl if I wanted to keep her on my side, so I tossed some bacon and eggs onto a plate, along with some freshly baked bread from Milka's shop down the road, and passed it to Daella before making a plate for myself. By the time I sat at the kitchen table I'd built myself a few years ago, she'd already finished half her food.

"So what's the plan?" Daella asked between bites. "We've got four challenges to do, right? When do we get started?"

"Let's not get ahead of ourselves. First, I have to get chosen for the Games. The opening ceremony is today."

Her chewing slowed, and strangely, I could have sworn a flicker of disappointment went through her eyes. "You mean, we might not even get to compete in these Games of yours?"

"Suddenly eager to help me now, are you?"

"Well, we have a deal. If you don't get chosen, then what? Going to make me sleep curled up in the stables, after all?"

"Then you'll help me out in my shop for the summer until the next ship arrives."

"Hmm. I don't really know anything about smithing." She stabbed her last piece of bacon with her fork and popped it into her mouth.

I folded my arms and leaned back in my chair. "No, I suppose not. Your skill is more on the murdering side."

Her fork scraped against her plate, and she glanced up at me with narrowed eyes. But then the tension vanished, and she smiled—fake again. "Keep talking to me like that, and I'll give you a first-hand demonstration of just how skilled I truly am."

"Careful. Skoll doesn't take kindly to strangers threatening his master."

"Ha. Then why is his tail wagging?" Delight danced in her eyes as she lowered her plate to the floor to let Skoll have the crumbs. He greedily licked them up, and his tail was in fact thumping away with wild abandon. The traitor.

"Skoll," I called out.

He lifted his shaggy head, and I tossed my last slice of bacon toward him. With glee, he snapped his teeth at the air and gobbled it up, and then immediately went back to Daella's plate to thoroughly inspect it for any crumbs he might have missed.

"Competition aside," Daella said, lacing her hands on the table and leaning forward. She blinked her big brown eyes at me. "I have an exceedingly important question. How in fate's name do you have water coming out of a spout?"

"Ah. I should have known you'd wonder about that. It's called running water. We got it after one of the Games a few years back. The winner, our baker Milka, asked the island for an easier way to bathe. It gave us this, far beyond anything we could have dreamed up ourselves."

Her eyes widened. "You're telling the island gave you something as significant as that?"

"I told you," I said. "It can give us anything."

"Then why not ask it for something bigger? Something that could change the world?"

"Most people here don't want to change the world. They just want to improve our lives bit by bit each year."

"You could ask for the death of the emperor."

I draped an arm across my knee and eyed the distance between her hand and my knife. I hadn't given her one with her own plate for very obvious reasons. And now she was trying to lure me into saying I wanted the emperor to die. According to her laws, that would be worth my head. Isveig was a fucking tyrant.

"You can't ask for the death—or even harm—of *anyone*," I said carefully. "But especially not of someone who isn't on the Isles. The magic only works here, like I said."

"But that would solve all your problems, wouldn't it?" she asked. "The death of Emperor Isveig?"

"You speak very casually when your words could get you killed."

She raised her brows. "So you *have* heard about what it's like in the Grundstoff Empire these days."

I knew better than most.

Nodding, I shifted my hand to the left so that my palm covered the knife. "Every now and again, someone washes up on our shores, and that someone is usually from the empire. We've heard about his laws. He forbids anyone to even speak of his death. Doing so puts you on the wrong end of a scythe."

A ghost of a smile flickered across her lips. "The Isles of Fable are not a part of the Grundstoff Empire. So his laws do not apply here."

"You're one of his murks."

"Not by choice."

I sat up a bit at that. "It's in the name, Daella. Mercenary. You're his hired blade, doing his bidding for coin."

"You're right. I have a chest full of ice pennings and a bit of gold. Isveig has tried to keep me happy over the years, and he thought he could buy my loyalty. That doesn't mean it was ever my decision." Her cheeks were bright pink.

My heart pounded as I took in that fire in her eyes. Could I have been wrong about her? Surely not. Daella was infamous around these parts for doing whatever her emperor asked of her.

"So you never signed a contract?" I asked.

She loosed a breath. "No, I did sign a contract, but—"

"Then it was your choice." I shoved back the chair and stood, gathering my plate and hers, before she could try to weave her words in a way that might get under my skin. I knew what she was doing. Fates be damned, I understood because I'd planned to do the same thing to her. She was trying to gain my trust by sharing *just enough* about her that I'd see her in a different light. Her words could be truths or lies. At the end of the day, it didn't really matter. She was here to hunt down Draugr, but she had nothing to go on yet. And so she wanted to reel me in so that I might reveal something to her—accidentally or not.

"You know, for someone who hates the emperor, you don't seem to have much empathy for a girl who has been forced to work for him against her will," she quipped.

"We should talk about the Games." Ignoring her, I moved over to the basin and dropped in the dishes before grabbing an old rag from the wood countertop. "As soon as the ceremony is over, the contestants are thrown right into the first challenge. We'll have to start immediately if we get a place, and I'll need your help."

Daella came over to the basin and leaned against the countertop with crossed arms. "Let me guess. You need my sense of smell." She tapped her nose.

Orcs were well known for their heightened senses, particularly when it came to fire magic. Sometimes, that extended to the other elements as well, but usually only earth and air. They clashed with water in more ways than one.

"I don't think your sense of smell will help us with this first challenge," I said. "We're dealing with water, and I'll have to go out on the lake in a boat."

She flinched. "A freshwater lake?"

"That's right. Last year, the contestants had to search

the lake for the best fish, dive, and capture it in a net. The entire village feasted on the catches at a midnight party afterwards. It likely won't be that again, but it will be something similar," I said, scrubbing the dish and then setting it down on the fresh towel beside the sink. "But you don't have to get in the water. I just need you to help me build the boat and make sure no one tries to sabotage us."

"You mean to tell me your idyllic utopia has saboteurs?" she asked with a laugh. "And here I thought HeartHappy was all sunshine and rainbows."

"Hearthaven," I corrected, wiping the soap suds off my hands. "And we've only had one saboteur over the years. Knowing his luck, he'll probably get a spot in the Games again."

"Again? Sounds like a cheat."

"In more ways than one," I said wryly. "The second time he won, he asked the island to gift him a new paramour every year and then make the previous one forget he binned her, just in case he ever wanted to have her again."

Daella's eyes went wide, her lips curling into a snarl. "And the island gave that to him?"

"Absolutely not. It's against the rules, as that hurts someone. A lot of someones. The problem is, he refuses to accept it." A simmering fire went through my gut. He'd tried it, partially, to gain my sister's affection. "So I'd watch out if I were you."

"Oh, don't you worry." She frowned. "If he broke the rules, shouldn't he be banned from the competition?"

"If only. His mother is Head of the Games, and she's convinced everyone in Wyndale to give him another chance. But mark my words, he won't be able to help himself."

Daella let out a light, tinkling laugh, though the smile on her face was still strained—still fake. I couldn't help but wonder when the last time she'd truly smiled was. Not even Skoll and his wagging tail had brought one out of her.

Her words whispered through my mind, though I knew I couldn't trust them. Still, I wondered…was what she said about Isveig true? Was working for him not her choice?

But as she moved away, she rubbed her hand along her hip—right where a dagger would normally reside. The dagger I'd taken from her and tossed into the sea. My heart hardened, and I shoved away all my softening thoughts. I couldn't trust anything she told me.

9
DAELLA

One moment, Rivelin was talking to me like a normal person would—in complete sentences that weren't wrapped in barbwire, with relaxed shoulders and loose fists. But as we moved out of the kitchen, the grumpy elf I'd met on the beach came roaring back to life. He glared at me as he motioned to the front door and practically barked at me to open it.

I sighed. For a moment there, I thought I'd started to soften some of his hard edges, but no. He had his guard up again. Thankfully, even if Skoll picked up on Rivelin's change in attitude, it didn't make him stop wagging his tail. Such a cute little creature.

A bell clanged in the distance, winding through the morning symphony of birdsong.

The muscles around Rivelin's eyes tightened. "It's

71

time for the opening ceremony. You need anything before we go?"

I plucked at the tunic's hemline. "I know you don't like to share much, but can I ask where you got this tunic? Does it belong to someone, like a sister or...an old lover?"

I didn't know why I'd asked that last bit. I mentally gave myself a quick kick in the head.

"Neither. Why?"

"Someone else, then. A friend?"

"Does it matter?"

"Yes."

"I got them from Tilda. She's about your size and has far more clothes than she knows what to do with. But they belong to you now. She doesn't need them back. Satisfied?"

"You're *certain* she doesn't want them back?"

He sighed. "Yes. Can we go now?"

"It's just, I'm not used to this style, and it's extremely warm. I need a pair of scissors and a moment of privacy." I smiled for good measure. "Please?"

He stared at me for a moment, his expression unreadable, and then he sighed again. "There's a pair of scissors in the desk drawer over there. Just hurry up. We don't have all day."

Before he could change his mind, I grabbed the scissors from the drawer he indicated, where it sat with a pile of parchment, returned to the bedroom, and pulled off the tunic. A few snips later and the tunic was much more bearable in the humid heat. I'd cropped the shirt and cut off the arms, sighing in relief at the soft caress of the air against my bare skin.

When I returned to the living room, where Rivelin was waiting for me, I could have sworn his breath quickened. But when I met his eyes, there was no indication he'd had any reaction to me at all. Which was just as well. I didn't want him getting any wild ideas just because I was exposing a little more skin than he was used to.

"Is that the standard of dress at Fafnir Castle?"

"For me? Yes." I shrugged. "I run hot."

"Hmm." His eyes flicked down to my exposed stomach, and something in his expression tightened as he dragged his gaze back up to my face. Something about the whole situation brought a flush to my cheeks, even though I'd worn outfits like this every day of my life. I'd never before felt so...seen. Not even when Isveig had ogled me. "Just watch out for Gregor. Knowing him, he'll try something when he sees you."

I cocked my head. "The saboteur?"

"The one and only." He opened the door and motioned me down the front steps. When I stepped outside, the gentle breeze brought with it the scent of lilacs and berries, of fresh grass and baking bread, of cedarwood and citrus and wet stone from the morning dew. I closed my eyes and breathed it in, letting the scents consume me, the soothing sensations chasing away the remnants of last night's pain.

Rivelin stepped up beside me, and I felt his eyes on

my face. But he didn't comment on my reaction. He just stood there and let me breathe.

Sighing, I opened my eyes and took in the sight of Wyndale in the morning light. Before the rain-drenched darkness had taken over last night, it had looked like a bustling, bright thing. That had been nothing compared to the sight of it now. Several dirt-packed streets wound through the cheery clusters of buildings—some homes, some shops, some both, like this one. Vines and colorful flowers wound across each one, draping around windows and curling across chimneys. Everywhere I looked, there was life. Even the streets were pockmarked by small bursts of grass, and blackberries seemed to consume the unused wishing well along the way.

Clothes rippled along washing lines. The sound of laughing children echoed from somewhere nearby. A few doors down, a small, squat dwarf perched on an oversized wooden toadstool and puffed from his wooden pipe.

My chest seemed to open up at the sight of it, and a raw ache spread through my soul. I'd dreamed of a place like this all my life. I hadn't been certain one really existed until now. But just as quickly as that thought occurred to me, I pushed it down. On the surface, this idyllic island village looked safe and warm and calm, but it might be nothing but a facade. A way to hide the villagers' use of dragon magic. Or at least *his*. I glanced up at Rivelin, who was still watching me.

"Not as fancy as your Fafnir, I'm guessing," he said in a gruff voice.

I jogged down the steps. "Nothing is as fancy as Fafnir, if your definition of fancy includes lots of stone and cold steel and empty castle halls with about as much soul as a dead man."

Rivelin followed with Skoll right on his heels. "Haven't you lived there all your life, even before your emperor took over?"

"Bit odd you know that about me."

He huffed out a laugh. "You're infamous, Daella."

"Good to know the world is aware of all my amazing qualities," I quipped, though something inside me felt unsettled by what he'd said. What, exactly, had Isveig spread about me? And how much of it was true? From what I'd heard so far, he'd definitely exaggerated when it came to my willingness to work for him. I should have expected as much. He wanted the world to think he had a half-orc under his thumb because she *wanted* to serve him, not because he'd stuck a deadly ice shard in her skin and threatened her.

I opened my mouth to say just that, but we took the corner and ran smack dab into at least two hundred people crowding the road ahead of us. Several tented stalls were stationed along the perimeter of a cobblestone square, merchants selling freshly baked breads, bouquets of flowers, and piping hot tea, even though it was a warm morning at the beginning of summer. Women strode by with ribbons trailing from their hair, and a harpist plucked a tune from where she'd set up in the center of the square, right next to a stone statue of Freya, who embodied the elemental magic running through the bones of the earth.

"The Old Gods," I murmured. The ones my people had worshipped before the arrival of the ice giants, before Fafnir had been taken as part of the Grundstoff Empire, where they only worshipped one—Ullr, who Isveig insisted he was descended from. Not that many believed him, even his own followers.

"Are you surprised?" Rivelin asked, a step closer than I'd realized. At the sudden sound of his deep, husky voice, I almost squeaked.

"Did you really have to sneak up on me like that?"

"I've been standing here the whole time."

"Not that close, you haven't." I pointed at the statue. "And yes, I *am* surprised. Your island is called Hearthaven, and this village is Wyndale. Those names sound more like something you'd find in the human continents across the Northern Ocean. They have different gods than the elves, the orcs, and the pixies do, although the humans who live in Fafnir now worship Ullr."

He gave me an appraising glance. "Good catch. Humans were the first to settle here, ages ago. They named these islands and villages, but they did not bring their gods with them. The folk didn't find the Isles until many years later."

"Where are all the humans now?"

"Most developed wanderlust and left, though a handful remained. Their descendants are still here."

I looked around at the crowd, indeed spotting a small

number of humans amongst the folk. There were also plenty of elves, dwarves, pixies, fire demons, and shadow demons. Unease whispered through me at the sight of the horned creatures. They reminded me far too much of Isveig and his loyal court of giants, even if they were shorter of stature.

Swallowing, I tried to school my features into a mask of calm, but somehow Rivelin saw through it. "If you're looking for one of Isveig's ice giants, you're out of luck. None of them have ever reached this place."

"How disappointing."

Suddenly, a hush went through the crowd, and a tall, golden-haired elf clad in a breezy purple gown clapped her hands. She moved to the center of the square as the harp's song cut off and addressed the gathered residents —and visitors—of Wyndale with a beaming smile.

Rivelin leaned closer and whispered into my ear. "That's Hofsa, Gregor's mother."

She looked like she could be as young as twenty with her smooth, clear skin and those bright sunlit eyes. And when she spoke, her voice was as soothing as the sound of a trickling stream. "Thank you, everyone, for gathering here at our annual opening ceremony to signify the beginning of our Midsummer Games!"

Cries of cheer spilled through the crammed market square. A pink-winged pixie beside me lifted a ribbon above her head, bouncing on her toes. From somewhere nearby, someone tossed rose petals into the air. They rained down, kissing my skin with a soft caress, so unlike the poisonous waters of the sky.

Hofsa waited a moment and let the cheers die down. And then she continued, "As always, fate will decide the lucky seven who will participate in this summer's Games, all to win the coveted gift from our blessed island. If you'd like to put forth your name, please line up to give your blood to Freya."

Blood? I glanced up at Rivelin, my stomach twisting.

Beneath my breath, I whispered, "You didn't tell me I'd have to do this."

"You don't," he said. "I'm the one participating. You're just my assistant."

Rivelin moved off through the crowd, following the others who wanted to volunteer. At least thirty hopefuls lined up to make the sacrifice, Rivelin sandwiched between a dwarf with a long braided beard and a shadow demon who somehow managed to sport a grumpier expression than even Rivelin.

There was little for me to do other than watch the procession. Each potential participant stepped up to the stone statue, cut their palm, and then spilled their blood on Freya's bare feet. It didn't take long for everyone to get through it, and soon, Rivelin started back to my side. Truth be told, I'd expected far more people to present themselves. Why would anyone want to turn down the chance to compete for a gift like that? It wasn't as though the Games were dangerous. No fighting, no killing, no threat.

Rivelin squeezed through the crowd and stood beside me, edging a little closer when a few whispers went through the crowd. They'd finally noticed me, then—the outsider from the Grundstoff Empire. At least I wasn't wearing my armor with Isveig's sigil stamped into my shoulder. I imagined that would *really* get them talking.

"All right!" Hofsa clapped again. "You have all made your sacrifices to our blessed goddess. She will now choose who is worthy to compete in this year's Midsummer Games. Probably best for you all to spread out a little."

I opened my mouth to ask Rivelin why we'd need space when a flame suddenly burst from the top of an elf's head just in front of me—a woman who had been in the line. The flames consumed her brilliant red hair, but then they died in an instant, leaving behind nothing but a black smudge on her forehead. *Magic.* And it was the ancient magic of the Old Gods, the kind that didn't need Galdur sand. The island—or Freya's spirit—truly was choosing the participants for these Games.

The elf folded her arms and beamed. "It's about damn time I got chosen."

A flurry of fires ripped through the crowd, too fast for me to track every one, but I did spot a burly elven man with golden hair just to the left of Hofsa, who caught flame. His eyes were locked on my face, and when he saw me looking, he winked and smiled. From beside me, Rivelin let out a low growl.

Something about that sound sent a flutter through my belly.

Clearly, that was Gregor. I turned toward Rivelin to announce that I could, in fact, take care of myself, thank you very much, but his flaming head stopped the words from leaving my tongue. Relief shuddered across his face as the mask of disinterest—or gruffness, really—momentarily collapsed to show the truth of his emotions. He almost looked *pained* by his relief.

But then the furrowed brow returned. He folded his arms and ignored the applause that followed. I couldn't stop watching him, even as Hofsa droned on about the start of the Games and everything it entailed. I wanted to see another slip, another hint as to what, exactly, was going on inside his head.

I'd known he wanted to participate. From my perspective, anyone would, which was why the low number of volunteers made little sense to me. But Rivelin—he was desperate. He wanted this with every fiber of his being. Luckily for both of us, so did I.

IO

DAELLA

O nce the ceremony was over, the crowd's exuberance only surged more. Music piped through the small market square, and the dancing began. Everyone split into groups, chattering and laughing the morning away. Rivelin, on the other hand, led me to the side of a building where he leaned against the rough timber wall and just stood there staring off into the distance.

I propped my hands on my hips, careful to avoid touching the ice shard, and cocked my head. "Is there a reason we're lurking in the shadows instead of mingling with everyone else?"

"I'm waiting for my sister. She'll be here soon, and then we'll get started on making our boat." His voice was dull—bored.

"For someone who just got chosen to participate in

the Games, you seem pretty underwhelmed. In fact, if I didn't know better, I'd say you were annoyed."

"I don't like these ceremonies or big groups of people."

"I see. Is there anything you do like?"

"What?"

I sighed. "A lot of things annoy you. So what *do* you like?"

He reached down to his side, where Skoll eagerly accepted his pat on the head. "I like Skoll, and I like forging steel. And I like my sister. That's about it."

"That's really it?" I almost felt sorry for him. "This world is full of beautiful things."

"I'm not entirely sure I agree, so I'll stick with my three."

"You can like whatever you want. It's just a shame." I shrugged. "But the scents of this place…the baking bread that curls around you like a hug. The blooming flowers and the fresh grass. The birdsong and the laughter of children that fills the air. The soothing warmth of the sun on your face. All of it just reminds me I'm alive. And I will relish that. We're lucky to experience any of this. Life is a gift far greater than anything your island could give us."

I felt his eyes on me, and a moment passed.

"You're pretty poetic, for a murk," he said.

I sighed. "I told you, I'm not a—"

"Rivelin!" a woman called out.

A bright-eyed, silver-haired elf bustled toward us,

dragging a massive wagon behind her, its tires churning through the soft dirt. She looked so much like her brother, tall and clear skinned and achingly beautiful. But where he wore a frown like it was permanently carved into his face, her smile was like a new summer's day.

A pair of brown trousers hugged her curvy frame, and she wore a pair of sturdy leather boots. She'd have to, dragging that wagon behind her. It was as large as a cottage. I had to admit, I was impressed by her strength.

At the sight of her, Rivelin visibly brightened for the first time since I'd met him. Smiling, he opened his arms as the elven woman dropped the wagon yoke and rushed toward him. He grabbed her around the waist and pulled her in for a hug, but when her eyes caught sight of me, she stopped and swatted at his arm.

I braced myself for her reaction. Just like everyone else in this village, she'd know who I was and where I came from. Even without Isveig's sigil, I stood out in a world where half-orcs were a rarity. Her eyes flicked up and down, but then she held out a hand and smiled.

"Hello. I'm Rivelin's sister, Lilia. Are you..." She slid her gaze sideways at her brother with merriment dancing in her eyes. "Well, I don't know how else to put this. Are you his lady friend?"

"No," he cut in with a frown. "This is Daella Sigursdottir."

I braced myself. If she hadn't known who I was before, she did now.

"Lovely name," she said in a singsong voice. "For a lovely orc. I'd say it's a shame my brother isn't courting you, but it's probably for the best. He can be a bit of a grump."

The corners of my lips twitched. "Only a bit?"

She laughed and elbowed Rivelin's side. "I keep thinking he'll cheer up if he meets someone. You sure you aren't interested? He—"

"Lilia," Rivelin said.

"Oh, come on. Don't frown at me like that. I'm just trying to look out for you." She glanced up at the ash on his forehead, her eyes widening. "You finally got chosen for the Games."

"And it's about fucking time."

"Gregor?"

His eyes darkened. "You were right. He's in it again."

"He *has* to be cheating. No one else has ever been chosen more than once."

"How? He has no Fildur sand to fake the flames. I checked."

Lilia shook her head, her brows pinched. "I refuse to believe Freya legitimately blessed him a *third time in a row*, especially after what he asked for last time."

"You mean the lover thing, don't you?" I asked.

"Rivelin told you about that? Good." She nodded. "He'll probably try to go after you next, and he's persistent. Anyway, enough about bastards. Riv, where can I set up shop?"

"I'll go clear some space in the square for you." Just

before he turned to go, he clasped her shoulder, and that rare smile returned to his face. "I'm glad you're here. Don't make it so long next time, eh?"

She beamed at him. "I make no promises. The Traveling Tavern goes where it's needed."

Rivelin moved off to find somewhere for her wagon, his broad frame pushing through the crowd. I couldn't help but watch him. Even though there were a variety of demons and other elves, he somehow managed to tower over everyone else, and the bright morning sun illuminated the silver in his hair.

Lilia cleared her throat. "So how long have you known my brother?"

I dragged my gaze away from him. Lilia was pulling her long hair back from her face and fanning her neck. It was a hot day already. I felt it deep in my bones, but it didn't bother me quite the same way, as long as I was wearing the right clothes.

"About twelve hours," I said.

"Twelve *hours*? That certainly explains why he's never mentioned you before."

"I was in a shipwreck, and I washed up on shore last night. Rivelin...found me."

Her eyes widened. "Fate be damned, are you all right?"

I rubbed at my arms, still sore from all the rain. "I survived."

"Freya must have been smiling down on you for you to have survived the Elding. Listen, you deserve a fun

85

evening after what you've been through, and my brother probably isn't going to give you one. Stop by my tavern tonight when the sun goes down, and I'll give you a drink on the—"

"Lilia."

The elf's face went bone white as Gregor sauntered out from behind the rear of the wagon. His eyes zeroed in on her, sweeping across her curves and the cleavage highlighted by her low-cut tunic. Lilia's entire demeanor seemed to change in a breath. Her body went taut. Her eyes went hard. Tense lines bracketed her lips.

I shifted a little closer to her, my hand instinctively going to my belt. But there was no dagger there, of course. That damned Rivelin.

Gregor slowed to a stop only an inch from Lilia. With a wicked smile, he propped one hand against the wagon and leaned in to whisper into her ear. I didn't hear his words, but I had a pretty good idea of what was said. Lilia hissed through clenched teeth and then slapped his cheek.

He flinched and reached for her wrist, but before he could touch her, I was there. I slid between the two of them, palmed his chest, and then shoved him up against the wagon with the lethal speed and dexterity I'd honed over the years.

"You can't do this," he growled. "This kind of assault is against the law here."

I smiled as he tried to shove against me. "I know violence is frowned upon in this village, but the thing is,

I'm not from here. Now leave the girl alone, eh? I'd hate to cause a scene in your idyllic utopia."

"You heard her. Get out of here Gregor," a gruff voice said from behind me. My chest tightened. Rivelin was back. No doubt I would get reprimanded thoroughly for this. I just hoped he wouldn't decide to kick me off his Midsummer Games team because of it.

I dropped my hand to my side and stepped back, flashing Gregor a tight smile as he snarled and stalked away. And then I braced myself as I turned to face Rivelin's wrath.

His hard gaze met mine. I held myself still as he took a step toward me. He looked as if he were ready to rip the world apart. But then he lifted a gloved hand to his forehead, rubbed the soot with his thumb, and then reached out to me. His thumb swept across my forehead, the leather soft against my skin, and everything within me went painfully tight. I held my breath, heart thundering, until his hand dropped back to his side.

"Thank you for that." He turned to his sister. "I take it you're all right?"

She nodded, though her face was still pale. "Yes, I'm fine. Thanks, Daella, though I'm sorry you had to do that. He'll have his eye on you now, and he doesn't forget things easily. He hasn't left me alone since I turned down his advances last Midsummer."

"It's fine. I have a lot of experience dealing with bastards like him."

Rivelin gave me another considering look, the kind that felt like he could see straight through me. Based on everything he'd said to me so far, he probably thought I'd only stood up for Lilia to gain his trust, but that couldn't be further from the truth. My instincts had taken over the second Gregor had wandered out from behind the wagon.

"Let's go get you set up, Lilia," Rivelin said, reaching for the wooden yoke that jutted out of the front of the wagon. "Everyone's excited the Traveling Tavern is here. They can't wait to have some of your signature brew."

Together, the elven brother and sister pulled the wagon to a corner of the square, where a crowd was already gathering. I started toward them to help when the intoxicating scent of *dragon* washed over me. My heart jerked into my throat as I whirled in the direction of the breeze, trying to pinpoint the source of it. But then it was gone, almost like a dream.

Pressing my lips together, I fought to remain calm, even as that old familiar fear burned through my veins, flushing my cheeks. In the excitement of the ceremony and from the magic of the morning air, I'd loosened the grip on my priorities. I'd forgotten why I was here. The people of this village might seem decent, but they were hiding a secret that could burn the whole world down.

An hour later, Rivelin took me down a winding dirt path that led out of the village. He went back to his gruff silence, and I went back to covertly searching for any sign of dragon magic. If he was a Draugr, there should be signs. There always was. His eyes could show a hint of it—a flash of orange when he got angry. His skin might feel hotter than expected, even on a summer day. The smell was an obvious indicator, but except for that earlier whiff, the pungent odor was nowhere to be found now.

I thought about reaching out to brush my fingers across his arm, but...my chest tightened at the idea. No, I would not be doing that, thank you.

"So," I said, our boots crunching on some fallen leaves as we passed beneath the lush canopy of the woods near the village. "You're a blacksmith."

"Very clever observation."

"Curious profession, what with all the heat and fire. Elves have an affinity with water. Don't you have some strands of Vatnor magic in your blood?"

"A little. But I like the way heat feels against my hands."

A strangled cough scraped from my throat, and I tried to hide it by stumbling on a tree root and falling flat on my face. Unfortunately, that wasn't the best idea. Pain radiated through my cheek, where it had hit the ground hard. Rivelin wrapped a gloved hand around my arm and hauled me to my feet, our chests brushing because of the closeness. His fingers pressed into me. Even through the gloves, I could tell they were warm and strong but not blazing hot like a Draugr's.

And he held on, still, even though I was back on my feet.

I swallowed.

He shifted closer. I tipped back my head to keep his eyes in my field of vision, taking note of the ripple in his jaw and the slight flare of his nostril.

"Don't think I don't know what you're doing." His breath whispered across my skin, nearly making me shudder.

I tried to take a step away from him, but my back hit a tree. "I don't know what you mean."

"Don't play coy. You're trying to root out information to take back to your emperor. You are a mercenary, Daella. You even admitted you signed his contract."

"And I told you. It wasn't by choice."

"It's always by choice."

"Not when you're me," I insisted, fisting my hands. "His army destroyed the last of the orcs, and there weren't that many of us in the first place. Do you really think I would want to work for a monster like that?"

"They say you live in his castle—that you're his protected little pet."

I flinched. His attention zeroed in on me, like he'd noticed the reaction.

"I've lived in the castle most of my life. Before he came along, I was a serving girl for the king; a very kind, very generous orc. My parents were killed when I was young, and he took me in. Isveig used to visit the castle with his family. We were...friends. And so when he took Fafnir as his, he spared my life—but not my freedom. He keeps me hidden away in a tower when I'm not out on a quest for him. The doors are always locked. None of this was my choice."

The words spilled out of me and left me breathless. With the rough bark scraping against my exposed skin, I lifted my chin and silently dared Rivelin to make another snide remark about my willingness to become one of Isveig's murks. I didn't know why I even cared. I didn't need his approval.

I did need his trust, though.

Still, the idea he might laugh in my face made my heart twist into shredded ribbons. I was not the person he believed me to be, and I desperately wanted him to see it. If he trusted me, maybe he'd lower his defenses a bit, and I could find out where the Draugr were hiding—and if he was one, too.

He exhaled and stepped back, his eyes hooded. "Isveig kept you in captivity?"

"Look at me. I'm half-orc. The only reason he didn't have me killed was because we were friends once."

"And all those quests you do for him...?"

The ice shard throbbed in my hip. "If I don't follow his orders, he'll make sure I never take another breath."

He ground his teeth and moved away, running his fingers through his silken silver strands. "I shouldn't believe you. This could be some story you've made up to gain my trust."

"You're right. It could be."

"He sent you here."

"No, he sent me to the Glass Peaks."

"Why?"

I folded my arms. "Why do you think?"

91

"To track down Draugr. That's what you do. It's what you're good at. Don't try to pretend it's not."

"Oh, I am excellent at it. Is that a problem?"

"It is when it gets innocents killed."

"Innocents?" I let out a bitter laugh. "Please. I've seen what Draugr can do. The magic burns them up, along with everyone else who made the mistake of being near them."

His eyes swept across my face, and I took the opportunity to search the yellow for any sign of that fire. The kind that consumed someone until there was nothing left of them but ash. Those who used the magic—even just once—became corrupted by it. It was impossible to turn away once you had a taste of it. I understood why. The power of it was intoxicating, far greater than even the four elements combined.

Rivelin towered over me. He pulled a dagger from his belt and pressed the tip against my chin. The sharp point dug into my skin, but I did not flinch away. I just kept my hard, steady gaze on his face.

"Do you know why I'm here?" he asked with lethal quiet.

I swallowed, my throat bobbing against the blade. "To win the Midsummer Games."

"No." He leaned in closer. "I'm here to protect the Isles. That includes the Glass Peaks. And I'll protect them from anyone Emperor Isveig sends our way."

"So then he's right. There are Draugr in those mountains. Why would you ever want to defend them? Don't you know what they can do?"

He shook his head. "I shouldn't let you walk away from this."

"And yet you still haven't shoved the tip of that dagger into my neck."

With a growl, he dropped the blade and slammed it into the sheath. "Only because I vowed never to spill blood here unless mortally provoked."

"So you didn't bring me into the secluded woods to stab me? That's a relief, though I think you'll find I'm not that easy to kill."

"We need to collect some wood for the boat."

"Ah yes, for the competition you want me to help you win, just after you threatened me with your dagger."

"I don't trust you," he grunted.

"I don't trust you, either, especially after that."

"Good."

"Fine."

He narrowed his gaze. "You say you've spent your entire life in captivity, except when you're out on quests?"

"Yes. Lucky me."

"On these quests of yours, did you ever spend an evening at a tavern?"

I blinked at him. "Pardon?"

"Have you ever gone out for the night, drinking and dancing at a tavern?"

"Only a moment ago, you were poking my chin with your dagger, and now you want to know if I've ever been out drinking?"

"Well?" He arched a brow. "What's the answer?"

"The answer is no, Rivelin. Isveig always sent guards with me. Or mercenaries, depending on what he was after. They never let me out of their sight."

"Good." He nodded. "Best get moving, then. We have a lot of wood to gather, if we want to make it back on time."

"Time for what?" I asked, but he moved down the path without answering.

II

RIVELIN

I followed Daella out of the woods, my arms loaded up with logs. Her hips swayed as she walked, the curves of her lower back tantalizing where they dipped into her well-fitting trousers. I tried not to look but fates be damned. She might be working for the enemy, but she looked delicious doing it.

Her story today had surprised me, and even though I knew it all might be a lie, I leaned toward belief. Isveig had always been a murderous bastard who had tried to paint his war crimes as noble and just. When he'd invaded Fafnir, he'd been "saving" the world from the dragons and their terrible magic.

He hated orcs. I'd always assumed he'd conquered Fafnir so easily because he had a spy in the court, someone who helped him learn their defenses and how to best them. That person had been Daella, or so I'd thought. Now I wasn't so sure. The look in her eye...that flicker of pain and defiance. The haunted ghost of her fake smile.

It was impossible to feign that kind of pain. I would know.

When we reached the edge of the village, music and laughter already drifted through the air from the market square, where everyone had gathered to celebrate the evening away. Daella and I had been in the woods for hours, gathering branches and sawing logs. She'd spent the time helping me without complaint. In fact, she'd been uncharacteristically silent. I couldn't help but wonder if I'd taken it a bit too far with the dagger. I'd only been trying to get the truth out of her— see if a little extra intensity would get her mask to crack. She was an infamous murk, that kind of thing wouldn't be new to her. I'd assumed she'd take it in stride.

And she had. Until the silence.

A strange sensation clenched my heart, and I frowned. There was no reason to feel guilty. Maybe Lilia's arrival in Wyndale had made me softer than I usually was. That was the only logical explanation.

Back at my home, I unlocked the door to the shop on the ground floor. Hollowed out inside, the room held a brick forge along one wall, where I spent hours of my life surrounded by flickering sparks that filled the air like fireflies. Horseshoes and decorative bracelets hung along the timber beams, and my work table held various hammers and tongs. I motioned to an open spot on the floor beside the anvil.

"Just dump the logs there. I'll sort it all out in the morning."

The wood tumbled from her arms, logs thudding. "Nice shop."

I pulled off my gloves and ran my hand along the smooth steel of the anvil, pride unexpectedly blooming in my chest. "I've worked real hard on it."

"What do you make most of here?" she asked in a too-casual voice. That was when I caught the slight flare of her nostrils, quick as a snake. I kept my expression blank, but inside, my heart kicked my ribs. She should not be able to smell any hint of dragons, and yet...there was that flash in her eyes. That knowing glint.

I fought the urge to search the room for any clue as to what had set her off, but I forced myself to appear relaxed.

"A lot of horseshoes. Candlesticks are also a favorite around here, plus the wagons that roll in for every Midsummer Games always need new fixings."

"Seems like such a waste, what with all this space and your tools. You could craft some incredible daggers and swords."

"You and your fixation on weapons."

"I have a right to be. You threw my mother's dagger into the sea."

I leveled my gaze at her. "I thought we were being more honest with each other now."

"I swear to Freya that's the truth. The dagger you stole from me was once my mother's."

"You don't worship the Old Gods in Fafnir."

She hissed at me—*really* hissed. "I'm tired of arguing with you. I'm going to bed."

Daella, with her fierce, wild eyes and her vibrant intensity, spun on her feet toward the door. I caught her arm. The heat of her body seeped into my hands like a furnace. Steam hissed where we touched, and the collision of our skin sent a thick fog sweeping across us.

She glanced back at me, and her cheeks bloomed like spring flowers. "What's happening?"

"I'm an elf from Edda. We have a bit of Vatnor magic in our blood, and orcs run hot, like you've said. Have you never touched an elf before?"

"No, I can't say I have." Her eyes narrowed. "You go around touching orcs on a regular basis?"

"Unfortunately not," I drawled.

The pink of her cheeks deepened. "If all this is true, shouldn't your touch burn me like fresh water does?"

"It seems not." I cleared my throat. "I want to take you to Lilia's tavern tonight."

The thought had been rattling around in my head ever since she'd told me about her captivity. She'd never been out dancing, and she'd never spent the evening surrounded by rowdy storytellers and their booming laughter. Me, I'd rather sit in the quiet of my living room with the fire blazing and a book in my hand, but there was something in the way Daella carried herself that told me she'd enjoy the magic of these midsummer nights.

Not that her happiness mattered. But I'd promised the others to make her fall in love with this place, so she'd be less likely to tell Isveig about us once she returned to Fafnir. She'd already made it clear she didn't care for her emperor. I was starting to think it wouldn't take much to get her on our side. Hopefully. She seemed pretty dead set on hating dragons.

She scoffed. "You want to...take me to a tavern?"

"The Traveling Tavern. Everyone loves it."

"You are a very confusing person, Rivelin the Blacksmith."

"You're going to be here for weeks. Might as well settle in and enjoy it."

"Fine, let's go to your sister's tavern," she said, swiping aside the steam still fogging the air. "Mind letting go of my arm now?"

I loosened my grip, and instantly, my hand felt cold. The heat of her had been far more welcome than I wanted to think about.

"Shall we go?" she asked in that fake chirpy voice of hers.

I motioned at the door. "After you."

Almost everyone in the village had turned out for the celebration. Paper streamers looped from one end of the square to the other, and lanterns hung from the tree limbs that snaked overhead. Several wooden tables had been crammed into the space, and there wasn't an open spot at any of them. Dozens of attendees wandered through the crowd or broke off into small groups to gossip the night away.

A small stage had been erected just beside Lilia's tavern, where the dwarf bard stomped his foot and sang a tune about the Old Gods. Fireflies darted about, buzzing with the same cheerful energy as everyone else.

Beside me, Daella took it all in, her cheeks flushed. I'd noticed her looking around the village with that same expression a few times now. Her eyes snagged on my sister's tavern, and a slight smile tugged the corners of her lips. I understood why. Lilia's Traveling Tavern was infamous.

She lugged it with her everywhere she went—alone. Her wagon was heavy, but she was strong as fate, and unlike me, she seemed incapable of staying in the same place for long. Ever since we'd found our way to the Isles fourteen years ago, she'd gone from village to village, and even from island to island, searching for something I did not think she even knew.

The wagon itself was decorated with lanterns and silver tapestries that were embroidered with a sigil of two tankards clanking together. A matching awning hung over the open door that led down a set of wooden steps. She stored the extra tankards, ales, and spirits inside, but she had a bar set up outside. Several of the younger elves and dwarves of the village perched on top of the wagon. I knew Lilia didn't like them hanging about up there, but she never reprimanded them. All she'd ever wanted was to make people smile.

We'd turned out so different, she and I.

"Well." Daella's fake smile spread across her face.

Even now, there was no sign of a real one. "I can see why you thought I might want to come here."

"Beats your tower, eh?"

"Everything beats my tower, but especially this. I doubt most taverns are so…"

"Bright and cheery."

The corners of her eyes crinkled. "The opposite of you, really."

"Which is why I'll be leaving you here to enjoy yourself while I return home to start work on the boat. Stay as long as you like. I'll leave the front door unlocked."

Her hand snaked out, quick as lightning. She grabbed my arm before I could turn away. The heat of her blazed through me, and steam filled the space between us. "Not so fast. If anyone needs a night out enjoying themselves, it's you."

I leveled my gaze at her. "I don't do parties."

"Neither do I. And yet, you brought me here."

"Because *you'll* enjoy it."

"Will I?" She motioned at the celebratory square with her free hand. "I don't know anyone other than your sister, who looks very busy, and that bastard Gregor, who I'd rather avoid. So it looks like I'm stuck with you, and you're stuck with me."

I glanced down at her hand on my arm, at the steam hissing from our skin-to-skin contact. Her fingers were softer than I'd expected, and her smooth sage skin was so vibrant and alive next to my tan. So ridiculously beautiful.

I cleared my throat. "All right, I'll stay, but you'll

101

likely regret it. I don't like these kinds of things."

"Maybe that's why I want you to stay. I like the idea of tormenting you." She winked and let go of my arm. The cold air that followed chilled me to the bone.

Without another word, she spun and took off into the party. I sighed and followed, slinging my hands into my pockets and wondering how deeply I'd regret this in an hour or two. As the night wore on, the drinks would flow and the raucous energy of the crowd would become unbearable. Every year, I'd listened to the sounds of it from my open bedroom window. And every year, I'd slammed that window down and tried to sleep despite the noise. I never did.

Daella approached the bar, and Lilia's face visibly brightened, especially when she saw me in the background trying my damndest not to attract much attention. Every single person here knew I hated these kinds of things. I'd really rather they didn't make a fuss.

"I can't believe it," my sister said in her trademark singsong, swiping her hands on her apron. "Freya's fires must have frozen over, because that right there looks like my hermit of a brother."

Daella laughed. "Inside that head of his, you just know he's kicking and screaming."

"How'd you do it?" Lilia asked as she grabbed two tankards from the rack behind her. She lifted the first to a barrel of her infamous brew and arched a brow at Daella.

"I threatened him with a dagger to his throat. Oh, wait. No, that was what he did to me. Something about being the big bad protector of this place."

"Rivelin!" Lilia exclaimed, her frown drawing down the corners of her eyes. "You can't just go around threatening people with daggers."

Daella glanced over her shoulder and smirked. "See? Your sister agrees with me."

"I think I'm going to head home now," I said flatly.

"No, come on. I'm just messing around." Daella passed one of the tankards to me and lifted hers, as if awaiting a toast, brushing aside the whole bit about the dagger. Clearly, it hadn't upset her earlier. I felt relieved, then frowned. Why did it matter if it had?

"I think I might need to separate you two or you'll make life unbearable." Still, I took the offered tankard and knocked mine against Daella's. Froth flowed over the side, coating my fingers, and Daella deftly avoided getting it on her skin. Then she stared at me expectantly, waiting for my toast. Something about the look in her eye made me momentarily forget my frustration.

"To...new alliances," I said.

"To new alliances," she repeated, and then she drank the whole thing down. When she finished, she gasped for air and then coughed, pounding her fist against her chest. Froth covered her top lip like a mustache, and a few droplets of the brew clung to her chin. She winced as if in pain.

"Ah." I reached out and swiped the froth away. She stiffened beneath my touch, steam rising, but she didn't flinch away. "You've got it on your face. You do know it's more enjoyable if you just sip it, right?"

She stared up at me, her eyes bright, then rubbed the

spot with her shirt. "No, I did not know that. I've never had ale before."

"You've never—that is absolutely unacceptable," Lilia interjected with a quick shake of her head. She snatched Daella's empty tankard and poured her another drink. "The first one was on the house for you saving me from that bastard's grubby hands. This one's on the house because every woman deserves to have a little fun sometimes. Drink up and enjoy yourself tonight."

"It's different than what I expected," Daella said, lifting the tankard to her lips and sniffing. "I heard ale was bitter, but this is quite sweet."

"That's Lilia's brew for you," I said with a smile. "It's the best ale in all the Isles, maybe even beyond. I doubt any tavern in the Grundstoff Empire can compare."

She nodded as she took a smaller sip this time. "I believe you must be right."

A few other patrons stumbled up to the bar, and my sister shooed us away with a fond smile and an unfortunate wink in my direction. I knew what she was thinking. She'd said as much before. Daella was a beauty, and there was a spark about her. Lilia had always said I needed someone in my life like that. Someone with edges rough enough to understand me but soft enough to bring a little brightness into my 'dreary hermit life', as she liked to call it.

But what Lilia just didn't understand was that I was happy on my own. I didn't want or need anyone else other than Skoll. In fact, upending my life to make room for someone else would only get in the way of what I needed to do most in this world: protect Hearthaven and the other islands. And even more than that, I couldn't risk trusting the wrong person, let alone one who worked for the emperor—even if they were forced to.

Still, I understood what Lilia saw in the half-orc. With the fireflies dancing around her head, their yellow glow illuminating her brilliant sage-green skin, she looked achingly beautiful tonight.

I cleared my throat and motioned at a nearby elf with long auburn hair. "That's Kari. She's one of the contestants this year. Smart as a whip."

"Good to know. Who else?"

I scanned the crowd and picked out a purple-winged pixie chattering with her partner, a dwarf who, incidentally, had also been chosen this year. Should be interesting. "Those two are in it this year. The pixie's name is Nina. She's a firecracker who loves to cook. Her partner there, Hege, is a carpenter, and she's stronger than she looks."

"She looks pretty damn strong," Daella said, taking another sip of her ale.

"Then we have Godfrey." I pointed to the lanky human lurking by the bar. He was new to the village, and I didn't know much about him. Then I shifted my attention to the fire demon, one of the earliest residents of Wyndale since the humans left. "And that's Viggo. Strong, powerful, determined. I'd say he's the most likely to win, other than me."

"And Gregor of course," Daella said.

"Yes, if he cheats."

"And what's the likelihood of that happening?"

"High. That's why we'll keep an eye on him."

Suddenly, the bard began singing an upbeat tune, his voice wailing through the market square. Half of the folk crammed into the tables leapt to their feet and made space in the center for the dance floor. It was early in the night, but we'd already reached this point. Things were about to get rowdy.

Once there was a northern troll
Whose face looked like a big blue mole!
He pranced around as if to rule
But he was nothing but an icy fool!

Daella turned to me, her eyes sparkling. "This is about Isveig. I've heard rumors that people call him a mountain troll when they think they can get away with it."

I nodded. "Bards are particularly fond of the nickname."

"I have to dance to this," she said in an excited whisper. "It's too fun of a song to pass up."

"You really do hate him," I said with a bemused smile as she downed the rest of her drink.

After handing me her tankard, she joined the dance floor and spun in circles with the others. I found myself tapping my foot after a few moments, watching her whirl and dip and clap to the beat. I was so caught up in the music I didn't notice Gregor approach until his shoulder slammed against mine.

I stiffened as I turned on him, liquid anger racing through my veins. He wore a fitted midnight blue tunic with the sleeves rolled up to his elbows and a glittering golden crown atop his head—the first gift he'd won from the island. The magic of this place hadn't made him king, but it had allowed him to have a crown. What a waste of a gift. Out of instinct, I reached for the dagger at my belt, but he held up his hands in mock surrender.

"Whoa now," he said with a guttural laugh, though there was no merriment in his eyes. "I'm just coming to say hello."

"You never say hello to me, Gregor."

"You got me there." His teeth flashed as he smiled. "Mostly, I wanted to give you a warning. Because of who you are, I'm willing to overlook what your orc friend over there did earlier, but Rivelin, lad, you need to keep her in line. If she attacks me again, I'll be forced to do something about it."

A low, simmering anger swept through me. Fisting my hands, I took a step toward him. "Are you threatening her?"

He tsked. "She was the one threatening me."

"Stay away from Daella."

Gregor shook his head. "You know she's one of Isveig's murks, don't you? Surely her ass isn't sweet enough to make you forget that, although..." His eyes drifted toward the dance floor, and an eager glint lit his golden eyes. "I did ask for Freya to gift me with a new lover. Interesting how the lass showed up right in time for Midsummer."

"I said stay away from her." My hand went to my

dagger hilt. "And if you make me say it a third time, you'll sorely regret it."

Tension curdled the air between us. He stared at me, and I stared at him, and I couldn't be sure which way this would end. He'd either back down, or I'd make my move. Gregor had been here for a few years longer than I had, but at the end of the day, I protected this island. I'd gladly protect it from him, if need be.

After a long, excruciating moment, he loosed a breath and stepped back. "Speak of the fucking devil." And then he wandered off.

A body collided into me before I could turn, but somehow I knew—*I felt*—it was her. I turned and caught her arms just in time. Her knees buckled, and her flushed face aimed for the ground. A hiss went through the air as I held her up, pulling her against my chest.

"Think I drank. Too much," she slurred as she looked up at me with bleary eyes.

I couldn't help but chuckle. "You downed two pints in the space of ten minutes when you've never had a drink before."

She nodded. "In hindsight. Bad idea."

"Let's get you home."

"Mmmm. Far. Legs no work."

A pause. "I'll carry you."

"*What?*"

"Don't overreact." Before she could try to talk me out of it, I looped my arms under her legs and hauled her from the ground. Her head dropped against my chest, and she sighed.

"Embarrassing."

"Don't be. It happens to everyone at least once."

"Not you, I bet."

"You'd be surprised."

She lifted her head for a moment to pin her narrowed gaze on me. "But. Grouchy and brooding."

Shaking my head, I carried her away from the dance floor and toward the road that led back to my shop. The laughter and music and buzz of conversation faded into a dull roar, and shadows crept around the corners of the buildings to replace the lantern light. Daella relaxed into me, closing her eyes.

I carried her up the steps and through the door, and then went straight to the bedroom. When I lowered her onto the bed after pulling back the quilt, she grabbed my hand. Steam whorled between us.

"Thank you," she whispered.

My heart clenched. "You're welcome, Daella."

Almost instantly, she fell asleep. I pulled the covers across her body, and then grabbed a glass of water from the kitchen. I tried not to think too much on what I'd done—that I'd spent my evening looking after someone who worked for the enemy, and that I didn't regret a single moment of it.

In fact, for the first time in a very long while, I didn't spend my midnight hours on the roof glaring at the stars. I went straight to the sofa, and I slept. Perhaps it was because I might have my enemy right where I wanted her.

12

DAELLA

My head felt as if it had been sawed in half, like the logs I'd spent all yesterday collecting. Blearily, I cracked open my eyes and squinted up at the ceiling. Wooden beams crisscrossed overhead, illuminated by the orange glow spilling in through the windows. Ouch. The light hurt, too.

Last night…it had been achingly brief, thanks to my drinking a measly two pints too quickly. But my heart swelled when I thought of the market square. All those lanterns filling everyone's faces with light. The bard and his silly song about Isveig. The taste of Lilia's brew on my tongue, sweet and intoxicating. And Rivelin…

My heart beat a little faster. He'd carried me home and tucked me into bed, and there, on the bedside table, he'd left water.

The irritable, angry elf who hated everything I was and everything about where I came from. He'd taken care of me. Obviously, it hadn't been an entirely selfless move. I was his assistant for the Games, and he needed my help to build the boat. If he'd left me there to down a few more pints, I'd be nothing short of useless for the entire day. I'd never been drunk myself, but I'd seen plenty of the castle denizens back in Fafnir vomiting up their lungs after a particularly raucous feast.

It was the only explanation that made sense—he didn't want me to be a burden when he needed my help. Only hours earlier, he'd trapped me against a tree and put a dagger to my throat. And then he'd decided to *carry me*.

With a steadying breath, I threw aside the quilt and put my bare feet on the floor. I didn't remember taking my shoes off last night. Had he done that, too? I blinked at the water on the bedside table, my mind struggling to make sense of the past few days. It all suddenly felt too real—too big to comprehend.

I'd spent so long in captivity or traipsing through the empire doing Isveig's bidding that freedom always felt like an impossibility—even a brief moment of it. And now I was here in a strange land surrounded by strange people, and I'd never felt more light, like a heavy weight had finally fallen from my shoulders. I hadn't seen it coming. I'd never even dreamed something like this could happen to me, and since being here, a part of me had tried to avoid thinking about what this could mean.

That there truly was a life outside of Fafnir Castle. That, if I played my cards right, a place like this could be my future, not just a passing dream.

Sighing, I drank the water and then wandered out of the bedroom, following the scent of food. The living room was silent and empty, and there was no sign of Rivelin or Skoll, though the blanket on the sofa had been folded into a neat little square and placed on top of his pillow.

I nibbled on my bottom lip, a guilty twang going through me. Perhaps we should take turns on the sofa. It only seemed fair.

The scent of crispy bacon and fried potatoes led me through the archway into the kitchen. A plate of food had been left on the counter, covered by a cloth. While I'd been sleeping the drink away, Rivelin had been up and at 'em, cooking me breakfast and getting a head-start on the day.

Perhaps...perhaps I'd been wrong to judge him the way I had. He might not walk around with a smile on his face, but neither did I—at least not a real one. And there might be the scent of dragon in his room, but...well, I couldn't think of a good explanation for that one. He didn't act like a Draugr, at least any I'd met. He didn't have that wildness, that cruelty in his eyes. And his hands, when they touched me...I shivered just thinking of the steam that hissed between us.

In the privacy of my own thoughts, I could admit something about it felt thrilling. Toe-curling, almost.

As I ate, I heard a hammer thudding behind the building. I finished my food, carefully rinsed my plate, and left it to dry on the counter before looking out the window. Rivelin was out back with yesterday's wood piled around him. He'd lined up the larger of the logs in a row and stood above them, his bare chest glistening in the baking sun.

My stomach flipped as a delicious heat seared me. His broad chest was home to mountainous peaks that spoke of hard-earned strength and power. Fingers tensing, I couldn't help but wonder what those ridges felt like. Would just one touch be like the spray of the storm-tossed sea? Would those muscles rumble against my hands like thunder?

I blinked and sucked in a breath when I realized the torrid direction of my thoughts. What in fate's name was wrong with me? It wasn't as if I'd never seen a man's bare chest before. In fact, at court, Isveig liked to parade around half-naked with his entourage, making certain every woman in the castle got a glimpse.

"Right." I wiped my sweaty palms on my trousers, and my palm brushed a splatter of dirt. I was still wearing the same thing I'd worn all day yesterday. Rivelin likely expected me to join him after I bathed, and truth be told I probably owed him that, at least.

And then I remembered.

As soon as I'd stepped inside his blacksmith shop last night, the scent of dragon had been so strong I'd almost gagged. In the haze of the celebration, I'd forgotten all about it. After everything he'd done—and who he was showing himself to be—I didn't want to think the worst of him. I wanted to trust him, fates be damned. I shouldn't want it. I really, truly shouldn't.

Just like I never should have trusted Isveig.

A whistling breath escaped from my throat, and I stole across the floor to the door that led down the stairs and into his blacksmith shop. While he was busy building the boat, I'd just take a quick look around, more to confirm he wasn't playing with fire than to confirm he was. I didn't want to find any evidence, but my nose had never lied to me.

I just had to hope there was a good explanation.

The steps creaked as I inched into the shop. I quietly shut the door behind me, and the scent of dragon hit me like a punch. My eyes nearly watered from the force of it, from the all-consuming pull I'd always felt toward that power. As I tiptoed past the anvil—almost as tall as me and twice as wide—I breathed through my mouth to give me some relief from the onslaught.

But my throat burned and my gut twisted and every hair on my arms stood on end.

I shuddered, sweeping my eyes across a collection of hammers and some horseshoes hung along the wooden beam to my right. The truth was as thick and cloying as the scent. I'd wanted to give Rivelin the benefit of the doubt, but there was no mistaking the depths of his involvement with this. He couldn't have picked this scent up by accident. For it to be this strong, he'd been near a dragon or he'd used their volatile magic himself. Very recently.

If he was using dragon magic, he was a Draugr, and I had to stop him. And the entire village, too, if they were involved. All the kindness he'd shown me, it had been nothing but a lie to get me to trust him, to look the other way.

I stole a glance over my shoulder to make certain he hadn't wandered back into the house. The heavy thud of his boots would give me enough warning to get out of here, but thankfully, the only answering sound was distant birdsong.

He'd only shown me his shop for the briefest of moments. And he'd been acting oddly, too, likely suspecting I might sniff out the truth. Perhaps he'd hidden some evidence somewhere amidst all the horse-shoes and hammers and tongs. If I could find that, I could be certain I was doing the right thing by telling Isveig about this place when I left—if we didn't win the Midsummer Games, of course. Then I'd have to take care of the dragon magic problem myself. How? I had no idea, but I'd cross that bridge when I came to it.

There were few places in the shop someone might hide something. Inside the forge itself was a possibility. What better way to throw someone off the scent than by burying any contraband beneath a pile of charred coals? Of course, then I likely wouldn't scent dragon at all. Coal hid smells extremely well.

Rivelin also had some barrels packed full of various tools: axes, long-handled hammers, and a couple of spears. I shoved my face into the barrel and took a long sniff but found no dragon magic there.

That left the closet in the corner. With furtive steps, I crossed the room and reached the back wall with one ear still listening for footsteps. I frowned as I looked at the closet's door handle. There was no lock.

This felt wrong somehow, but if I didn't check, I might never confirm the truth.

And so I yanked open the door and looked inside.

Rows upon rows of swords lined the closet walls. Each one was unique and expertly crafted. Designs swirled across the blades, gemstones had been inlaid along the hilts, and some pommels had been carved in the shape of various animals. I was struck by the beauty of it all—the incredible talent needed to create these. Each and every one was like a piece of art.

"Trying to find the perfect weapon to wield against me?" Rivelin said from behind me.

I yelped, my heart leaping into my throat. As I turned to face him, I braced myself for the angry lines that would bracket his mouth, but instead, his eyes roamed across my face, almost...curious.

"I'm sorry, I was just having a look around," I said. It was close enough to the truth.

"In my weapons closet?"

"Well, I didn't know it was a weapons closet until I opened it. A pretty impressive one, I'll admit. Have you made all of these?"

He nodded warily. "I'm a blacksmith. That's what we do."

"True. It's just...you made a big deal about this island and your no-weapons law. I'm surprised to find you have so many swords."

"I don't use them, nor do I announce their presence.

They're supposed to be safely hidden away in my closet."

"There's no lock on the door," I pointed out.

"I don't normally have intruders poking around my shop."

"I'm offended. I'm not an intruder. I'm a..."

He raised his brow, waiting for the rest of my sentence. Truthfully, I kind of was an intruder, at least to the island at large. I'd been sent here by the enemy emperor to find some people to capture. Maybe not this specific island, but close enough. And I had every intention to keep up my end of the bargain if we didn't win these Games. Because if I didn't, I'd never go free.

So Rivelin did have a point.

I decided to change the direction of the conversation. "These aren't just any swords. The craftsmanship is incredible. The pommel here—is that a dain?"

"I'm surprised you know of dains."

"I came across some in a forest once when I was...anyway, it is a remarkable resemblance."

Dain were deer who feasted on a particular type of plant only found in the deepest parts of the forests of Edda. They had elven features with their sharply pointed ears and long lives. Some said they were somehow distantly related, though I'd always thought that story was more myth than truth. Perhaps I'd been wrong.

Rivelin gave me a long, lingering look before he replied. "Thank you, I think. I spent a long time on that one."

"It looks like you spent ages on all of them. How did you learn to do all this?"

A shutter went over his eyes. "My parents."

"Are they here on the islands, too, like your sister?"

"No, not here," he said, his voice clipped. "They're dead. The emperor's murks killed them."

Oh.

I stared at him, my heart thundering, unable to find the right words. I should have known as much with the way Rivelin spoke about Isveig and his mercenaries. His feelings toward the emperor went far deeper than mere dislike. He held a grudge. A big one. And I understood far better than I could ever explain.

Isveig had killed a lot of people. And if he hadn't done the deed himself, his warriors, his guards, and his mercenaries had done it for him. *I* had done it for him. Regret wound through me.

Rivelin grabbed a leather satchel from the table beside his anvil and made for the shop's front door.

"Where are you going?" I asked, my voice hoarse from the conflicting emotions pumping through me.

"Out," he tossed over his shoulder. "Don't follow me."

I frowned. "Don't we need to work on the boat? The first trial starts tomorrow, doesn't it?"

"We'll work on it later. I need some space." He reached the door and shoved it open.

"Rivelin, wait," I felt compelled to say, though I didn't know why. The scent of dragon made it clear he was my enemy. I shouldn't feel so eager to smooth things over, and yet, the words had come of their own accord.

He paused, one hand on the door. "Close the closet and don't touch anything in there. I'll know if you do."

And then he was gone.

13

DAELLA

hen Rivelin returned, he reeked of dragon. I'd spent a good twelve hours in his back garden assembling the boat, with rivulets of sweat trailing down the back of my neck. Skoll had sat with me for a time as if observing my work, occasionally growling his approval. It had taken the entirety of the day, but eventually I finished the boat as best I could. My hands looked like they'd gotten into a fight with a cat, and my muscles ached, but I felt damn good. Useful and tired in the best kind of way—like I'd earned the cup of tea that now steamed in my hands. Funny thing about orcs, fresh water burned our skin, but we could drink it easily enough.

And so I'd helped myself to Rivelin's herbal tea bags, choosing a chamomile and lavender mix, and then settled into the armchair in the living room while Skoll curled up on the rug beside me. The second I'd tucked my feet beneath me, the front door flung wide open and the elf charged in like he was itching for a fight.

And he smelled like a fates-damned dragon.

Skoll lifted his head and sniffed. Could he smell it, too? He probably could.

All my senses went on high alert, but I schooled my features into an easy smile.

Rivelin narrowed his gaze at me as he kicked the door shut. "What are you doing?"

"Having a cup of tea," I said sweetly. "Would you like one?"

"Tea."

"Yes, tea..."

"You're still here. Drinking tea."

I blinked, taken aback. "If you wanted me to leave, you should have said so. I just thought you wanted some space after the weapons closet incident. Since that's, you know, what you said."

"The weapons closet incident," he repeated.

Slowly, I put down my mug and unwound myself from the armchair. "I think I've missed something."

"You had access to all those swords," he said with a frown. "I assumed you'd take one, or even a few so you could sell them for coin, and then you'd be on your way out of Wyndale."

"And why would I do that?"

"To find somewhere else to stay until you can leave this island to sail for the Glass Peaks. If you took the swords and sold them, you wouldn't have to stay here and help me with the Games. You had an easy way out. I assumed you'd take it."

"I see," I said quietly. "And did you want me to take it?"

A tense silence hung between us as I waited for his reply. My breathing went shallow, not that I cared if he'd hoped to find his house empty when he returned home. If he wanted me to leave, so be it. It was a shame I'd miss out on the Games, but I had options. I would still find out the village's secrets. I would still track down the source of that scent. And Isveig would free me. That was the only thing that mattered.

Still, my sweaty palms and thundering heart made the wait for his answer almost unbearable.

"I need your help. With the Games," he eventually said.

"So you *don't* want me to leave?"

"Not particularly." He eyed the nightclothes I wore and the mug on the table, almost like he was seeing them both for the first time. "You look like you're settling in for the night."

"It's late, and I'm tired. Is that a problem?"

"The first event kicks off in the morning." He frowned and rubbed his jaw. "The boat's only half done. I'll need to—"

"*Fully* done. I finished it while you were out doing... whatever it was you were doing." Sitting in a dragon's nest, probably.

"You..." He narrowed his eyes. "You're telling me you finished building the boat by yourself?"

123

"And it's a good thing I did. I doubt your neighbors would be thrilled with noisy pounding all night."

Something flashed in his eyes. "If it came from inside the house, I doubt they'd hear."

"Well, yes, but I don't think you want to build a boat inside your living room."

The corners of his lips twitched, and then he motioned at my tea before I could ask him what, exactly, was so funny. "I didn't take you for a tea drinker."

"And I didn't take *you* as someone who would have fifteen different kinds of tea in his cupboard." Speaking of, it was probably starting to get cold, and I *hated* cold tea, much like I hated most cold things. I grabbed my mug and took a sip. It was no longer piping hot, but it would do.

"And I didn't take you for someone who would pass up stealing my swords."

I lifted a brow. "I'd say I didn't take you for someone who would have a secret stash of swords, but that pretty much fits. They are a lot more...*artistic* than I would have expected, though."

"It seems we've both made snap judgements."

"Never judge a book by its cover."

"I don't know if I'd go that far," he said. "If a book has an intriguing cover, I'm much more interested in opening those pages and finding out exactly what awaits me inside."

There was something in his voice. It was almost as if it had dropped an octave. And his tone had shifted into something that reminded me of a velvety caress. Flushing, I took a quick sip of my tea to mask my reaction, along with the fact that I'd just noticed how he'd rolled up his sleeves to reveal his powerful forearms. Why in fate's name was I looking at that?

He took a step toward me, and my body tensed. I still had my tea mug to my lips, and the liquid flew down my throat. I choked, sputtering up all over my shirt and making an absolute fates-damned idiot out of myself.

The lukewarm liquid dripped down my chin, leaving a trail of pain in its wake. I brushed it aside with my shirt and lifted my gaze to find Rivelin practically grinning.

"Everything all right, Daella?" My name rolled off his tongue like a decadent piece of chocolate.

"I think I'm done with my tea for the night."

"Probably for the best since you're spilling as much of it as you're drinking."

"Very funny. I'm glad I can be a source of amusement for you."

He chuckled as I left the living room to rinse the cup. When I returned, he was already spreading his blanket across the sofa. His bed for the night. I hadn't planned on going to sleep just yet, but I couldn't very well stay in here now. The idea of sitting in the armchair while he lay down…it felt far too intimate.

Because he smelled like a dragon. That was why. There was no other reason I felt on edge.

And so I wandered toward the hallway as Rivelin called out behind me. "Good night, Daella."

I swallowed. What was wrong with me? "Night, Rivelin."

After I walked into the bedroom and shut the door, I noted the dragon scent had faded. And it had been so strong, so spicy and intoxicating, it felt odd now that it was gone. Like something essential was missing.

T he next morning, Rivelin was practically vibrating with intensity. I found him in the back garden looking over my handiwork from the day before. Based on the shadows beneath his eyes, he'd clearly struggled to sleep. He ran his massive hands along the ropes I'd used to tie the logs together. Admittedly, the thing was more like a raft than a boat, but it wasn't as though I'd ever built a damn ship before.

"This is going to be a problem," he said in a gruff voice that prickled my irritation.

"You're welcome, Rivelin. I know you ran off to waste all of yesterday grumping around wherever it was you went. Probably the woods." Or a dragon lair. "You really are lucky I took it upon myself to finish your boat. Otherwise, you'd have nothing."

"You're my assistant," he said through gritted teeth. "The rules state that you have to engage in every challenge."

"And I did. I built your fucking boat."

"You built a raft, Daella. And you have to come with me onto the lake."

My blood ran cold. "Pardon?"

"You can't stay on shore. You have to come. If you don't, we forfeit our place in the Midsummer Games."

It was then I truly understood the depths of his aggravation. I stared at the raft, seeing it with new eyes. Yesterday, I'd pieced it together imagining a single person—Rivelin—maneuvering it across the lake without worrying about water spilling through the cracks between logs and seeping into his trousers. Or splashing over the side. Or potentially capsizing if the thing was just a tad on the too-small side. He would right it and climb back on and all would be well.

Me, on the other hand...

"I can't go on that."

"I know."

"My skin is *allergic* to fresh water."

"I know."

I started pacing. "We have some other logs I didn't use. If we pile some on top of what we already have—"

"The raft will sink." He ran a hand down his face and sighed. "This is my fault. I should have come out here last night to see how it looked instead of waiting until this morning."

"Well, what you should have done was not storm off yesterday."

"I didn't *storm off.*"

"You did."

He glared at me, but I just smiled back. After a moment, he shook his head. "You know, I can tell your smile isn't genuine."

"What else do you expect? I'm about to have a grand old time on your raft."

"No, you're not," he said quietly.

"What?"

"We may not get along well—"

"You think?"

He narrowed his eyes. "If you would just let me finish."

I motioned for him to continue, and then mimed buttoning my lips.

"We may not get along well," he tried again, "but I'm not going to put you through that. I'll forfeit my spot in the Games and try again next year."

Panic clawed its way up my throat—funny I felt more alarmed by losing the chance at the island's gift than getting drenched by lake water. "No!"

He frowned. "Daella, you will get wet."

"Yes, but..." How could I phrase this? "I believe in your mission. You want to protect everyone from Isveig. So do I." Just as long as they weren't Draugr.

"There isn't room for both of us on that raft," he pointed out.

"Well." I flushed. "I'm sure there's a way to make it work."

He propped his hands on his waist and stared at the ridiculous contraption I'd spent so many hours building. In the light of everything else, it looked a mess. The edges of the logs weren't lined up, and the rope was frayed and far too thin for my liking. The last thing I wanted was to share the thing with Rivelin, but what else were we to do?

"You'll have to sit on my lap," he finally said.

Rivelin heaved the raft into his arms and carried it through the house and out onto the front steps, like the thing weighed no more than a feather. A moment later, he came back inside and rooted around in a trunk before handing me some leather oilcloth—it was waterproof, apparently, though I wasn't convinced. The material was thick and far too warm for summer weather, but I'd rather be sweaty than shivering in pain.

After changing into the oilcloth, I stomped outside in waxed leather boots. Instantly, the morning sun baked me. Rivelin looked me up and down, then nodded in satisfaction. "You sure you don't want something to cover your face?"

"As long as you don't tip the thing sideways, it should be fine," I snapped, scowling.

He chuckled.

"What?"

"It's just nice to see your true nature come out."

"And what true nature would that be?"

"You try to pretend that you're cheerful all the time, but inside, you're just as prickly as I am."

I scoffed. "*No one* is as prickly as you are."

A bell chimed in the distance, and a flock of blackbirds scattered into the air, their retreating bodies flecks of black against the clear sky, like grains of peppercorns.

Rivelin's smile dropped as he gathered the raft in his arms. "That's the signal. We need to go."

"All right." Nervously, I pressed down the front of the oilcloth, thick and clammy against my skin. My gloves made it so I couldn't feel the material at all, and my senses seemed dulled because of it—like I was blind in one eye.

Rivelin paused. "You can still say no to this. If it's too much, I'll understand if you want to back out."

I shook my head. "I never back out."

"Then we've got a trial to win."

14

DAELLA

We found the lake beyond a copse of trees on the other side of the village. Everyone else had beaten us there, and it felt like the entire village had spilled out of their packed homes to bask in the sun along the shore. Hundreds of spectators milled through merchant tents scattered across the hill, including the Traveling Tavern, where Lilia was already busy with a long line of patrons.

Six other boats of various shapes and sizes were lined up on the bank where the contestants were gathered. A couple of them were rafts, though they were much larger than ours. Some were proper boats. Gregor stood with crossed arms sizing up the competition. His boat was twice as large as any others and looked far sturdier than anticipated.

"He couldn't have built that in one day," I muttered to Rivelin as we approached the lake.

"You're right. But he'll have made sure there's no way to prove it. That's how he wins."

"Shouldn't the magic be able to tell? If you cheat, why would it give you the win?"

"The magic isn't what gives you the win," he said. "It's everyone else, all these spectators. If they vote him the winner, he's the winner. The only way he's out is if he fails to finish a task, breaks a village law, or gets caught cheating."

I frowned. "So even if we do better than him, he could win on popularity alone."

"The last thing Gregor can call himself is popular."

Rivelin carried the raft to the end of the line and deposited the mangled thing on the sand. A flash of guilt went through me when I saw how small it looked compared to the others. I truly had done a terrible job.

Hofsa whispered in from the crowd, wearing another glorious gown that flowed around her long, lean legs. This time, it was a blue as brilliant as the sky. As she approached the contestants, the roar from the spectators dropped to a pregnant silence. Everyone stopped what they were doing to divert their full attention to the fourteen of us readying ourselves for the Games. Seven contestants. Seven assistants.

A nervous tingle lit up my insides. Rivelin had explained these challenges were just for fun and that no one took it too seriously, but there was lightning in the air. I could feel the scorch of it, even through the thick oilcloth coating my skin.

Hofsa clapped and motioned to the fourteen of us.

"The Vatnor Trial is officially upon us and will launch this year's Midsummer Games. Contestants, including their assistants, must board their homemade ships and sail to the other side of the lake where the water meets the woods. There, they will hunt for one of the many flags we've left there for you to find." She paused and smiled. "When the drumbeat sounds, go."

The roar of the cheering spectators washed over me. Swallowing, I grabbed one side of the raft and helped Rivelin tug it closer to the edge of the crystalline blue water. My heart thundered; tension spiked me like a deadly spear. As soon as I climbed on that raft, there truly was no turning back. When we were out on the water, I would be fully submerged in this task, and I'd have no choice but to see it through. It wasn't as if I could swim back.

Rivelin seemed to read my mind. He leaned forward and cupped my elbow in a reassuring grip. "You ready?"

"No." I swallowed again. "So whoever is fastest wins, right?"

"Not necessarily. If someone doesn't play fair, they won't vote for him to win," he replied in a low voice, his gaze drifting over my shoulder. I knew who he was looking at: Gregor. If anyone would try to shove me in the water, it'd be him. Possibly because I hadn't exactly been...polite, shall we say?

"Does he know about my condition?" I whispered.

"The entire world knows. Orcs like you are things of legend, Daella."

I didn't want to be a thing of legend. I just wanted to

133

get through this trial without having a rush of water close in over my head. Swimming had never been my strong point. Yes, Isveig had trained me to paddle in the sea, but I'd never been particularly good at it. Even with the salt protecting me, I'd never been able to fully relax. I could manage for a few moments at a time but that was about it.

A thread of silence wound through the waiting contestants and their assistants. Sweat trickled down the back of my neck and into my oilcloth as the sun beat down on my head. I flared my nostrils, breathing in the collision of scents all around me. The sweetness of the flowers blooming along the bank of the lake. The intoxicating scent of Lilia's brew from the hands of a pixie only a few feet away from us. The freshly baked bread from one of the market tents. I let it all fill me up until nothing else existed, least of all my fear.

It was a trick I'd learned a long time ago, every time Isveig sent me on a quest I did not wish to complete. Scents soothed me. They steadied me. They made me feel like I could take on any enemy, and win.

Just not Isveig. Never Isveig.

One day I will be free of him.

The drumbeat sounded, and everyone on the beach sprang into action. Rivelin grabbed the raft and shoved it out onto the water. A second later, he wrapped his arms around my waist and hauled me into the air. A squeak shot from my parted lips.

"What are you doing? This is not part of the plan." I swatted at his arm.

He kept his grip on me, wading into the water and shoving the raft further out with his boot. "I knew you'd argue if I told you about it."

"This is ridiculous." Still, it was keeping me dry. He pushed the raft a little further, and then somehow flipped in midair, violently plopping the both of us on the wood. My teeth snapped together, but only a small rush of water spread over the logs. It receded just as quickly, barely skimming my trousers.

But only a moment later, the raft started bucking around like a wild horse as Rivelin tried to find the right position. I found myself with a death grip on his thighs. His strong hands enveloped my waist, and he tugged me closer. My backside slid right into the center of his crossed legs.

My heart fluttered through my chest. I tried to focus on anything other than the way his muscles shifted against me, the way his strong, powerful body pressed against my back. And I tried to shove away the thought that roared through my mind.

This was not entirely unpleasant.

All my life, I'd been on my own. I'd had to depend on myself. No one else. I liked it that way. Anytime I'd ever trusted someone, he'd betrayed me. Or used me. In Isveig's case, he'd done both. But the way Rivelin had formed this protective cocoon around me to shield me from the lake's water...felt *nice*. Even if he was only doing it so we could win.

"You going to help?" He barked the words and

shoved an oar into my hands, breaking me free of my ridiculous reverie.

I blinked and dipped the large end of the oar into the lake, though I truly had no clue what I was doing. Rivelin used the rear paddle to steer us in the right direction while I put my brute force behind my row. Much to my surprise, this tactic seemed to work. Our little raft aimed right toward the opposite bank, where several deer scampered away from the rocks and vanished deep into the woodland. A handful of trees seemed to sprout from the very water itself, their reflections elongating their spindly forms and the kaleidoscope of orange, red, and green leaves.

It was a beautiful sight. Except for the fact every other boat but one was ahead of us.

I narrowed my eyes and rowed faster. Gregor was right at the front. In moments, he'd reach the shore far before everyone else. His assistant was a shadow demon, long and lean with shoulders the size of my head. He sat in front of the boat, rowing furiously, while Gregor lounged in the back barely breaking a sweat.

With a low growl, I paddled even faster, but we barely skimmed across the lake, even as my arms began to ache and the sweat thickened beneath the clammy oilcloth.

Rivelin leaned forward, and his breath whispered across the exposed skin on my cheek. "Keep rowing like that, and you're going to flip us over."

"We can't let that bastard win," I said through clenched teeth.

"Even if he wins this one, that doesn't mean he'll win the whole thing." But despite his words, there was a sense of resignation in his tone, like he'd known the second we got on this raft that we'd never win. All the other contestants had split away from us almost immediately. I craned my head over my shoulder. The boat behind us must have broken just after leaving the shore. Nina, the purple-winged pixie, was paddling back to the festival while her assistant was trying—and failing—to rid the boat of water. They wouldn't even finish the task.

"See?" Rivelin said in a too-calm voice. "We won't come last."

"I don't know why you're not more upset about this. This is *your* competition. Don't you want to win?"

"More than anything," he said quietly, his words nearly drowned out beneath the rush of my oar through the water. "But right now, I want to focus on getting through this without you getting hurt. So just row, Daella. I'll take care of the rest."

My breath stilled in my lungs. There it was again. That strange, intoxicating feeling that someone else besides my own damn self was looking out for me. But the strangest part of it all was who it was coming from. I shouldn't like it. And I shouldn't embrace it. Even now, I could smell the hint of dragon on him.

Still, I kept rowing, my eyes narrowed on the boats ahead. After a few moments passed by, Gregor reached the shore and sent his shadow demon assistant off into the woods to find the flag. It didn't take long for the rest of the contestants to arrive behind him. Most left their assistants to wait while they dashed through the towering oaks.

By the time we reached the bank ourselves, one of the contestants—Viggo, the fire demon—had already returned with his flag. He leapt into his boat as his dwarf assistant shoved them back into the water. And then they were off. Gregor shouted obscenities in the air, his pale face growing redder as he watched.

"Don't pay attention to him," Rivelin murmured beneath his breath. "Focus on the shore and get ready to jump."

"Jump," I repeated, attempting—and failing—to keep my voice light.

"You're going to aim for that rock and get off the raft as soon as you can. I'll get in the water and drag the raft the rest of the way to the shore myself. You can keep guard of it from the rock."

I nodded. "All right. I'll do my best."

"I don't doubt you for a moment," he said, his tone no longer sharpened by his usual gruffness. A little flutter went through my chest.

This part would be the hardest for avoiding the water. Everyone else could leap over the side of the boat and slosh onto shore. Rivelin would have been able to do that, too, if we weren't on a raft only big enough for one of us. As it was, if he got off, I was going with him, whether I liked it or not.

But I was Daella Sigursdottir, for fuck's sake. I'd survived the Elding when few did. Throughout my time working for Isveig, I'd fought a score of armed shadow demons, and I'd beaten every last one single-handedly. And far before those days, I'd hidden in the rubble when Isveig had attacked Fafnir. Many had suffocated. Others had been scorched.

I had survived all that and still come out fighting. I could survive a sprinkle of fates-damned lake water.

I put all my strength behind the next row, and that final push brought the front of the raft within a few meters of the rock. As I pushed up onto my feet, Rivelin gave me a tiny nudge, hand splayed across my backside. Heat stormed through my belly, but I forced myself to focus on the rock. And then I leapt.

My boots collided with the stone, and the force of it snapped my teeth together. A few feet down the bank, Gregor guffawed, clearly taking pleasure in my clumsy dismount. I turned to give him a piece of my mind, but Rivelin tossed me the rope that would keep the boat anchored to me.

"Hold on to this," he said, turning toward the bank, but then he paused for a moment to catch my gaze. "Don't rise to his bait."

And then he was off, moving so fast that he was nothing more than a blur of silver amidst the dense woods. As soon as he was out of sight, I tightened my hold on the rope and settled down on the rock cross-legged. I could feel four pairs of eyes on me, and I could only imagine what the other contestants must be thinking.

Daella, the intruder from Fafnir sent here by the horrid emperor, had completely ruined any chance

Rivelin had of winning this challenge. They would probably all clap me on the back when this was over and thank me for my service, because I'd pretty much handed one of them a win—if they could manage to catch up to Viggo.

But out of all of them, I felt Gregor's stare the most, like his eyes were made of the lake water itself, and he was trying to burn two holes right through my skin. Rivelin's words echoed in my mind. *Don't rise to his bait.*

Shifting my attention to the woods, I blocked him out, hoping against all hopes that Rivelin would beat the others back. In the canopy overhead, songbirds danced and chirped out a tune that sounded like an ancient song I'd heard all my life—a call to those above who watched down on us all. The Old Gods. The warm and earthy scents of birch and cedar curled toward me on a soft breeze that ruffled the ends of my ponytail hanging across the back of my neck. It was so soothing, so peaceful here.

Of course Gregor had to ruin it.

"Say, Kari," he barked out so loudly it made me jolt. "You and your assistant, you were the first boat here after me, weren't you?"

"Yes..." Kari said, frowning. "What's your point?"

"That means he's the most likely runner to return next, don't you think?"

"No, that's probably your assistant. You lot got here first. So he has a head start," Kari said. I watched the exchange out of the corner of my eye, careful not to let Gregor see I was paying attention. Kari was clever,

Rivelin had said, and I could tell she was choosing her words carefully, all the while trying to sound calm.

Unfortunately, her white-knuckled grip on her oar and her flattened lips caught Gregor's attention just as they did mine. Clever but not good at masking her emotions, it turned out. Gregor's boat creaked as he shifted forward. "Something wrong, Kari?"

"Nothing's wrong. Just leave me out of whatever it is you're plotting," she said tightly.

There was a flash of movement in the corner of my eye. Water splashed.

I finally turned toward them. Gregor had launched into the water and was wading through the marshy grass toward Kari's smaller boat. He had an oar in his hands. So did Kari. Weapons, I realized.

The two other boats had been quietly and slowly easing away from the rest of us. They were both sliding behind a cluster of weeds that would hide them from view until the others returned. Smart move. I, on the other hand, knew that if I slid onto the raft, it would be like setting off an explosion. Even as Gregor sloshed toward Kari, I swore he was keeping one eye locked on me.

"Just stay back, Gregor," Kari said. "I don't want to fight you. I never have."

"Oh yeah? What are you going to ask the island to give you if you win?"

Kari didn't answer. Only the continued slosh of water kept an unbearable silence at bay, but that wouldn't last much longer. In another moment or two, Gregor would reach Kari's boat.

"No need to answer," Gregor snarled. "I already know you want to ask it to get rid of me."

Kari's hands trembled as she gripped her oar tighter. "I can't do that. No harm to anyone else, eh? That's one of the island's rules. Even if I want to get rid of you—and I've never said I do—it wouldn't give me that."

"Get rid of." He moved forward. Slosh. "Not kill." Another slosh. "I bet it would give it to you. The island hates me."

"I don't think an island can hate someone."

"Well, maybe that's just you." He grinned. "Since I made your sister fall madly in love with me. Too bad redheads aren't my type."

Kari growled and swung her oar at Gregor's head. Gregor whirled to respond with a blow of his own, as if he'd anticipated the move. He dodged to the left and swung down and to the right before bringing the paddle up to slam into Kari's face. Blood sprayed; Kari's gurgling scream rent the peaceful quiet.

She fell, her back punching the water. Shouts of anger echoed from the far shore, where spectators were watching.

I jumped to my feet. "What the fuck? You can't do that. It's against the rules."

"She came for me first. I was just defending myself, now wasn't I?" he asked with a sneer, wiping the blood spray off his face with the back of his sleeve. "Now sit back down, orc. Or I'll defend myself from you next."

"Yeah? Go on, then. Let's see how you fare against someone who actually knows how to fight." I spread my lips into a wicked smile, flashing my elongated canines. I didn't have tusks, but close enough.

He narrowed his gaze as I stood to my full height, throwing back my shoulders. I knew I looked absolutely ridiculous wearing all this oilcloth on a hot, humid day, but I didn't care much about appearances right now. Let him underestimate me. It would only make his defeat that much sweeter.

He must have read the deadly glint in my eye and realized going up against Isveig's "infamous murk" would only end in pain—his pain—because he started sloshing his way back over to his boat.

"Go on and attack me if you want," he called over his shoulder, "but you'll only get Rivelin disqualified since I didn't provoke you. Something tells me that's the last thing you want."

I snarled at his back, then eyed the water. Kari still hadn't resurfaced yet, and blood spilled across the lake like red paint. My heart kicked my ribs.

"She's going to die if you don't do something," I said.

Gregor shrugged and launched himself into his boat, water jetting onto his seat. I dropped the rope and pinched the bridge of my nose.

"Fine. Someone else?" I called out to the others hidden behind the weeds, but they were too far away now to do a damn thing.

No, you can't! my mind screamed at me.

But no matter how many Draugr I'd tracked down,

no matter how many throats I'd cut over the years, and no matter how many monsters I'd slain for the empire, I'd never harmed or turned away from an innocent when they needed help. Even if I suspected some of the people in this village of dealing in dragon magic, I didn't have proof. There was no way to be certain they were *all* involved. And Kari did not smell of dragon.

I closed my eyes. "Fuck."

And then I jumped.

The first thing I felt was the cold and the way it squeezed the air in my lungs like a fist was wrapped tight around my chest. For a brief moment, I opened my eyes and peered through the crystal blue, marvelling at the lush green of the cattails and the reeds, the coating of algae along the lake bed, and the schools of orange fish darting away from the disturbance.

And then, there—Kari floated ominously a few feet away, her eyes closed, her blood staining the blue a deep, dark red, the same color as her hair.

I started splashing toward her. That was when the pain hit me like a piercing rod.

I screamed, and bubbles swarmed my face. Still, I kept swimming toward Kari, my determination numbing the pain. I reached her a moment later, grabbed her arm, and tugged.

My lungs ached along with every inch of my skin. Black spots stormed across my vision.

I blindly swam, shoving aside thick pocketfuls of reeds. My mind warred against me with wave after wave of unyielding pain. It felt like I was on fire now.

My boots hit dirt and rock. Shuddering, I crawled forward, dragging Kari behind me. We rose from the depths of the lake, emerging on the bank where Rivelin had darted into the woods to hunt for the flag.

Water dripped into my eyes, blurring my sight. I pulled Kari up beside me and tried to find the strength within myself to check her breathing, but the scalding pain knocked me sideways. My body hit the ground.

A strong hand palmed my cheek. Steam hissed. "Fates be damned."

And then the darkness took me.

15

RIVELIN

B y the time I got Daella back home, she'd started to wake, which made me more relieved than I wanted to consider. At first, I'd thought she might not make it. Her cheeks, the only bare skin I could see, were a blazing red, and I could only imagine what the rest of her looked like. Her breathing had gone shallow; she'd been limp in my arms as I'd made the long, slow trek back across the lake.

No one knew what medicine to give her. We'd never had an orc in the Isles, and her wounds were unlike anything we'd ever seen.

I kicked open the door and settled her onto the bed. Her waterlogged body hissed as I brushed the strands of wet hair out of her eyes. A hoarse breath spilled from her pale lips as she blinked up at me.

"Tell me what to do," I said quietly.

She moaned and writhed on the bed, clawing at the clothes.

I nodded. "You need to get out of those so we can get you dry."

Coughing, she weakly picked at the bottom hem of her shirt, but then she shook her head.

"Help," she croaked out.

"Fucking Gregor," I muttered as I moved to her side. He was the reason she was like this, and if I hadn't hated the elf already this would have been the final straw. He'd always pushed things too far, but this was on an entirely different level. If the people of Wyndale couldn't agree to boot him out of here, I'd find a way to get rid of him myself.

As gently as I could, I undid the clasps securing Daella's oilskin leathers in place, and then tugged them off her arms. Beneath, her sleeveless tunic was soaked through, and angry red welts enveloped her arms. She hissed through clenched teeth, barely conscious. Rage burned through my veins.

"Please get the rest of it off me," she whispered up at me.

"Are you certain? I could go get Lilia. I know you don't trust—"

"No time," she breathed. "Just take it all off. It's only skin."

And so I did, taking care to avert my gaze as I pulled the tunic over her head. I passed her a towel, which she clutched to her chest while I moved on to her boots and her trousers. The wet material was hot in my hands as I tugged it from her trembling body. I continued not to look, as best I could. Until a flash of blue snagged my attention.

An angry red mark stretched across her right hip. Embedded just beneath the skin was a large shard made of ice, its blue glow throbbing ominously. It looked like someone had cut her open and shoved the thing in. Years ago, judging by the scar. But it had never fully healed.

A preternatural stillness took over my body, a remnant of my battle training from before my life in Wyndale.

"What," I asked in a deadly calm, "is that?"

She closed her eyes and tugged the towel over her hips to hide the scar. "It's a magicked ice shard."

"What does it do? And who put it there? Who cut you open like that?"

But I already knew the answer. I'd known the second I saw it. There was only one being in the entire world would could have done it.

"Isveig."

I sat back and averted my gaze as she finished toweling off her body. She was shivering less now, but her occasional gasps told me she was still very much in pain. I stalked off to the cupboard down the hall and brought out some fresh linens for the bed. The ones on there now would be soaked through, still irritating her back. I also pulled out another pair of nightclothes, the last clean set I had. At this rate, I'd have to ask Tilda for some more.

When I returned to the bedroom, Daella had inched

off the wet patch to the drier side of the bed, and she'd covered her front with the towel. I set the fresh linens on the trunk and swallowed at the marks all over her legs. Those had to hurt like hell.

"Do you need me to help you get dressed?" I asked.

"No, just give me a few moments. Do you have any more of that salt? For the welts."

"I can find some."

"All right." She sighed. "Can you just...give me half an hour or so? This is going to take me a little time."

"You sure you don't want help?"

"No, no. I just need to rest for a bit. I'm in quite a lot of pain."

I frowned. "I'll get you that salt."

I stormed into the village square, where everyone had gathered after the challenge. Unlike the days before, the celebration tonight was muted. Groups were gathered at the tables, drinking ale and talking amongst themselves, but the lack of laughter and cheerful bard tunes felt like an ominous cloud had settled over Midsummer.

Lilia spotted me from her ever-present spot beside her wagon. She rushed over and grabbed my hands. "Is Daella all right?"

"No," I said, my voice clipped. "Where's Gregor?"

She shook her head. "Haven't seen him."

"And Kari?"

"She's got a broken nose, but she'll be all right."

"Good." I started to move away.

Lilia called after me, "Don't do anything foolish, Rivelin."

I just grunted and kept walking through the square. The cheerful paper streamers and flowers only dampened my mood even further, particularly when I found Odel and Haldor covertly perched on some crates in an alley just beyond the square, whispering excitedly like the day had borne some drama-filled gossip.

I scowled as I approached them. "Enjoying this, are we? Maybe we should change the rules and allow assault during every Midsummer Games."

Odel fell silent and gave me a frank look. "Kari has a busted nose, but she's fine."

"Gregor attacked her. He needs to be disqualified from the Games, and then kicked off Hearthaven."

"Well." Haldor sucked on his teeth for a moment, squinting up at the sky. "Problem is, Kari went for him first, and you know the rules. Technically, she's in the wrong here. She's withdrawn from the competition."

"You must be joking," I said flatly.

"Rules are rules, Riv," Odel sighed. "If we bend them for this, you know that'll mean others start pushing the boundaries of what they can and can't do."

"Someone is already pushing the boundaries. And if we let him get away with it, he'll do something else. Something that could get someone actually killed. And next time, we might not have an orc willing to jump into a literal lake of fire—as far as she's concerned—in order to stop it."

"How is Daella, anyway?" she asked, her voice going soft.

"In a lot of fucking pain."

"Thank her for us, will you?" Haldor cut in. "That took a lot of moxie."

"And compassion," Odel added. "Think we might have been wrong about her?"

I thought back to what she'd told me about her captivity and what Isveig had put in her hip. But I also remembered the hatred in her voice when she'd spoken of dragons. "Perhaps."

"I suppose this won't have endeared her to us much," she said, furrowing her brow. "Can you manage to turn it around? You two looked pretty cozy on that raft. The plan to charm her must be coming along well."

"I'm not having this conversation. I came here to ask you about Gregor. Where is he?"

They exchanged a glance. Haldor rubbed the base of his horns. "He vanished after the challenge. No one knows where he's gone, not even his mother. At least, that's what she says. Could be lying."

"You tell her I'm looking for him. Tell everyone you see."

"Don't do anything foolish, Rivelin," Odel said, edging closer with a frown. "I know you're angry, but he technically hasn't done anything wrong. You can't touch him."

I narrowed my gaze at her. "Why does everyone keep saying that to me?"

"Your anger has a short fuse and you have a violent past. We all know that."

"I've never lifted a finger against anyone on this island."

"And let's keep it that way, eh?" Haldor clapped my back.

I shook my head at the both of them, shrugged his hand off my shoulder, and left them to their gossip. I shouldn't get so irritated. They only wanted to keep the peace, like all of us did. That was why we had our rules in the first place, and no need for a prison. Everyone yearned to keep our safe haven the way it was: a calm oasis tucked away from the brutal realities of the Grundstoff Empire. A place where there was no fighting, no bloodshed, no crime and punishment and all the dirty work that went with it. And most of the time, it was exactly that.

On my way back home, I stopped by the apothecary to pick up some more salt, noting the evening chill now that the sun had crept behind Mount Forge in the distance. The sky was streaked with periwinkle blues and crimson reds, and most of the village would be watching from the square.

Back home, Daella was curled up in the armchair with Skoll pacing beside her. Her face was still red, but her eyes were a little brighter now. As I approached, she pushed up from the chair, grimacing.

I held up the bag of salt. "Got your medicine."

She nodded and motioned toward the kitchen. "I just need a bowl of water and some mud, or even dirt, to make a paste."

"I'll get it." I handed her the bag and walked into the kitchen, grabbing a bowl from the cupboard and filling it from the spout. The mud was next. I took a handful from the back garden and tossed it into a second bowl. When I returned to the living room, I found Daella peering out the window, her body still trembling from her ordeal.

"Your skies. They're beautiful." She sighed and turned around. Pain lined every inch of her red-stained face. "Best get the salt paste on these welts or they may leave scars. I was in the lake too long."

I couldn't have explained why the thought popped into my head, but I found myself saying, "Think you can climb a ladder?"

"What, now?"

"We can watch the sunset from the roof while we fix up your wounds. Might make this whole ordeal seem... well, less terrible, I suppose. I know nothing will really make it right, but—"

"Let's do it," she said firmly.

And there it was. That spark in her eyes—the *real* one. The orc liked sunsets. Noted.

I motioned for her to follow me outside, where I'd propped an old ladder against the house. It was a rickety thing that shook as we climbed, but it did the job well enough. Balancing the supplies, I followed Daella as she gingerly edged her way upward. More than once, I thought about suggesting we do this another day, but she seemed determined as fate to make it up there.

When she reached the top, she clambered across the brown slates and stood gazing toward Mount Forge in the distance. Her entire body seemed to exhale, like she'd just released a breath she'd been holding all her life. A little surge of pride went through me. I knew she'd like this.

I put the bowls on the roof and hauled myself up behind her.

"You come up here a lot," she said, still gazing ahead at the vibrant sky.

"Most evenings," I admitted.

She turned toward me and motioned at the village square a few streets over. From here, it was easy to see the packed tables and the bustling Traveling Tavern. A bard had taken to the stage now, and lilting music drifted toward us on the wind.

"And what about them? Do they sit there watching the skies every night?"

"When the weather's good, a lot of them do."

"But you stay here and don't join them. How come?"

"Let's focus on getting your wounds tended," I said, changing the subject. "What do we need to do?"

She sighed and settled down on the roof, kicking her legs over the sloped side. "Just hand me the bowls, and I'll sort out the paste."

So I did, and she got to work. Dropping some salt in the water first, she waited for it to seep in, and then she added some of the salt water to the dirt. She tested it with a timid touch, gave a satisfied nod, and then mixed it all together.

While she spread some of the paste across the welts on her arm, I decided now was the time to broach the subject. "So what happened out there, Daella?"

She stiffened and then slathered another welt with some paste. "Gregor attacked Kari and then left her to drown. The others were hiding from him, I think. No one else was around to go after her."

"You saved her life."

"Anyone else would have done the same thing," she said, still dabbing the saltwater mud onto her wounds.

"I'm not sure that's true."

"Hmm. Is he gone?"

"Gregor? I don't know. Some hope he's gone, but he's not out of the Games. Rules say he was just protecting himself. I hate it, but that's how it is."

She sighed and moved on to her legs, rolling up the soft linen trousers. There were at least ten welts marring her green skin, but they weren't as angry as the ones on her arms. "He's not gone, not with that determination to win. Whatever he wants to ask the island, it must be big. Any idea what it is?"

"No, it's against the rules. No one ever shares what they plan to ask. We don't want it to influence the spectators when they put in their votes."

"So he could want something terrible."

"Knowing him, he most certainly does."

Silence fell as she continued to work with the paste, but it was an easy kind of quiet, the kind that felt like a long nap in the sun. I leaned back against the roof and laced my hands behind my head, watching the pinks and reds of the sky succumb to the midnight blues of night. We sat like that for a good long while until Daella was done with the medicine. The fireflies had come out to play, darting overhead beneath the silver of the moon. Down in the market square, the bard still sang. This time, he was on to a tune about the dwarven city deep inside the Glass Peaks.

Daella settled onto the roof beside me. "Thanks for giving me this."

"The sunset? Can't say it's mine to give, but I'm glad it could ease some of...today's shit."

"The sunset, yes. But everything else, too. I was in bad shape."

"I'm sorry, Daella. If I win, I *will* make sure he's gone, if I can't find a way to get rid of him before then. He doesn't deserve this place."

She slid her eyes my way. "What exactly is it you're going to ask for if you win? I know you said you don't share that with anyone before the end of the Games, but...well, I'm your assistant, and I think I've earned it after today."

I chuckled. "That you did."

"So?" She raised her brow, and I couldn't help but notice how the moon's glow amplified the shine of her eyes. "What is it, then?"

"I told you. I'm going to make sure Emperor Isveig can never harm anyone who is a part of this place."

"And you can just ask that? 'Dear Isles of Fable,

please ensure Emperor Isveig never hurts anyone who lives here.'"

"No, others have tried that kind of thing in the past," I admitted. "You have to be more specific with your wording."

"You're not going to tell me, are you?" She sat up and wound her arms around her rolled-up trouser legs, gazing ahead at the twinkling lanterns of Wyndale. From up here, I often thought the sprawl of it across the hills looked like a reflection of the starlight above. A distant marvel, one I could survey but never quite know— always just beyond my reach.

I sat up beside her. "I'm going to ask it to make an unbreakable rule for those who find these islands. No one can come or go who will cause us harm if they do so. That way, Isveig will never step foot in Wyndale nor will he know what's here."

Daella stiffened.

I frowned. "And that bothers you? If what you've told me is true, you will cause us no harm."

She hastily stood, the roof tiles wobbling beneath her bare feet. "You know why I'm here. I'm to track down Draugr in the Glass Peaks and take them to Isveig. I was *ordered* to do it, which means I have to. You don't think that's *harm*?"

I rose beside her, noting her tortured expression. "Well, then you won't be able to leave if I win. Is that really so terrible? You'd be free from him if you stayed."

Tears filled her eyes. She yanked up her tunic to reveal the ice shard embedded in her skin.

"You asked me what this is and what it does," she whispered furiously. "Well, at the moment, it does nothing, as long as I do what the emperor commands. But if I don't..." She closed her eyes, and a tear streaked down her reddened cheek. "If I don't return to him within six weeks—five weeks now, I think—then he will use the power of the shard against me. It only takes one whispered word from him, and it will turn me into a block of ice. He will kill me."

16

DAELLA

The pity in Rivelin's eyes hurt more than the welts did. Physical pain I understood, but not this...this rawness around my heart. I'd spent so much of my life trying to pack all the emotion into crates inside my mind, nailed shut forever so that no one like Isveig could use them against me. Could use *me*.

The people at court in Fafnir Castle had often stared at me with mocking smiles or blatant curiosity. The Draugr I'd tracked down gaped at me in fear. No one had ever looked at me like they felt sorry for me, especially not someone who would happily condemn me to die in this place. This situation had damaged those carefully sealed crates, and the emotions burst through.

I started to shove past Rivelin. I couldn't let him see me cry. But he gently grabbed my hand before I made it to the ladder.

"Daella, wait," he murmured as the steam rose between us.

I blinked, trying to keep the tears at bay. "I can't have this conversation with you."

"Isveig is the enemy. Not me."

"Aren't you?"

He pressed his lips together. "I don't have to be."

"Then don't ask the island to prevent people from leaving. Don't force me to stay here if you win."

"Isveig can never know anything more about us than he already does."

"But why?" I asked. "If he can't come here, what does it matter?"

"I cannot say."

I swallowed as he stepped in close, and I tipped back my head to meet his stare. "I know you want to protect these islands from Isveig's conquering army, but it's more than that. There's something here you want to hide from him, and even if I hate him—even if I balk at his every command—I agree with him about the Draugr. Dragon magic users are volatile and dangerous. They will burn this whole world down if someone doesn't stop them. Not just the Grundstoff Empire. The Isles, too. And you would stand in my way if I tried to prevent it."

He released my arm, but he did not step back. "There are no Draugr in the Isles."

"You expect me to believe that?"

"Believe it or not, but you won't find them here."

"The dwarves said—"

"The dwarves were lying. They were probably trying

to lure Isveig to their mountain city. Most don't know this, but they were once great allies to the orcs. To your old king. He knew about the Glass Peaks when he was still alive."

My brows shot high. "*Lure* him here? To kill him?"

"Perhaps."

"I thought you had a law against violence and bloodshed on the islands."

"On *Hearthaven*. The dwarves do things differently over in the Glass Peaks."

My heart pounded as I gazed up at him, at the line of silvery moonlight that ran along his defined, angular jaw. A part of me wanted to believe him—desperately so. I did not want to doom the folk of Wyndale.

But I knew Rivelin was lying. He had to be. Why else would the stench of dragons be so strong?

As if in answer to my thoughts, the ice shard throbbed, but the pain was nothing compared to the welts.

"I'm tired. I'm going to bed," I said.

Rivelin's luminous eyes searched my face. "This shard in your hip. I'll help you figure something out."

I could only shake my head and laugh bitterly. "I've been trying to figure something out for years. There is no solution."

He watched me go as I wearily climbed down the ladder. I hadn't been lying. Everything inside me ached for bed. And despite all the thoughts and warring emotions tumbling through my mind, I fell asleep the second my head hit the pillow.

The next morning, we ate breakfast in strained silence before heading to the market square to see the results of the Vatnor Trial. The distance between Rivelin's front door and the main thoroughfare was far too short for my liking, even though my pace was slow. I was still recovering from the day before.

As far as I could determine, there was no winning in my current situation. If we came in last place, and we might have, any hope I had of asking the island for freedom would drift away like smoke in the wind. But, if we somehow got enough votes to be in the top half of the competition, Rivelin would be closer to his goal, which was at odds with my future. Rivelin seemed to think he could find a solution, but I wasn't convinced.

When we walked into the square, we found a crowd milling around the center stage, blocking our view of whatever it was they were looking at. Lilia pranced over to us, though there were storm clouds in her bright yellow eyes.

"Gregor's back," she whispered fiercely, latching onto Rivelin's arm with white-knuckled hands.

A muscle in Rivelin's jaw ticked as he scanned the crowd. "Where?"

"He came by a few moments ago to check out the votes. Then his mother dragged him away toward his house. I think she's been keeping him hidden until everyone forgets to be angry."

"Hmm," was all Rivelin said.

"How are you feeling today?" Lilia asked as she pointedly avoided glancing at my exposed skin. Rivelin had produced yet another change of clothes for me. This time, he'd provided me with options. I'd gone with simple brown trousers and a sleeveless black tunic that left my skin exposed, rather than choosing to cover my arms. The welts weren't pretty, but fabric rubbing against them was too painful.

"I'd feel a lot better if Gregor was eliminated from the competition," I said.

"You should see the votes, then." She grinned.

I perked up a bit at that, though I still wasn't sure which way I wanted this to swing. Lilia took off toward the stage, and Rivelin's hand brushed against my back to urge me to follow. Hot steam hissed from the touch, and I was acutely aware of every single inch of his strong, calloused palm. Rivelin cleared his throat, and his hand dropped away.

Cheeks hot, I marched away from him and refused to look in his general direction. That damn steam kept getting me flustered, and there was no reason for it. It was nothing.

I shook my head and focused on the stage. The votes were what mattered right now.

The crowd parted before us, their murmurs and whispered conversations receding like the tide. Lilia eagerly tugged me forward and motioned at the line of glass jars set out on the stage. Seven in total, each filled with blue pebbles. A plaque was set out in front of each of them with the contestant's name written in a loopy, artistic scrawl.

Rivelin's jar was on the far end. It was the second most full out of all of them.

My stomach twisted.

"See?" Lilia motioned at the other end of the stage. Gregor's glass jar was almost empty, which would have put him last if it weren't for the two entirely empty ones. Kari had withdrawn from the competition after the fight, and Nina hadn't even made it across the lake, which meant she was out.

"So we're in second," I said slowly, heart thumping a painful beat. My welts seemed to throb in rhythm with it.

"Because of you and your courage," Rivelin said quietly.

I didn't know what to say. My conflicted emotions were too much to bear. Swallowing, I moved away from the stage, wandered down the street, and found a crate to sit on beside the overgrown well. Skoll trotted over to me, his tongue lolling from his mouth. I hadn't even noticed him following us.

He sat on his haunches and blinked at me. With a sigh, I ran my hand along his fur and tried to think. Perhaps winning really was the only way to solve this. I would just have to snatch the victory away from Rivelin before he could ask the island for what he wanted.

Rivelin found me and sat beside me on the crate. "No fake happiness this time, then?"

"You know why I have mixed feelings about this."

"I'm guessing that means you don't believe me about the Draugr."

My heart pounded as the words itched to escape my throat. If I came clean, it could doom me—*really* doom me. He would understand me as the threat I was, and he would happily trap me here, regardless of what it meant for my life.

"Rivelin." I sighed and leaned back against the stone well, kicking my feet up onto another crate. I gave him a flat look. "I thought you understood what orcs can do, what *I* can do. You called me infamous, as a matter of fact."

"Everyone in the fates-damned world knows your name. Wouldn't you say that makes you infamous?"

"I'd say that's a tad alarming, but that's not my point. You know...." I tapped the side of my nose. "I can scent dragons. Their magic, too."

He folded his arms and rested against the well, his shoulder brushing mine. "What are you getting at?"

"Rivelin, your shop reeks of it. So did your bedroom when I first arrived. Every now and then, I get a whiff of it on the air, too. There are dragons somewhere nearby, and you've been in contact with them. Or you're a Draugr."

"I see," he said quietly.

"Rivelin!" A pink-haired pixie landed before us, her wings fluttering. She wore a bright smile and an interesting assortment of clothes: a breezy shirt that moved like clouds around her legs, a cropped tunic the color of sunshine, and at least a dozen multi-colored gemstones in each ear. It created a particularly flamboyant effect. "Well done on coming in second place. You should be thrilled." She looked at me and stuck out a hand. "Hi, I'm Odel. I'm on the Village Council with Rivelin here."

I shook her hand. "I'm Daella."

She let out a tinkling laugh. "Oh, honey, I know who you are. How are you liking Wyndale? Sorry about the..." With a grimace, she motioned at my arms.

"It seems like a lovely village. For the most part."

"Yes, well." Odel sighed. "We're trying to find a way to deal with that whole situation. In the meantime..." She turned toward the corner of the nearest building and made a waving motion at the shadows. "Come on out, then. She won't bite."

I sat up a little straighter as an elderly human woman with white, frizzy hair hobbled around the corner, one hand clutching a wooden cane and the other holding a parchment-wrapped lump. With a watery smile, she approached and set the package on my lap. The warmth of it seeped through my trousers like rays of summer sun.

The woman bowed and backed away.

"Now Mabel," Odel said with an encouraging smile. "Don't just stand there and gape at her. Tell her what you told me."

Mabel shuffled her feet a bit. She then patted my hand, careful not to touch the welt near my wrist. "You came into my village fourteen years past. You likely don't remember me—you were so young. I was hiding in a pantry and heard Isveig's murks order you to kill every last one of us, just to be on the safe side. Even if you smelled no dragon magic on us."

My stomach dropped. I remembered her, all right, though the lines in her face had multiplied and deepened over the years, and her black hair had gone bone white. It had been one of my first "missions" from the new emperor.

The old woman sniffled and big blobs of tears rolled down her cheeks. "You spared me. You looked right at me, right in my eyes. And you told the murks barging into my house that there was no one inside."

There was something hot and scratchy in my throat, and my eyes burned. All these years, I'd often wondered about that woman in the pantry, if she'd escaped, where she'd gone, and whether the emperor had somehow known and tracked her down. But, against all odds, she'd made it here.

"I'm glad you got away from that bastard, too." Mabel nodded at the parcel on my lap. "Now you eat that up, you hear, and don't give none to Rivelin. I made it just for you."

As she turned to hobble away, I finally found my voice. "Thank you. It's good to see you again, Mabel. I've not forgotten you at all."

"Nor I you," she called out over her shoulder. And then she moved on, her cane digging into the ground with each labored step.

As I watched her go, I could feel the scorching heat of Rivelin's gaze.

"Well, I suppose I should see what this is," I

mumbled aloud, more to distract myself from the intensity of his stare than anything else. I peeled open the wrapping. Inside was a small square pastry of a sort, brown and crispy along the top. Unexpectedly, the savory scent of cheese and fried mushrooms wafted toward me. I cocked my head, curious.

Rivelin practically moaned, a sound that sent an unexpected shiver down my spine. "One of Mabel's famous mushroom pasties. She doesn't make those for just anyone. Eat up or you'll have the whole village coming to fight over it."

"Surely it can't be *that* good."

I took a bite. Creamy cheese and salted mushrooms coated my tongue in a dizzying explosion of taste. The pastry crumbled, creating the perfect texture to complement the filling. My eyes went wide. Fates be damned. It was one of the best things I'd ever eaten in my life.

Rivelin sat there smirking at me. "Told you. It's amazing, right?"

I waited until I'd swallowed to answer. "I've never had anything like it before."

"Human recipe," he answered. "Mabel grew up in the human kingdoms before moving to a village on the outskirts of Fafnir, after she met an orc and fell in love. When her husband died rebelling against Isveig, she fled on a ship and ended up here."

I swallowed that awful scratchy lump again. The guilt of what happened that day was almost unbearable. Try as I might, I hadn't been able to stop the murks from killing every innocent in that village. Isveig had been convinced there were dozens of Draugr and orcs hiding out in their homes. There had been many lives lost that day. Mabel seemed to see me as her savior, and I was anything but.

Her unexpected kindness combined with the trials and the future I didn't think I could escape…it was just all too much.

I brushed the crumbs from my trousers and stood, my throat tight. "I need to do something. What's the next trial? When does it start?"

Rivelin stood from the crate, his eyes locked on my face. I tried to avoid looking at him, sensing the pity I'd find there. After everything he'd said and done, I couldn't stand the thought of him feeling sorry for me. Not the grumpy elf blacksmith who seemed to dislike everyone, except for Skoll and his sister. If he, of all people, felt bad for me, then I truly was fucked.

At long last, he finally spoke. "It kicks off today, but we have over a week to prepare for the actual competition. And there's something I want to show you before we get started."

17

DAELLA

"Here." Rivelin handed me a sturdy pair of boots to replace the ones I'd soaked. He then grabbed a leather satchel from a hook beside the door and started filling it with a compass, a couple of canteens, and an emergency kit.

I watched him curiously. "I have some questions. First, you seem to have an unlimited supply of women's clothing that fit me perfectly. Second, how far are we traveling exactly? If we're going far, I'll need to pack salt and some kind of waterproof tent, if you can find one."

"I told you. The clothes are all from Tilda, who is about your size. I'll introduce you next time I see her. She won the Midsummer Games a few years back, and she asked the island for an endless wardrobe. She only ends up keeping half of it."

Well, that certainly explained some things. "Not particularly useful compared to the running water."

"It's keeping you clothed, isn't it?"

"You have a point."

Rivelin vanished into the kitchen. Clattering and thumping followed. When he returned, he carried a pouch of salt, some stale bread, and dried meats, which he unceremoniously stuffed into the pack with the other supplies.

"You didn't answer my second question," I said.

"We're going to the base of Mount Forge. It takes me less than a day to get there and back if I don't run, but I don't like going out there unprepared. Shit happens."

"That explains the boots."

"Are you up for this?"

I glanced down at the welts on my arms. They were still inflamed, and I was tired, but my curiosity had given me an extra dose of energy. "I can manage."

The elf attached a bedroll to his pack, then handed me a second one to carry along with a small tent that didn't look nearly waterproof enough. Without any more explanation, he moved to the door and motioned outside. I went along with it, though I found the entire episode increasingly odd.

I jogged down the steps and called out over my shoulder. "The Fildur Trial is starting today, right? Should we really go on a mountain hike that could take all day?"

"This is important." He joined me on the dirt-packed road. "We'll focus on the competition when we get back."

"It's more important than winning the Games so you can protect this place from Isveig?"

A moment passed before he answered. "No, but it's connected. Just come with me, Daella. I can promise that you'll want to see this."

I was exceedingly intrigued. Whatever this was, it must be big indeed. I thought back to his disappearance the other night. He'd returned smelling of dragon magic —*reeking* of it, really. Was that what he wanted to show me? Had he gone to Mount Forge that day? Admittedly, that put a slight waver in my step as I followed him out of the village, heading in the opposite direction from where I'd first arrived. I had no idea what lay ahead. If there were any Draugr in that mountain, they would want to stop me from reporting them to Isveig. Was that was this was? Rivelin realizing he needed to hand me over to them?

If only I had my mother's dagger.

We followed the path out of the village and into the forest beyond, Skoll scampering along beside us. The trees were full of birdsong and thick humid air that wrapped around me like a gentle hug. The brush rustled as rabbits and deer bounded deeper into the woods. Rivelin and I fell into a companionable silence only inter-rupted by the occasional thump of the satchel against my back. And even though I had no idea what lay ahead of me, the fresh fragrant air settled my nerves in a way that only being outside amongst the elements ever had. Even some of the residual pain from my welts faded.

After a few hours, we crossed a small wooden bridge

over a river and reached the foothills. Up close, the mountains were breathtaking. Low-hanging clouds scuttled across the jagged peaks, where the rich, verdant moss was lit up by the afternoon sun. There wasn't a speck of snow in sight.

The tallest mountain was flat on the top, and a plume of smoke curled from within. It was a volcano, I realized, just as a blast of dragon magic hit me: sulphur, salt, leather, and dust. The sight before me blurred as dizziness clouded my eyes.

"No," I choked out, stumbling away. "Why have you brought me here?"

To cause that potent of a scent, there must be hundreds of Draugr in these mountains. Thousands, perhaps. I'd never experienced anything like it before. No wonder I'd smelled them all the way back in Wyndale. Terror buckled my knees as I tried to run. I hated cowardice, but I wasn't a fool. I couldn't fight this many, especially unarmed, especially if they were as powerful as they smelled.

"Whoa, whoa." Rivelin wrapped an arm around my waist and tugged me into his side. I tried to squirm away, but his grip was firm. "Calm down. Nothing here will harm you."

I trembled and closed my eyes. The memories threatened to drown me beneath their weight. "Let me go. If you have any kindness in your heart at all, don't make me face all these Draugr. They'll know who I am, just as you did. And they will kill me."

"There are no Draugr here, Daella," he said softly. "I

was telling you the truth. There's nothing to be afraid of."

I flipped open my eyes and tried to wrench away, but he still held me tight. Steam hissed between us, but for once I didn't revel in it. I just wanted to get as far away from him as I could.

"My nose has never failed me. There are hundreds nearby," I said, tensing as I took another whiff. And yes, just there. It was coming from beyond the foothills, near the base of the largest mountain. Where Rivelin had mentioned we were headed.

He steadied me. "You're smelling dragons, Daella. Not users. *Dragons*."

My entire body tensed. I gazed ahead at the looming mountain and the smoke puffing from the volcano's summit. The heat seemed to throb like a living thing. When I'd first arrived on this island and scented the dragon magic, I'd thought there could be dragons nearby, but I hadn't *truly* believed it. Deep down, I'd doubted their existence in this place. Years ago, Isveig had his mercenaries kill them all. And they were the one thing he'd never ordered me to face.

"How is this possible?" I whispered as Rivelin finally loosened his grip on me.

"Just as hundreds of elves, dwarves, pixies, and humans escaped the Grundstoff Empire, so did dragons. They made this their home."

"*Hundreds?*" I asked incredulously.

"No. Just four."

"And they're in that volcano."

"There's a cave at the base of Mount Forge where they sleep. They like the heat."

I took a step back. "Their power is dangerous."

"It's dangerous when others try to bond with them and use their power as their own, but no one here does. We leave them in peace."

"No, you don't." Narrowing my gaze, I put some space between us. "The overpowering scent of them in your blacksmith shop proves otherwise. You come here all the time. This must have been where you vanished to the other day."

I waited, my breath held in my throat. Rivelin's hands tensed as he gazed down at me, and the soft breeze rustled the silver hair that hung to his shoulders. The elf who stood before me was the answer to all my problems. I'd been sent here to find someone steeped in dragon magic, and here he was. At the end of Midsummer, I could return to Fafnir and trade his freedom for mine. He was the enemy I'd been searching for, and I'd known it the second I'd laid eyes on him. At long last, I had the proof.

So why did it all feel so...*wrong*? There was no happiness, no relief. Just a grim resignation curling around my heart.

"Yes, I come here to visit them. At least once a week," he finally said. "They're my friends, and I vowed to protect them."

I swallowed.

He continued. "Their cave is only another half hour's

walk from here. Come with me. Let me introduce you to them."

Skoll trotted toward me and nudged my leg with a whine. I frowned down at him. "Not you, too. I thought you were on my side."

"See, Skoll trusts the dragons. He wouldn't encourage you to go with me if he thought it would put you in harm's way."

I couldn't believe I was taking the word of a *fenrir* over my own instincts.

"This could be some sort of trap," I said.

"If it was a trap, you'd already be stuck in it. Dragons fly fast."

I frowned but made no attempt to argue.

"So you'll come?" Rivelin asked.

I motioned him forward. "I will approach. *Cautiously.* But any sign of trouble, and I'm gone."

As promised, we reached the mouth of the cave not long after crossing the bridge. The pungent scent of dragons rolled toward me from the shadowy depths, like vicious waves on a stormy day. I clenched my jaw against the force of it, trying to ignore how it dug into my bones and called for me. I did not want to go any closer, but still I followed Rivelin inside, warring against the instinct to run.

Water dripped from somewhere deep within the caverns, and a thunderous heat throbbed against the walls. I stilled as I caught sight of four sleeping forms curled up along the far side of the cave, where a rocky overhang served as a shelter. They were larger than horses but only just. Laying on their backs, their round scaly bellies faced the ceiling above, revealing sleek, glowing gemstones—each one had its own unique coloring. Sparks shot into the air as they breathed, before drifting back down around them like falling snow.

"They're so...small," I whispered, my voice echoing. "For dragons, I mean."

"They're young and still spend a lot of time sleeping," Rivelin said softly. "I found them just after they hatched. Fourteen years ago. They won't reach full maturity until they're thirty."

Like elves and orcs, dragons could live for centuries. Or they had, before Isveig had killed them all. Killed them because they were *dangerous*, and their magnificent power caused those who bonded with them to lose their grip on their souls. The magic burned them up, along with anyone else in their vicinity.

I turned away. "I knew you were doing something like this. You act like you're this noble, protective man, but you have dragons, and you're hiding them from the empire."

"Because Isveig will kill them," he said, a sneer curling his lips. "And *you* have no place to tell me what's moral or not."

I flinched. "You going to call me a murk again?"

"If the shoe fucking fits."

"Dragons are dangerous."

He jerked a thumb toward the sleeping creatures. "Do they look dangerous?"

"Well, *not yet*, but—"

"If you could leave now and tell your emperor about this, you would, wouldn't you?"

My mouth dropped open, then I snapped it shut. I didn't know how to answer that question. Everything I'd seen and heard throughout my life screamed at me that this was wrong, that it needed to be stopped. But it was so impossibly hard to reconcile all that with what I'd seen since arriving on Hearthaven. And with the people I'd met in Wyndale—barring Gregor, of course. These people weren't wild and dangerous. These dragons were peacefully sleeping youngsters. No one was burning anyone up in a fit of uncontrollable rage. *Yet.*

I heaved a sigh. Why did this have to be so damn hard?

"I don't know. Maybe," I finally said.

A low growl rumbled from the back of Rivelin's throat. He took a step forward, and I took a step back, but my retreat was halted by the sleek stone wall of the cave. He leaned in and palmed the rock beside my head, his narrowed eyes churning with anger.

"I knew there was no getting through to you." His hot breath caressed my neck. "I hoped if you saw the dragons with your own eyes, something might thaw in that ice-cold heart of yours. But no. You're too stubborn for that."

I lifted my chin. "Don't act like you know anything about me."

"I know you hide your truths behind a false smile. And I know you'd rather bite off your own tongue than admit you were wrong."

"Well, *I* know you're an insufferable bastard."

"Unfortunately for you, this insufferable bastard is your ticket out of here. And right now, I'm not feeling particularly generous."

I shoved at his chest. He didn't budge. "Move."

"So you can kill innocent baby dragons?"

"Fuck you."

I glared up at him. His face was only inches from mine, and I could see every fleck of gold in his eyes. With his chest pressed tightly against mine, there was nowhere I could go. Nothing I could do but lift my chin in a silent challenge. He shifted against me, the ridges of his muscular chest hard and unyielding against the softness of my breasts. I hated that I noticed, and I especially hated how close his mouth was to mine and how the steam rising between us made something spark deep within me.

A spark of anger, of course. Nothing more.

My heart pounded when his eyes darted to my lips. His entire body tensed, and I stopped breathing. His face inched slightly closer. Our noses brushed.

Steam stormed between us.

Rivelin took a wide step back. "This was a mistake."

He could have been referring to so many things, but I didn't need to hear which one. He was right. Everything about my time on this island had been a mistake. I needed to get out of here and never come back.

18

DAELLA

I left Rivelin in the cave and found my own way back to Wyndale. But I didn't stop when my feet hit the path that snaked through the buildings. Despite the warm glow of lanterns and the sweet scent of pastries drifting on the evening wind, I bypassed the cozy village and returned to the beach where I'd entered this nightmare.

Though...had it truly been a nightmare?

Sighing, I kicked off my boots and rolled up my trousers. I left them in a pile next to my satchel a few feet from the surf and walked into the sea. The water lapped at the raw skin on my ankles and toes, surging and receding like the steady beat of a drum. I dropped my head back and stared up at the inky sky. The stars were so bright, so numerous. It was like looking upon a field of fireflies.

It was so beautiful here, so unhurried, so serene. Fafnir

had once been a gorgeous city, too, but it had a bustling, fraught energy about it, even in the dead of night. Until I'd spent my days trapped in a tower, I'd rarely had a moment to myself. There hadn't been time just to sit and watch and appreciate the beauty of the world.

As the cool evening wind whipped at my face, I tried to think. What was I going to do now? I couldn't leave the island yet unless I swam, and I definitely wasn't a strong enough swimmer to make it all the way back to the mainland. And that was *if* I didn't run into the Elding again. It would be lurking somewhere nearby.

There were other villages on this island. I'd heard Rivelin mention them. But would they accept a half-orc with no coin? I'd been lucky Rivelin had offered me a place to stay, though deep down I knew it had nothing to do with luck. He'd wanted to keep an eye on me so I didn't discover the dragons.

Even if I did leave, then what? When the ships came, could I truly sail back to Isveig's side and tell him about this place, about these people? About Rivelin? The ice shard throbbed painfully in my hip. Isveig had sworn not to kill anyone I found, and he was not an oath-breaker, but…

"Daella," a now-familiar voice called out from behind me.

I closed my eyes. I should have known he'd follow me. He would do anything to protect this island, which meant he would never let me leave.

"Daella," he repeated when he reached my side. Even

though he did not have an affinity for fire like I did, I could somehow still feel the heat of him invading my senses. "Listen, I didn't really handle that well. I'd foolishly hoped you'd set your eyes on the dragons and instantly fall in love with them. And when you didn't, I...reacted badly. Why don't we try this again?"

"Try what again, Rivelin?" I asked tiredly.

"Don't ruin this place," he said in a gruff voice that sounded pained, like the very thought of it was a knife in the heart. "Please."

Please. The word shuddered through me.

He continued. "You know what will happen if Isveig finds this island."

"I'm all too aware."

"So then don't do it. If not for me, then for Lilia. For Odel. For poor Mabel, who finally found a safe haven after Isveig took *everything* from her." The ragged emotion in his voice rattled the reinforcements around my heart. "This place is all we have left."

I lifted my eyes to his face. "And what about the dragons? Is this what you wouldn't tell me earlier, when we were on the roof? You don't want Isveig to find out about this place because of them."

Sighing, he nodded. "The dragons can't be protected the same way the folk of this island can. As they grow, they'll start flying further and further, exploring their world. I have no control over them. None of us do. If Isveig learns they exist, he'll wait for them to roam, and he'll find a way to kill them all."

I hung my head. "Draugr killed my mother and father."

A long moment passed, the only sound the steady rush of the waves.

Rivelin finally said, "How did it happen?"

I was surprised he bothered to ask. "It was before Isveig invaded, back when Fafnir wasn't part of his empire. Mother and Father had gone to the market. While they were there..." I swallowed the lump in my throat. "Draugr attacked. Three elves who had bonded with dragons and filled themselves up with their power. They burned down the entire market. Hundreds died."

"I heard about that. It was an awful thing that happened. You couldn't have been more than..."

"Six years old. The king took me in after that, gave me a place in his castle. I remember his face so much better than theirs, as hard as I try to picture them."

"I understand far better than you know."

I frowned and looked up at his distant eyes. "What do you mean?"

"I lost my family when I was only fifteen."

"You and Lilia..."

"We had three other siblings, and our parents, of course. Plus, cousins and aunts and uncles. Grandparents, too. They're all gone. Only Lilia and I got away."

"I'm sorry. You mentioned Isveig and his mercenaries before. What happened?"

The muscles around his eyes tightened. "Isveig sent murks to our city when he heard the Kingdom of Edda was planning for war. We wanted to stop him from conquering any more lands. But he attacked us before we had a chance to do a damn thing."

I'd heard about their plans. The Elven Resistance had risen up when the world learned what Isveig had done to my kingdom. But stories of the elves had dissipated as quickly as they'd appeared when Isveig had invaded *their* lands, too, in retaliation.

Rivelin sighed. "And then, three years later, I tried to get my revenge. I sneaked across the border and started killing every ice giant I could find, even those not involved. I let my rage get the better of me until I was nothing but a shell of who I'd once been."

I looked up at him, surprised. "By yourself?"

"I've been by myself for a very long time. If Lilia had known, she would have tried to stop me. Not that I would have listened. I would have kept going until it claimed my life, if I hadn't wandered into the wrong village at the wrong time, where a Draugr was hiding out—a human barely holding on to consciousness. She burned herself and the whole place down. I barely got out alive."

I shook my head. "If what you say is true, how are you so cavalier about these dragons? You've seen first-hand what they can do, same as me."

"Because the dragons are harmless, Daella," he said, suddenly reaching out to cup my cheek. I shuddered as the steam danced between us, at the feel of his strong hand against my skin. "They just want to live in peace, and they don't want anyone to use their power. No one truly can, anyway. They run too hot. You'll get burned just by being too near them."

"People did it before," I argued. "They bonded with them."

"Using Fildur sand. No one has any of that here on the Isles."

"Are you certain? Have you tried to bond with them without the sand?"

His hand dropped away. "I did try, but only when I first brought them here. They...chose me, I think. Infused me with some kind of protection against their heat. I was able to carry them without getting burned, but I'm unable to touch them now. They've gotten too big. I can go inside their cave, but I have to keep my distance."

I thought back to everything I knew about dragons and Draugr, which wasn't much. Most of what I knew had come from the emperor himself. Decades ago, orcs had lived in harmony with dragons, though they'd always kept their distance, choosing to live amongst the rural mountains away from civilization. They never took their fires to our people, to our lands. Until one day when elves and humans started bonding with them. That was what Isveig had told me.

"Have you ever seen someone bond with a dragon?" I asked Rivelin, uncomfortably aware that he still stood so close I could see tiny beads of water on his forehead. Not sweat, I realized. More steam, just from being so near to me. My heart pattered almost painfully.

"No," he murmured.

"Then how can we be certain someone here won't find a way to do it?"

He raised a brow. "*We?* Have you decided you're on our side, then?"

"I...I don't know." I twisted away. The luscious night breeze rushed in with the waves, bringing with it dark clouds, cooling my neck and cheeks. Suddenly, I felt far too hot.

Rivelin loosed a frustrated sigh. "How can you *still* want to tell your emperor about us after everything I've told you? I thought you were fucking different, Daella."

He moved away, and the sound of his footsteps faded as he left me there on the beach with nothing but my ruined heart to keep me company.

"Wait," I called out, fisting my hands.

He paused at the edge of the trees.

"I don't want to tell the emperor, but I don't know how to keep it from him when I go back. And I *am* going back because I have to, or I'll die," I found myself saying. "He'll find a way to get it out of me, Rivelin. I'm strong, but he knows how to break me down. And even if I manage to hold out, he'll be curious about where I disappeared to for so long and why I don't want to tell him much. He'll send others here." I sucked in a sharp breath and continued. "There's only one way forward. You have to win the damn Games and let me leave before you ask the island to protect this place. Then no matter what he does or what he makes me tell him, he can never reach you."

Rivelin strode across the sandy beach, his tunic

rippling in the wind. "You shouldn't have to go back there."

"No, I shouldn't," I said. "But unless you know how to remove this shard, then I'm bound to him for the rest of my fucking life."

"Have you tried?"

"Removing it? Well over a dozen times. It's impossible."

He opened his mouth, but he was interrupted by the crack of thunder overhead. A harsh wind suddenly blew in from the waves, more insistent than the steady breeze from before. I tipped back my head to see dark, angry clouds crackling with lightning. I'd been so focused on Rivelin and our conversation that I hadn't noticed the storm rolling in.

"No," I mumbled, my stomach twisting. "For the love of fate, no more water. I haven't even healed yet from the last time. I need to get that tent out quickly."

"Come on. Let me carry you." He held out a hand, and his eyes held far more meaning than his words. This was an olive branch. "Elves run fast. I can get you back to Wyndale before the rain starts."

"You can't be serious, Rivelin. I can't let you *carry* me. I'll just wait it out in the tent until the storm passes. I've done it dozens of times before."

"I want to help you." And from the intensity of his gaze, it felt like he was talking about more than just this storm.

But what could he do? What could *anyone* do?

"We won't get back in time. It's impossible," was all I said.

Rivelin suddenly scooped me into his arms before I could protest. His eyes were bright when he said, "Where'd all that smiling optimism go, eh?"

"You made it very clear you know all that's a lie."

"Perhaps it doesn't have to be."

Before I could find a suitable retort, he took off into the woods. He dashed through the trees with elegant speed, unleashing his full elven capabilities. The vegetation was nothing but a blur of verdant leaves and rustic brown, and loose strands of my dark hair whorled around my face. As I clung to his neck, I risked a glance at the determined set of his jaw and his eyes narrowed on the path ahead. There was a steady strength and power about him that he had not let me see until now. Rivelin, the stoic blacksmith, was a force to be reckoned with.

I had to admit it wasn't an entirely unattractive feature.

We reached the village and the steps of his home in no time at all. And as the clouds boomed, releasing their cascade of rain, Rivelin threw open the door and deposited me inside. The warmth of his home enveloped me as the steady patter drummed the roof. I didn't have a single speck of water on me.

"See?" Rivelin kicked the door shut and folded his arms, not even the slightest bit winded from his run. He smiled smugly. "Told you."

"You're going to be insufferable about it now, aren't you?"

The door rattled as the wind gusted through the village streets. Rivelin took a step closer, the shadows of the dark house curling around his jaw. My heart rattled, and for a moment, I forgot what I'd asked him.

"Well, I need to hold up my reputation as an insufferable bastard, now don't I?" he murmured.

A bubble of laughter popped from my throat, and I smiled.

His body went preternaturally still. "Ah. So that's what it looks like."

"That's what *what* looks like?" I asked him.

He smiled. "Nothing. We better get to bed. Tomorrow will be a long day prepping for the next trial."

Flushing at the sudden change in conversation, I shifted on my feet, suddenly realizing I'd left the boots back on the beach. That was the second pair I'd lost in a week, and they weren't even mine. "All right. Night then, I guess."

"Goodnight."

I watched him stride into the living room, toward the couch where his pillow and blanket sat waiting for him. For a moment, I hesitated, wondering if I should offer him the bed instead. But by the time I found the words, he'd started to undress. He tugged his tunic over his head, and the pale light of the moon slanting in from the window illuminated the hard, rugged panes of his chest.

My heart thundered.

I shook my head and dashed toward the bedroom at

the end of the hall. I hoped he hadn't noticed me standing there gaping at him like a fool. It was just...his physique was particularly impressive. Anyone would notice that.

Feeling far more flustered than I had any business being, I closed the door, stripped off my clothes, and climbed into bed. It wasn't until I was drifting off to sleep that I realized Rivelin had been talking about my smile.

19

RIVELIN

I tossed and turned all night. I couldn't stop thinking about what Daella had told me about her past—and her future. The bastard had bound her to him, and she saw no way out. It explained a lot. There had to be a way to get her out of this mess, but barring somehow removing the damn shard from her hip, I didn't know what it was.

She couldn't return to that life. That was all I knew for certain.

Skoll padded in from the back door I'd left cracked for him all night and nuzzled my hand. I sighed and sat up on the sofa, running my fingers through my hair. I'd hardly slept, and while elves didn't need as much rest as most, I still felt like my head was stuffed with wool.

"Dammit," I muttered to myself. Sometime in the past few days, I'd let myself soften toward the half-orc, and I didn't much like that. It always came back to bite me in the ass.

"Good morning," Daella said uncertainly.

I looked up to find her hovering in the doorway, still in her nightclothes. Quickly, I looked away. The thin material didn't leave much to the imagination, and her curves were a delicious temptation I could never indulge in. Still, the shape of her thighs—and everything else about her—hadn't escaped my notice.

I cleared my throat. "Morning. You hungry?"

"Starving. Should I make us something?"

I arched a brow.

"I do know how to cook, you know."

The offer was sweet, and pretty unexpected coming from her. "No, no. You get dressed. We'll break our fast at the Dreaming Dragon Inn. We can find out the details of the Fildur Trial there. They'll have announced it yesterday while we were in the mountains."

"The inn. Need I remind you, I got kicked out the first night I was here."

I found myself looking over at her, despite my every intention not to, and fates be damned, that nightdress showed off every inch of her mile-long thighs.

Her cheeks reddened. "Right, you have coin so it'll be fine. I suppose I should go get dressed now. Are you going to take a bath first or will you do it later? What about Skoll? Is he hungry? He should come with us, or do they not allow fenrir inside the doors?"

Her words came out in a breathless rush, and an unexpected satisfaction settled into me. She'd noticed me noticing her, and it had gotten her flustered. Her eyes darted down and then back up again. And that was when I remembered I was only half-dressed myself. She was noticing me right back. I smirked.

"I'll go get dressed." And then she was gone.

Skoll sat on his haunches and stared at me. There was judgement in his yellow eyes. Or was it encouragement? Fuck, I needed to focus. It wasn't the first time I'd seen her body, though I'd been careful to avert my gaze when she'd been hurt. And when I *had* looked at her that night, I'd been so focused on that damn shard...

No matter. Today's task loomed too large to get distracted by this kind of thing. Despite Gregor's sabotage, we'd done well in the first challenge, but we needed to win the next one. It was the only way to stop Isveig from getting his giant claws into this place.

M ornings at the Dreaming Dragon Inn were quieter affairs than the boisterous evening revels. The village of Wyndale, being as small as it was most of the year, didn't boast of a variety of delis, restaurants, and taverns. So if one wanted to break his fast somewhere other than at home, the Dreaming Dragon Inn was the place to do it.

A bell jangled on the door as I pushed inside, Daella just behind me. There were about a dozen patrons scattered around the many tables, each quietly digging into a full breakfast. Being a shadow demon, Elma's specialty was khlea—some dried meat—and fried eggs, along with olives, soft cheese, and bread to scoop it all up. The inn was the only place on Hearthaven to serve it. She'd won the Midsummer Games several years back and asked the island for a steady supply of ingredients, since olives didn't naturally grow around here. Food was always readily available, even if we still had to farm it.

Daella and I sat across from each other at a table along the back wall. Elma swung by only a moment later, wiping her hands on her faded brown apron. She shot me a smile but pointedly ignored Daella. Shadows pulsed from her skin.

"Morning, Rivelin. Rarely see you in here. What can I get you?"

"Elma, this is Daella, my assistant for the Games."

She pursed her red-painted lips and glanced at Daella. "Yes. The murk from Fafnir."

"Who saved Kari's life." I nodded at the corner where Kari quietly ate her meal alone. Every now and again, the red-headed elf cast a quick glance our way.

"Ah, yes. That is true." Elma's face softened a little. "Well, I suppose it's nice to meet you, Daella, but I hope you don't plan on telling your emperor about us. Otherwise, I'm going to have to kick you out again, even if you do have coin and one of my favorite patrons this time."

To my surprise, Daella laughed. "You're very blunt."

Elma grinned. "Gotta be, running a place like this. You should see what some of the rowdy dwarves try to pull in the evenings. They can sometimes get rather handsy, if you know what I mean."

"Something tells me you put them in their place easily enough."

"That I do. That I do. Now what can I get you? Can't say I know how to do a traditional orcish breakfast, but I can do a Full Eggs and Bacon—that's what the humans like—or I've got the one from my homeland. Demonika Breakfast."

"I'll have the Demonika Breakfast, thanks."

"The same for me," I said.

After Elma bustled off, I lowered my voice. "Where did that come from?"

"Where did what come from?"

"You charmed Elma."

"Well." She smirked, folded her arms, and leaned back in the chair. "Sometimes I can be quite charming. Sorry you don't know what that's like."

"Bet I could charm you."

Daella's eyes widened just a fraction of an inch. "Funny. Here I thought you'd already been trying. And failing miserably."

I couldn't help but laugh. Daella smiled—a real one that crinkled the skin around her eyes and brought a brightness to her face—and I didn't think she'd even realized she'd done it. And I knew, without a doubt, if she returned to Fafnir, she'd never smile like that again.

Instantly, my mood darkened and I remembered why we were here. I motioned Elma back over. I'd forgotten to ask her when she'd taken our order.

"Need something else, Riv?" she asked more sweetly than she had the last time.

"I was showing Daella the mountains yesterday, and we didn't get back to Wyndale in time to hear the details of the Fildur Trial. Mind filling us in?"

"Oh, right." She nodded. "Heard you weren't there. Gregor got excited, thinking you'd forfeited."

"Absolutely not," Daella said, sitting up straighter in her chair.

Elma nodded approvingly. "Good girl." She turned back to me. "Well, there's not much to it, like most of 'em. You just need to use fire to make something, and then you'll present it at the ceremony in a little over a week. Figure you've got that one handled just fine."

"Perfect," I said. "Thanks, Elma."

"You beat that bastard, you hear me? The both of you."

Elma bustled off again, and then disappeared through the swinging wooden doors to the kitchen. Daella was fidgeting with the bottom hem of her shirt, and I could tell she still felt uneasy about the dragon issue despite what I'd shown and told her. I understood, though. When you spend your entire life in fear of something, it's hard to let that fear go.

"Don't worry. It's normal fire, not dragonfire or actual Fildur flames."

"You know, I've never seen Fildur flames," she said quietly. "I've always wondered what they're like, being an orc and all."

"Wait, you haven't?"

"Isveig, he hates fire. He banned it from Fafnir once he took over the city, even normal flames. When I went

200

on quests with his mercenaries or warriors, we never used fire when we camped. Sometimes they would get so cold—not all of them are ice giants, you know. Still, no fire. They whispered about it like it was all cursed, like it *all* came from dragons somehow." She looked up at me. "But you don't think that's true, do you?"

"That all fire comes from dragons?"

She nodded.

"Hmm." I considered the question. "I think they were likely right, at least when it comes to the magical kind."

Elma soon hastened to the table, balancing two plates and two mugs of tea. She deposited the food before us and fussed over Daella for a few moments as she explained the perfect combination of olives, bread, and cheese. We ate in comfortable silence, occasionally commenting on the food and the brilliant sunrise slanting pink and orange light through the inn's windows.

Eventually, Kari approached. With her elf healing, there was no hint of the fight on her face. If I didn't know, I never would have guessed she'd almost died a few days ago. When she reached us, she dropped a small leather pouch onto the table and smiled timidly at Daella.

"I wanted to thank you for pulling me out of the water," she said, pushing her red hair behind her sharply pointed ear.

"You don't need to thank me," Daella said. "How are you doing? Looks like you healed up well."

Kari smiled. "Only because of you. I owe you one."

"I—" Daella tried to say, but Kari cut her off.

"I do, and that pouch there is the best I can come up with for now."

"You really don't need to give me anything," Daella said, her eyes churning with a darkness I understood all too well. She didn't think she deserved it.

"I know. But I'm giving it to you, anyway. Use it to win the Games, eh? Someone needs to beat Gregor."

And then she patted Daella on the shoulder and wandered back to her table.

Daella shook her head and lifted the pouch from the table, weighing it in her hands. "This smells like Vindur sand."

"It is," I said. "Kari brought a stash of it with her when she came here. She used to be a scribe, which meant she had access to all the different Galdur sand in the world. Brought Vindur and Jordur with her, though she doesn't have much left. It's a remarkable gift."

Daella fell silent as she finished her breakfast. Every now and then, she'd look at the pouch and shake her head, like she was thinking about trying to give it back. Thankfully, Kari left before she could.

When we finished eating, I left some extra coin on the table and thanked Elma on our way out. A short walk later, we were back home, and Daella helped me haul open the wide doors to my shop. It had been a few days since I'd opened the place, and the familiar scent of woodsmoke, iron, and fire rushed out into the street. Most weeks, I was open every day without fail, but the people of Wyndale understood things were different this year for Midsummer.

I did have some orders I needed to catch up on, though.

Daella followed as I ducked through the doors. Even though she'd been inside my shop twice already, she gazed at the towering brick forge with awe in her eyes. Pride swelled in my chest. I'd spent months getting this place into shape when I've arrived in Wyndale. I'd only been eighteen at the time, and it had been the first thing of my own I'd ever had.

"So what's your plan?" she asked, running a hand along the flat top of the anvil.

"We need to craft something beautiful and eye-catching." I watched her move through the shop like she belonged there, examining the hammers and tongs with keen interest. "Something beyond what anyone else will accomplish. Something that will clinch the win."

"One of your swords, then."

I folded my arms. "How did I know that'd be your first suggestion?"

"Tell me I'm wrong." She reached the forge and stuck her head inside to look around. When she pulled back, she caught my eyes on her, and she flushed. "An impressive forge can make impressive blades."

"No one here knows I craft swords," I countered. "Except you."

"You think they'll be angry with you if they find out?"

"No, I just don't want anyone to get any bright ideas.

203

Those blades are not for killing."

"What *are* they for?"

"I just…" I shrugged. "I like making them. It centers me and makes me feel like I'm doing something useful, even if they never get swung. But we're getting off topic now." I cleared my throat. I normally didn't bare these kinds of details with anyone other than Skoll, and certainly not with someone who was still very much a stranger.

Except Daella did not feel like a stranger, not anymore. I knew more about her past than I did about most of the folk who lived in Wyndale, people I'd spent the better part of fourteen years with, side by side, every day. It was a strange realization, one I didn't quite know what to do with.

Had I really kept myself that closed off?

I moved over to the wooden table along the back wall and held up a metal bracelet.

Daella frowned. "A bracelet? That's…nice. But it's not what I would call *impressive*. I saw your secret stash of swords. You can do much, much better than that."

"This won't be for the challenge." I smiled. "I'm going to teach you how to blacksmith, and we're going to start with something a novice can handle. That's this."

Her eyes darted from the bracelet to my face, almost eagerly. "Shouldn't you make something without much help from me? I didn't do an amazing job with the last trial."

I chuckled. "That's why we're starting with this bracelet."

20

DAELLA

Rivelin fired up his forge and flames engulfed the brick oven. Sparks danced in the air like fireflies, and wisps of smoke curled up the chimney. I watched, transfixed, as the orange heat poured through the shop. I'd never seen anything more beautiful in my life. And the scent of it all, the smoke and steel, it grounded me.

It took all day for Rivelin to teach me how to make a bracelet. Blacksmithing was a lot more complicated than I'd ever appreciated, but it was good, hard work. As minutes turned to hours, sweat drenched my shirt and hair, and every muscle in my body ached.

But at the end of it all, I earned a simple bracelet and a nod of approval from Rivelin.

"Here you go." I held out the bracelet. Crafted from iron, it formed the shape of a C with both ends tapered to a flat point. In the center, I'd twisted it four times so it had a decorative touch to the otherwise plain jewellery. Truthfully, it still didn't look like much, but I had to admit I was damned proud of my effort.

"No." Rivelin gently pushed my hand back, and an avalanche of steam gushed between us. "You worked hard for that. Keep it. Wear it, if you'd like."

I smiled and fitted the bracelet over my wrist. It was heavy and warm. I liked how it felt. When I looked up again, I caught the way he watched me with an intensity that made my soul match the warmth from the forge. A charming smile brightened his handsome face.

"Ah, I see what you do now," I said. "It's a good tactic, really. I bet it works more times than not."

He cocked his head. "I have no idea what you're trying to say."

"When I was dancing the other night, I overheard someone calling you a charmer, and I thought they were making a joke. But now I understand. You bring potential lovers into your forge and teach them how to make a bracelet. It's a simple task so they feel good about their efforts, and then they have a piece of pretty jewellery to remind them of you. Very clever."

"I've never taught another woman to make a bracelet, Daella. I don't like other people poking around my forge."

My breathing went shallow. "What?"

"I'm not a charmer," he said, lowering the tongs to the anvil, all the while keeping his eyes locked on my face. "Who did you hear that from?"

"The pixie with the pretty wings I met the other

206

day?"

"Odel. She only said that because she thinks I'm handsome."

I unintentionally snorted, then instantly coughed, hoping I could cover it up.

"Well, that's not the reaction I wanted to get from that statement," he said, though he sounded amused and his eyes were doing a twinkling thing that made my stomach feel funny.

"You're not *not* handsome," I admitted.

"High praise."

"You're an elf, and you're a blacksmith. It's a given that you'd have some...appealing attributes."

"Is that so?" He inched closer, and I stumbled a step away but my backside pressed into the edge of the anvil, halting my retreat. "And these appealing attributes would be...?"

I smiled. "You misheard me. I said *appalling*, not appealing."

He leaned in close and braced his hands on the anvil, one on either side of my hips. "You can try and backtrack all you like, but I heard you. What was it you said the first night? I should keep my hands to myself?"

I swallowed. "Yes, that's what I said."

"Hmm." His eyes swept across my face and lingered just a moment too long on my mouth. Suddenly, my lips felt impossibly dry, and it took all my self-control not to sweep my tongue across them. The moment stretched into another, the room silent but for the crackling flames from the forge. Was he going to kiss me? What a wild, ridiculous idea. Still, the tension between us felt palpable, so tangible it rose between us in a haze of steam.

And then suddenly, he shoved away from the anvil and stepped back. I nearly sagged forward—from relief or disappointment, I wasn't certain. Perhaps neither. Perhaps both. Fates be damned, I didn't *want* him to kiss me. I just...I shook my head to free myself from those kinds of thoughts.

"Something wrong?" he asked in a voice just a little lower than usual.

"No." I moved away from him and looked for something to busy myself with. A pair of metal tongs sat on the lip of the forge. We needed to clean things up before we went inside the house. As I reached for them, Rivelin let out a strangled yell.

Frowning, I lifted the tongs and glanced back at him. "What?"

He stared at me, his eyes wide. "That's been sitting by the fire. It's too hot to handle without gloves. Put it down, Daella."

"Oh." I set down the tongs and looked at my hand. The skin on my palm was perfectly fine. "Look, no burn. The tongs are hot, but they must have cooled off enough to touch."

Rivelin shook his head and moved to my side before poking at the tongs. "No, they're still burning." Gently, he lifted my fingers before his eyes and examined the skin, but I didn't know how well he could see with all the steam billowing everywhere. The air seemed to crackle, or maybe that was just my stomach. After a long moment of inspection, he let go of me. My hand tumbled heavily to my side.

"You're fine," he murmured. "Are orcs immune to fire?"

"No," I said quietly, my heart twanging. The moment suddenly dissipated like the steam. "My mother died in a fire, remember? From the Draugr."

"That's right." His face softened. "Perhaps just immune to heat, then."

"Perhaps."

Where a moment ago, an intoxicating tension had hung between us, now I just felt awkward. I shouldn't have touched anything. It only reminded us both of where I came from and what I'd come here to do. And the future that awaited me.

Quietly, we tidied away his things. I left him to handle the hot tongs with his gloves. We didn't have much to say for the rest of the night, even when we sat down for dinner in the kitchen, hand feeding Skoll our scraps. In the morning, we'd start working on the item we'd enter for the competition. Not a sword, he said, but something just as magnificent. I went to bed with images of fire and sun-kissed eyes in my mind, and I was so exhausted from blacksmithing I slept like the dead.

At the crack of dawn, I found Rivelin in the middle of the road staring at the shattered hinges of his shop's doors. They hung half-open, revealing carnage within. Splintered remains of wooden crates and barrels littered every inch of the once-polished floor. The racks that had held his hammers and tongs were now empty. Even the decorative horseshoes were missing. His metal sign rattled in the wind, creaking ominously.

Someone had completely ransacked the place.

Rivelin jammed his fingers into his silver locks and sank to his knees. The anguish on his face cracked some of the defenses that guarded my heart, especially the new ones I'd erected last night after our...moment in the forge. Slowly, I approached and knelt beside him on the dirt street.

"What happened?" I asked quietly.

A muscle in his jaw worked as his hard gaze never left the forge. "What does it look like?"

I ignored the snap in his tone. I would have snapped, too.

I stood and held out a hand. "Come on. Let's go inside and see what can be salvaged."

He looked up at me, his eyes dark and hollow. After a moment, he accepted my hand and let me tug him toward the broken doors. The interior was just as damaged as it had looked from outside. Most of his tools were missing, and it would take hours, if not days, to clean the place up. I kept those thoughts to myself, though. No need to make him feel any worse than he already did.

Rivelin picked his way through the debris to the closet door in the back. I noticed a heavy-duty lock now hung from the latch, and whoever had ransacked the shop hadn't managed to break it. There were a few dents in the wood surrounding it, though.

"If it wasn't for the lock, he would have taken the swords, too," he said wearily. "Just don't say 'I told you so.'"

I ran my hand along the top of the anvil. It was coated in a thick layer of sawdust, but it only needed a good clean to be as good as new. Same for the forge itself. The thief had only taken small things they could haul out of here easily, like the horseshoes. Anything else, they'd smashed to bits or left alone.

"I'm surprised you didn't hear anything," I said after a moment. "The sofa where you sleep is just on the other side of that door."

"I wasn't on the fucking sofa."

I glanced at him, surprised. "Where were you, then?"

I suddenly got the unwanted image of Rivelin sneaking into Odel's house and spending the night in her bed. He'd mentioned she found him handsome. What if they'd been an item all this time? What if they'd chosen to hide it so that I would accept Rivelin's offer to stay in his house, so he could keep an eye on the 'murk'? And now that he knew more about me, they'd gotten a little more relaxed about seeing each other.

He said he never brought women over to his forge. Was it because he was already taken?

And why was I even thinking about this right now?

"Patrolling the beach," he said.

"Patrolling? What for?"

"For any unwanted visitors."

"Ah." Relieved, I leaned against the anvil. "Is that how you found me when I washed up on the beach? You patrol there all the time?"

"The Elding rages just offshore all through Midsummer. Ships get caught up in it. Sometimes, folk manage to survive and end up on our beach. I like to be there when it happens."

"Most ships know better than to sail through the Elding. I doubt anyone will want to risk it for a while, especially after what happened to the craft I was on."

He gave me a long, hard stare. "You're valuable to the emperor, and you've been missing for a good while."

"Surely you don't think he would send a ship after me."

"You don't?"

"He sent me to the Isles of Fable knowing there was a good chance I'd die at sea. By now, he'll have heard the Elding smashed the ship to pieces. There's no reason for him to think I've survived. Why risk another ship?"

"What about the shard, then?" he asked.

The shard angrily throbbed in answer, and my hip ached.

"Oh, he'll use it if I don't show up in time, just in case I'm still alive somewhere. He's not the type to renege on his threats."

"Hmm." He glanced around the shop. "Well, you can be relieved about one thing. I'm not winning the Games, not now. The tools I need are gone."

"I'm not relieved about that. I want you to protect Wyndale," I found myself saying. The moment the words left my mouth, I frowned, and then realized I'd meant it. Somewhere between one week and the next, I'd come to understand these people weren't harboring the deep, dark secret I'd first believed. Yes, there were dragons around, but right now, they were harmless. And if Isveig invaded this place, he would destroy the peaceful tranquility everyone had worked so hard to create.

If Rivelin won, I did not know what that would mean for me, but I knew what it would mean for them. I would just have to find some other way to survive.

"Do you truly mean that?" he asked quietly.

"I do." I gazed around the destroyed shop. "And we can fix this. You can still win."

He held his hands out to his sides. "I'm all ears."

"The saboteur, Gregor. It's obvious he did this."

"Of course it was him. This is payback for saving Kari's life and turning the entire village against him. He likely thinks the only way he'll win now is by taking us out of the competition."

"Exactly. And what do you think he did with all your tools? He's not smart enough to get rid of them. I bet he even thinks he might use them to craft his own item from fire." I gestured at the missing rack of tools. "He'll be hiding them. In his house, I bet. I say we take them back."

Rivelin shook his head. "We can't just storm into his house in the middle of the day. He'll expect it."

"Exactly. That's why we go tonight."

21

DAELLA

After breakfast, we hauled the doors off the hinges and collected the debris from the shop floor, placing the wooden shards in piles out front. A few neighbors popped by to help. Milka, a dwarf from down the road, wandered over with some freshly baked bread that was much appreciated. Mabel brought us some mushroom pasties, and Tilda finally introduced herself.

She was a human of about thirty with deep brown skin and sleek black hair, and like Rivelin had said, she was about my height. I thanked her for the steady supply of clothes, but she just waved me away and carried off some of the broken crates to mend. Even Odel and Haldor joined in once the news travelled. They didn't say a word about who'd done it, but I could tell by the looks on their faces they had their suspicions, too.

In the late afternoon, Lilia swung by with jugfuls of a

sweet, lemony concoction that tasted like sunshine itself. As she watched me sweeping the floor, she folded her arms with a deeply troubled look on her face.

"Gregor did this, didn't he?" she asked.

I paused my sweeping and nodded. "We don't have any proof, though."

Lilia shook her head and gazed at the villagers sorting through the rubble we'd pushed out into the road. "I should leave Wyndale for the rest of Midsummer. This all started because of me, and I don't want Rivelin to lose the competition because Gregor is still angry I don't want anything to do with him."

"Leave? And go where?"

"Back up to Milford, and then Riverwold eventually. They're lovely villages, too. And then after the Elding moves along, I can sail over to Oakwater for a while. It's one of my favorite places in the Isles."

"But Lilia...everyone in Wyndale adores both you and the Travelling Tavern. From what I can see, it's an integral part of the Midsummer Games."

"My presence is agitating him."

"Fuck Gregor," I said firmly. "I'm going to prove he was the one who ransacked this place and stole Rivelin's tools. That means he broke the law, and he's out of the competition. You don't have to go anywhere."

The sides of her lips turned up. "You mean that?"

"Absolutely."

She nodded. "All right. If you're going after him, I want to help."

Out of the corner of my eye, I caught Rivelin's stare

from where he was polishing the anvil. A little tremor quaked my heart when he smiled. I found myself smiling back.

B y the end of the day, we'd cleared out half the shop. Weariness had settled over me like a fog. My body was still healing from my swim in the lake, and I wanted nothing more than to take a bath and climb straight into bed for a long, long sleep. But the idea of getting revenge against Gregor rejuvenated me enough to keep me from nodding off while we waited for darkness to swallow the last remaining dregs of sunlight.

I sat on the roof sandwiched between Rivelin and Lilia, two silver-haired elves I hadn't known two weeks ago but now felt like part of my crew. Together, we were going to resolve this Gregor issue, once and for all.

"You know you don't need to do this, Lil," Rivelin said, taking a swig of her infamous brew from a tankard etched in swirling elven designs. "Daella and I have this handled."

Daella and I. My heart thumped a little faster at the sound of those words.

"You two are very capable," the elf replied crisply. "However, you're not invisible. You need someone to distract him while you're rooting around his house. That someone obviously has to be me."

"I don't like it," Rivelin replied.

"Don't worry. We'll be in and out quickly," I said,

gladly taking the offered tankard. The brew went down sharp but sweet. "She won't have to talk to him for long."

"I don't want her talking to him *at all*. He'll think he's won her over and start harassing her again."

"That's true." I frowned and turned to Lilia. "You're certain you want to do this?"

She leaned in and clinked her tankard against mine. "It's worth the risk."

R ivelin and I lurked in the shadowy alley behind Gregor's house. He lived on the eastern side of the village, where single-story timber homes were packed together in neat little rows. Vines crept up the back wall and twisted around a chimney that puffed smoke into the sky, even at this late hour.

He was still awake, and judging by the looks of things, he'd gotten started on the Fildur Trial.

I exchanged a silent glance with Rivelin, and I swore I could read his thoughts just by the spark in his eyes.

Let's get the bastard.

We listened to the sounds of clanging and hammering, and then the boom of a fist on a distant door. That would be Lilia, interrupting Gregor's work. She'd lure him away from his house long enough for us to get a good look around.

Their muffled voices filtered through the walls. A moment later, the sound began to fade as Lilia led

Gregor to where she'd parked her tavern in the market square. There, at least half a dozen revellers still sat around the tables, trading tales and downing their ales. She might not get much help from them if they were that far into their spirits, but at least she wouldn't have to be alone with Gregor in the dark.

"Come on." Rivelin jammed his fingers beneath the window frame and hauled it open. A screech echoed into the night, but he didn't slow down. He threw his legs over the ledge and eased inside the house. My heart thundered as I waited. A moment later, he reappeared at the window and motioned for me to join him.

Once inside, I glanced around. Gregor's home was somehow simultaneously messy and sparse. In his one-room space, he had no more than a single cot squeezed into a corner, a small table and chairs, and a water basin beside a crackling fire. The orange glow illuminated a pile of familiar tools beside the hearth. Clothes and maps and empty bottles covered almost every inch of spare surface.

"Looks like we got our answer," I said.

"So strange," Rivelin said with a frown. "I thought this would feel far more satisfying. He'll be out of the Games because he's fool enough to leave my stolen tools scattered around his house? I always thought I'd have a real fight on my hands when it came time to defeat him. Preferably armed."

"I understand how you feel. In Fafnir, support was growing for Isveig's sister, Thuri. She's a good person, and she'd turn the Grundstoff Empire around—if she survived the shipwreck. The emperor's support is waning. And that's a good thing. It's just...I would rather see him go down with a sword through his heart."

"Vicious," Rivelin said, but there was no judgement in his tone. He moved to the tools and started collecting them from the floor.

"Aren't you a little vicious, too?" I asked as I joined him.

"Yes, but not mindlessly so like I was in the past. Now my rage is focused on Gregor, and anyone else who would threaten this place."

"And that's what all those swords are for." I hauled his hammer from the ground and propped the end against my shoulder. "You follow the rules of Hearthaven, but a part of you itches for a fight. And so you've made sure you're ready, if it ever comes to that."

"Wouldn't you—"

The door hinges creaked. Rivelin grabbed my arm and tugged me to the floor. I stumbled on all the mess, twisting sideways and barely catching myself as I face-planted on his broad, sculpted chest. He grunted and shifted beneath me. And as my heart thundered, I lifted my head and met his eyes. My face was only an inch from his, my lips nearly skimming the bottom of his chin. Fog rose around us like a cloud.

For a moment, I forgot what we were doing and why we were here. I didn't even try to move, my mind jarred senseless from the fall. He shifted beneath me once again, and every plane of his body pressed against me, from his chest down to his thighs, and *everything* between. I swore he was as hard as steel.

I shuddered out a breath.

"Gregor, where are you going?" Lilia exclaimed from the street just outside.

"I hate to disappoint you, Lilia, but I'm not interested in what you have to offer anymore, which is..." Disgust laced his every word. "...so little I don't know what I was thinking."

A low growl rumbled in the back of Rivelin's throat, and I hastily pressed my fingers to his lips. That single touch seared me with an intoxicating heat. His lips were so soft, so...*warm*, even though he was an elf. Everything within me coiled tight.

"Just...wait!" Lilia shouted.

In one fluid motion, Rivelin stood and somehow swept me to my feet, grabbing the last few tools from the floor beside the hearth. Five steps later, we were by the window. I went first, wriggling outside with Rivelin just behind. He landed beside me just as the sound of Gregor's footsteps echoed through the house.

Neither of us moved. I stared up at him, and he stared right back, the moonlight cutting a sharp line across his jaw.

"We should hurry back to the forge," he murmured.

Swallowing, I nodded. "Of course."

"In the morning, I'll report this theft to the others on the Village Council," he said, making no move to leave the alley. "It should be enough to kick him out of the competition."

"Yes, it will."

His eyes swept across my face. "Thank you, Daella. I—"

Lilia took that moment to rush around the corner. She waved at us feverishly, and whatever Rivelin had been about to say got left behind in the shadows of that alley. As we took the return route to the forge, Lilia apologized profusely for failing to keep Gregor's attention, despite the fact we'd scored the loot. Every few steps, I cast a furtive glance at Rivelin. Had he felt what I'd felt, back on that floor? What had I even felt, anyway?

Perhaps it had been nothing more than the excitement of the moment. We'd almost gotten caught, and both our hearts had been racing. Of course it was normal to get lost in that. It hadn't been anything more.

And it never could be.

22

DAELLA

"**I**'m telling you, I did not steal Rivelin's tools!" Gregor threw up his hands and paced before the small crowd, including his very stern-faced mother. He jerked his thumb at Rivelin. "It's him. He's framing me to knock me out of the Midsummer Games. I'm his biggest competition, and he knows he can't hack it unless I'm gone."

Odel's wings twitched as she frowned at the golden-haired elf. "Rivelin would never trash his forge. He loves that place."

Hofsa sighed. "I'm afraid I have to agree with Odel. We all witnessed what you did to Kari, and while you made sure to stay within the laws of the competition then, you have quite blatantly broken our laws this time. You're no longer a contestant in the Midsummer Games, and we'll have to think if you need an additional punishment. We do not *destroy* and *steal* another's property

223

here, son. That's the kind of behavior we'd expect in the Grundstoff Empire. And we will not allow it."

I could not hide my surprise. All this time, I'd assumed his mother was in on his schemes to win the Games and that was how he'd cheated to compete on three separate occasions. So if she hadn't been the one to aid him, who was? I glanced around at the crowd. Who would actually want him to participate, and why?

His mother walked purposefully to the stage, where five jars of pebbles still stood. She removed Gregor's and poured out the contents, her eyes never leaving her son's furious face.

"I didn't do this," he said through gritted teeth. "And one day you'll find out the truth and look like a fool. Your precious Rivelin isn't the saint he says he is."

After shooting a glare in my direction, he stormed out of the square. Gregor was out. But Rivelin was right. It didn't feel nearly as satisfying as it should have.

R ivelin and I fell into a pleasant routine over the next week. After we'd finished clearing his shop, he fired up the forge to start on our item for the Fildur Trial, and every morning at dawn we shared breakfast at his kitchen table—and with Skoll—before starting the work for the day. We enjoyed easy conversation as the flames roared around us, and then we broke for lunch where we often met Lilia, Odel, and Haldor in the square. Occasionally, we'd visit Elma at the Dreaming

Dragon Inn, and she always put some extra olives on my plate. The afternoons were dedicated to more forging, some of which included working through Rivelin's long list of commissions for the villagers: horseshoes, candlesticks, and a new plow for one of the local farmers. At the end of every day, I was so exhausted I often went straight to bed after dinner.

A couple of times, I offered to swap the bed for the sofa, but Rivelin firmly refused.

On the sixth night of all-day blacksmithing, I sat on the roof and tipped back my head to gaze up at the stars. There was a gentle breeze this evening, and there was a whisper of a chill in the air. I sighed and then breathed it in. Hard work felt good. I'd gone on a lot of missions for Isveig, but I'd never done physical labor quite like this.

The sky rumbled, a signal that rain was on its way. I hugged my arms to my chest and frowned, wishing I could have just a few more moments outside. But another rumble soon followed the first. Sighing, I moved to the ladder. Before I could make it back inside, big droplets of rain roared down from above.

I winced as the water made contact with my arms and cheeks. I'd only just healed from the lake. Gritting my teeth, I descended the ladder. Rivelin rushed out from the rear door of his shop—where he was still working—and tugged me inside, his face etched with concern.

He scanned me from head to toe, lingering on where my cheeks sizzled from the skyward attack. "How bad is it? Do I need to get some salt?"

I pressed my fingers to my cheek and winced. "I was only out there for a few moments. I've experienced far worse, as you well know."

"Hmm." He strode over to his worktable and flipped open a small trunk. A moment later, he returned to my side with a bag of salt, a bowl, and some dirt in his hands. "Have a seat. I'll sort it out."

I hopped up on the anvil, watching him pour a bit of salt in a bowl. "Where'd that bag come from? And the mud?"

"Swung by the alchemist's yesterday when you were in the bath. Thought I should stock up on salt and keep some in here, just in case. Looks like I was right."

My chest warmed as he dipped his fingers into the mixture and then spread the salve across my cheek. It didn't even hurt anymore, but I didn't have it in me to tell him, not when he was being so kind.

"You keep a special bag of salt in your forge for me."

He set down the bowl beside me. "I don't want my assistant to be hurt."

I smiled. "Careful. At this rate, you won't live up to your reputation of being a grumpy, insufferable bastard."

"Best keep it to yourself, then," he said in a low murmur. "How's your cheek feeling now?"

"Better."

"Have any other wounds that need tending?"

I shuddered as he dipped his fingers into the salve and then slid the mixture across a spot on my neck just below my ear. His touch was soft and gentle, and the steam from our contact erased any lingering pain, not that I would have been able to think of anything but the closeness of his body to mine.

My thighs spread instinctively, and without a word, he edged his body between them. Angling his head, he continued to rub the salt down the side of my neck, stopping only when he reached my collarbone. I held myself very still, scarcely daring to even breathe. My heart was rapturous thunder in my chest.

"How is that?" he asked.

"I…" A furious heat filled my cheeks. "I think a little rain may have gotten into my shirt."

What in fate's name was I doing? Rivelin was the *enemy*, except…he wasn't. Not anymore. He never had been. He was an angry, grumpy bastard, but he was also inexplicably kind, courageous, and protective of his people. And he was not *not* handsome. In fact, he was extremely attractive, even more than all the other elves I saw here every day.

He moved his hand to my tunic and popped one of the buttons. A tremor went through me as his fingers moved to the next. I palmed the smooth steel of the anvil and hung on as if I were seconds away from plunging over the side of a cliff. If I fell, I'd never recover.

He reached the bottom button and stared so intently into my eyes that several seconds ticked by before I could breathe. There was a silent question in that look, a search for confirmation. Swallowing, I nodded.

With an almost feral glint in his eye, he snapped free the final button. The tunic fell open, and the warm air from the fire caressed my bare nipples. A muscle in

Rivelin's jaw tightened as he gazed down at me, his lips curling in wicked satisfaction.

"I see a spot that needs healing," he murmured.

He dipped his fingers into the salve once more, then ran them along the curve of my cleavage. I tightened my grip on the anvil and struggled to stay still as he slowly stroked my breast, his touch more tantalizing than before. With darkening eyes, he continued to rub the spot where the rain had seemingly burned me, and then he swept his thumb across my peak.

A storm of pleasure engulfed me, and I bit my lip to keep from moaning.

"Oh, is *that* the right spot?" he asked in a deliciously sultry voice I'd never heard from him before.

"Mmm hmm. That's one of them, yes," I managed to say.

He dragged his thumb across my swollen nipple, and despite my every attempt to remain still, I arched against him. Sudden need clenched my thighs, tightening around his hips. He edged a little closer, and something hard pressed against my core.

"I think I need a closer inspection," he said roughly.

He cupped my breast, leaned in, and stroked his tongue across my peak. I couldn't contain my moan. It spilled from my throat as I reached out and dug my fingernails into his arm. The steam was a hazy fog now, so thick I could see nothing but Rivelin's face and those bright, brilliant eyes that lit up the dark.

He continued to caress my breast with his tongue,

teasing me, tasting me, causing a need unlike any I'd ever felt to pound through me.

When he pulled back, I thought he might stop there, or he'd return to his pretend wound tending. We'd crossed a line, but we could still pretend there was nothing to it. He was merely soothing my aching skin. He had accidentally spent a few moments too long on the wrong spot, that was all.

But then he cupped my face, leaned in, and kissed me. His mouth melted against mine, and an intoxicating heat burned the last of my inhibitions away. This was it, everything I'd secretly wanted for days—Rivelin's mouth against mine, the heat of our touch steaming between us, and his arms on either side of me, protective and strong. I reached up and clutched his tunic, tugging him closer to me. The hard length of him pressed against my core, and something primal awoke within me.

I arched against him, grinding my hips against his. The low growl that rumbled from the back of his throat lit every inch of me on fire. He pulled back, and I gasped for air as he tugged my tunic over my head. The warm air of the forge caressed my bare skin, but it was nothing compared to the heat in Rivelin's gold-flecked eyes. No one had ever looked at me like that. My heartbeat roared in my ears.

Rising from the anvil, I gathered the soft material of Rivelin's tunic in my hands and slowly, methodically, lifted his shirt to reveal the generous planes of his well-muscled chest, only marked by a key dangling from a chain that hung around his neck. I leaned in and kissed one of the many ridges, relishing in the steam that clouded around us and in the feel of his smooth skin against my lips. He slid his fingers into my hair and gripped tight, holding me there.

A delicious thrill went through me.

I kissed him again and again, moving from one sculpted pinnacle to the next, the mountainous peaks of muscle just as breathtaking as I'd expected. But I wanted more. So much *more*. I lifted my hands to his belt and undid the clasp, then raised my eyes to meet his.

The intensity of his gaze made the world drop away. The only thing that mattered was this.

"Ladies first," he murmured as his hands palmed my hips and tugged down my trousers. I stepped out of the material, now exposed before him, and then his trousers joined mine on the floor. His hooded eyes raked across me. "You are the most spectacular creature I've ever seen."

I let my eyes drift south. His swollen cock was larger than I'd expected, and by the way it strained toward me, he felt the same delirious heat I did. Swallowing, I sat back on the anvil and spread my legs for him, tossing my hair back from my shoulders.

"Fuck," he murmured, coming closer to me, so close his tip brushed against my aching core. "You're already soaking wet for me, Daella. But I need to know how you taste."

He knelt between my thighs and gripped my hips. I sucked in a breath, my entire body coiled so tightly I felt like I might shatter into a million pieces if he so much as breathed on my skin. But Rivelin wasted no time. He leaned in and caressed the inside of my thighs with his lips. I shuddered against him, clutching the side of the anvil behind me. Sparks of pleasure filled my eyes.

"That's right," he murmured against my skin. "Spread your legs for me like a good girl."

I eagerly obeyed his command and spread them wider, enjoying the bite of the metal against my backside. Rivelin's fingers dug into me, then he flicked my clit with his tongue. A moan escaped my throat, and I nearly broke just from that small touch. Shaking, I couldn't breathe as his tongue swept across me once more.

Fates be damned. Was this what I'd been missing all my life?

"Your taste is intoxicating," he said in practically a growl. As if he'd been unleashed, Rivelin drove his tongue across me, licking my opening as if he wanted to lap up every last drop of the wetness I'd conjured just for him.

The pressure in my core built. Everything within me narrowed to that point, where Rivelin was devouring me. I gasped as my very soul itself seemed to crackle like flames. And then suddenly, the roar of it consumed me, burning through me, tearing me up like fire. I shuddered, coming hard against Rivelin's mouth as the moans spilled out of me.

My tremors slowed, and as I tried to catch my breath, I finally noticed the dense fog swirling through the shop. It was as thick as a cloud on a stormy day now, and I could barely see Rivelin's face as he rose to stand before me.

"Rivelin," I murmured, light-headed from my climax.

He took my hand and wrapped it around his cock. I shuddered as he dragged my fingers along the hard length, stopping only when my thumb brushed the tip that was coated in his need for me.

"Turn around," he said roughly. "And hold on to the anvil."

I swallowed and turned, presenting my backside to him as I palmed the cool steel of the anvil. A moment later, his swollen tip pressed against me. The quakes nearly started anew.

He gripped my hips and slowly inched inside me, not stopping until he filled me to the hilt. My walls spread for him, taking him in eagerly. With a soft groan, he pulled back, then thrust inside me once more. I lifted my hips and ground against him, desperate for more of him.

Having him inside me, this man who had somehow stolen past the walls around my heart, made me come undone. I was his to take however he wished, at least for this one night. My moans mingled with the thickening fog as he thrust harder into me. My thighs knocked against the steel.

Rivelin's pace quickened, and his primal groan captured my breath and held it in my throat. I curled my fingers against the anvil, my nails scraping the steel, as that delicious pleasure built inside me once more. I wanted to hold on, I wanted to feel his cock inside me for hours more, but it felt too good. Every single thrust brought me closer to the brink of combustion.

"Let go, Daella," Rivelin said as his fingers dug into my skin. "Come for me."

He plunged his cock inside me once more, releasing his own grip on his pleasure. As his groans filled my ears, everything within me shattered. I came even harder than I had before, and wave after wave of intoxicating heat flowed through me. I couldn't breathe or think or even feel anything other than Rivelin and the way he held on to me as I shuddered against him.

When the internal flames finally died, I slowly breathed and released my grip on the steel. Soot stained the anvil in the shape of my hands.

23

DAELLA

"**G**ood morning." Rivelin's voice cut through my dreamless sleep, and I awoke curled against his chest, my hip cushioned by a blanket that hadn't been there when I'd fallen asleep on the workshop floor. Another blanket was draped across my body, soft against my bare skin.

Memories of the night before rushed through my mind, and my cheeks heated. I didn't regret one moment of it, but...what did we do now? Did we discuss what had happened between us? Or did we ignore it and return to how things had been before? I'd fought battles against Draugr, and had dispatched monstrous trolls twice my size, but I was lost on how to navigate this.

Almost certainly, this had been one night of hazy lust and nothing more.

Rivelin seemed to note my silence, and he slowly extracted himself from our makeshift bed on the floor.

He ran his fingers through his mussed hair, his jaw tightening. I opened my mouth to say something, but I didn't know what. I'd never been in this situation before.

"Thank you for the nice time. I, ah, should get dressed." As soon as I spoke them, I instantly regretted my words. They sounded so distant and hollow, so devoid of warmth. But what else was I to say?

"Of course." He held the blanket around his waist while he gathered his clothes, avoiding my eyes. "Best get up, then. We have a few pieces to finish up before the Fildur Trial ends tonight."

And that was that.

Awkward silence supplanted the blissful routine of the past few days. Rivelin and I moved carefully around each other, like a dance where neither party was allowed to touch. Any time I got close, he found something else to busy himself with, even if it was rustling some papers on his worktable. When it was clear we were mostly done with our preparation and he didn't need my help anymore, I excused myself to take a bath before tonight's event.

I hated how unstrung I felt, like I was a pool of tangled ribbons with no beginning or end. Truly, I needed to get it together. I still had a few weeks left here, and that was only if I couldn't find a way to stay permanently. I didn't want to spend the rest of my time in

Wyndale on constant edge just because I didn't know how to act around a man who'd seen me naked.

Easier said than done.

After a long soak in the saltwater tub, I felt a bit more like myself. I'd gone round and round the situation in my mind, and I'd decided I could just pretend we were friends who had gotten carried away. *Good* friends. Affectionate friends. But still, friends. And if I thought of him as nothing but a friend, I might not stammer and blush every time I looked at him.

Still, when I stepped into the living room after brushing out my hair and donning a violet silk dress with a slit to my mid-thigh, I was almost struck speechless by the sight of him. He wore a finely tailored tunic with looping silver threads forming an intricate elven pattern along the V-neck collar, which also had the added effect of exhibiting his chiseled physique. Wet strands of his hair curled around his tipped ears, and droplets of water clung to his skin. He must have taken a bath after I did, while I was getting dressed. The idea of him naked in the tub only moments after I had been...

His eyes heated as he stared at me. "You look beautiful."

"I..." I looked down at the ground.

"I see. Are you ready to go? I want to get this spectacularly boring evening over with," he said curtly, dousing any hope we might regain our footing here.

"Rivelin."

"Daella."

I blew out a breath. "Can we...start acting normal again?"

"Are we not acting normal?"

"You're being a bit of a grump."

That had been the wrong thing to say. His expression darkened almost instantly. "This is who I am. Is that a problem?"

I sighed. "Thank you for the compliment. You look nice, too."

"You're welcome. For the compliment and the sex, though it appears you'd like neither of those things from me."

"Is that what this is? You regret last night?"

He raised his brow. "You tell me."

"*No.*" I crossed the room to stand before him and almost instantly wanted to take it back. Not because I wanted to avoid him, or because I regretted anything at all. But because being near him made my nerves tangle in my belly. It was hard to think straight around him. "I've never done this before. Couldn't you tell last night?"

The corners of his lips tipped up. "Are you telling me I'm the only man who has ever explored those exceptional curves?"

I let out a nervous laugh. "Don't get cocky."

"No, I couldn't tell." He tucked a wayward strand of hair behind my ear and brushed his lips across mine. "You were incredible."

I fisted his tunic in my hands and tugged him closer, relishing in the feel of his skin against mine and the rising steam that never failed to burn between us. I could get lost in that kiss, could forget about the Midsummer Games and spend the rest of the night exploring every inch of his skin.

But not now. Tonight's festivities were far too important to miss.

He groaned as he pulled back, a sound that sent a delicious thrill down my spine. "Keep this moment in mind. We'll revisit it when we get home tonight."

My heart pounded. "I hope that's a promise."

He tucked a finger beneath my chin. "Oh, it most certainly is."

I n the hills just beyond the village, spectators had sprawled across the grass on checkered blankets, and several tables had been carried over from the square. The caravans and stalls had followed, including Lilia's Traveling Tavern where the atmosphere had taken on a very boisterous nature. Booming laughter drifted on the light wind that rustled the flowing skirt around my legs. Beside me, Rivelin carried the majestic dragon sculpture he'd been toiling over for the past several days. I'd helped as best I could with the larger pieces of the structure—the tail and the head—but the delicate, artistic wings and teeth had needed a practiced hand.

Several *oohs* and *ahhs* followed us as we approached the stage, where the others were already waiting. Gregor was nowhere to be seen, of course, though that did little to calm the pit of nerves in my stomach. He would be angrier than ever now, and it wouldn't surprise me if he retaliated. Tonight would be the perfect moment to make his move against us, smashing Rivelin's dragon into broken bits.

Hofsa nodded from where she stood overseeing the festival as Rivelin gently set the dragon atop the stage. Down the row, I could see what the others had created for this night. Beside us, Godfrey had created elegant candles in various pastel shades. Further down the row, Hege, the dwarf, had a plate of grilled fish. She'd gone with an interesting take on the fire theme, though not one I would have chosen myself.

Now that we were down to only four contestants, there was only one other left on the far end, and from what I could see, no item had been delivered to the stage just yet. Viggo, the winner of the previous challenge, stood there quietly beside his assistant, his red hands folded in front of him.

I leaned in and whispered to Rivelin. "What do you think that's about?"

Rivelin frowned and shook his head. I knew what he was thinking. It was almost impossible Viggo had decided to forfeit his place in the Games, especially after winning the first. That could only mean he had something up his sleeve. Judging by his relaxed posture and the hint of smugness on his face, he clearly thought whatever he had could win.

And if he won two out of four...that could effectively clinch the entire competition for him.

"You don't think—" I started to say just as a sharp, high-pitched whistle rent the night.

Bright orange light streaked through the sky and exploded in a confetti of sparks overhead. A hush went through the crowd as the first blast was soon followed by another—this time in a brilliant red. Then another in golden yellow. Again and again the sparks filled the sky, the light reflecting on the awestruck faces of the spectators.

Movement caught my attention down the row of competitors. Viggo smiled and lifted his hands to his sides, motioning at the display and mouthing something I couldn't hear over the blasts. I didn't need to, though. It was clear this was his submission for the Fildur Trial.

Something stirred in my chest. It truly was breathtakingly beautiful, and it was almost impossible not to revel in it. I looked up at Rivelin, noting the tightness of his jaw and the furrow of his brow. Whatever this display was, it would win, and I didn't know what to say to ease his frustration.

When the final spark blinked out of the night sky, the crowd cheered. Then came the presentation for the rest of us. The others went first, showing off their grilled fish and their candles, which only resulted in a mild, scattered applause. Rivelin held up the dragon when it was our turn. The cheers were louder this time but nothing compared to the response to Viggo's sky of sparks.

We wandered away from the stage when it was over. One by one, spectators came to add their votes to the glass jars. It didn't take long to see there would be a clear winner.

"I'm sorry," I said to him as we grabbed two bowls of bread and stew from one of the many market stalls. "I know how hard you worked on that dragon."

"I can't be angry when someone wins by besting my own effort," he replied.

"I don't think it's your effort he bested. He just made something...well, remarkable. What *was* that?"

The tables were packed, so we found a couple of crates stacked up near the line of merchant stalls and settled in to eat our dinner. Rivelin took a few bites before finding an answer to my question.

"I've never seen anything like it before, and I daresay no one else has, either. Must be something only fire demons know how to make. That's why he'll win."

"Looks like we'll stay in second, though." I nodded toward the stage in the distance. Spectators were still making their votes, but from here, it was clear to see we'd remained the runner-up. Unfortunately for the other two contestants, Hege and Godfrey, very few had voted for them. They didn't stand a chance any longer.

"Those votes won't be enough, not unless we win the final two challenges by a landslide," said Rivelin.

"Vindur and Jordur. Air and Earth."

"And I can't say I have anything good up my sleeves for either of them, unless you use the Vindur sand Kari gave you," he said. "Even then, I don't know what we'd do with it."

We finished our dinner, and Rivelin went to say hello

to his sister. I offered to return our bowls to the merchant, telling him I'd catch up when I was done. I was halfway to the stall when a weird hiss sounded from the bushes nearby.

"Psssh. Daella," a harsh voice whispered.

Frowning, I edged closer to the bush. A hand shot out from the branches, grabbed my arm, and tugged me through the scratchy plant. I cursed and spun away, only to come face-to-face with Gregor. He looked terrible. Purple stains rimmed his bloodshot eyes. His golden hair was askew, like it hadn't seen a brush in months, and dirt splattered his trouser knees. Had he been crawling in mud? No matter. The worse shape he was in, the easier it would be to defeat him.

He held up his hands as I launched my fist toward him. "Stop. I'm not trying to hurt you."

I froze. "Right. You just ambushed me when I was alone because you want to make nice."

"Actually, I do. We need to talk about Rivelin."

I narrowed my eyes. "What about Rivelin?"

"He's using you."

"You're a couple weeks too late. He's helping me. I'm helping him. Neither of us is using the other." Not anymore.

"Oh yeah? Helping you with what, exactly?"

"None of your business," I snapped.

With a shake of my head, I turned to go.

"I didn't destroy his shop and steal his tools," Gregor called after me.

I froze. "You don't actually expect me to believe that."

"Think about it," he said, moving to stand beside me. "Why would I be so blatant about it? Wouldn't I hide the tools if I stole them so that it couldn't be traced back to me?"

"You provoked Kari in front of everyone," I pointed out. "Don't forget. I was there. And she wouldn't be alive if I hadn't been."

He folded his arms. "All right, I did provoke her. I didn't outright attack her, though. Not until she attacked me. Because I play the game within the rules. Leaving stolen tools lying around is something only a fool would do."

"So someone framed you, is what you're saying." I patted his arm. "Nice try."

"Wait," he said quickly, digging into his pocket and producing a folded piece of parchment. "I thought you might want to see this."

I narrowed my eyes at him. "What's that?"

"I've got friends in Fafnir. I sent them a letter via raven when you first got here, asking them about you."

"You did *what*?" I advanced on him, horror snaking through me. If Isveig got wind that I was here and very much alive...

"Don't worry. They're loyal to his sister, Thuri. Turns out she survived the whole ordeal." He passed me the parchment.

I didn't want to look at it, fearing this was some kind of trick. But the roaring in my head was too loud for me to ignore. Without another word, I unfolded the note.

The heir is alive.

That was all it said. I lifted my eyes and looked Gregor. "You expect me to believe this is from Fanfir, and it's talking about Thuri?"

He shrugged. "Take it as my truce. I made a mistake, but I'm trying to make it right—starting with warning you about Rivelin."

I backed up and shook my head. "I'm returning to the celebration now."

"Just think about it," he said as I parted the bush. "Why didn't Rivelin hear someone destroying his things? Who wants to win this competition more than anyone else? Perhaps Rivelin sabotaged his own damn shop to set me up. It wouldn't be the first time he's tried to get rid of me, especially after I tried to romance his sister. He holds a grudge."

"I'm done listening to this." I shoved through the shrub, ignoring the scratches along my arm. When I stumbled back into the celebration, I searched the crowd for Rivelin and found him beside the stage frowning at the glass jars. It looked like everyone had cast their vote now. As expected, Viggo was still in the lead.

With narrowed eyes, Rivelin shifted his gaze from the jars to where Viggo stood surrounded by a gaggle of pixies. He glowered at the fire demon in a way that sent a chill down my spine. I recognized that look. I'd seen it on Isveig's face before. He was angry, and he was out for blood.

24

RIVELIN

D aella was contemplative for the rest of the night, and when we returned home, she went straight to bed. I'd hoped to continue our earlier encounter, but I had to admit my mind was elsewhere, too. Viggo's spectacle was odd. Where had he come up with something like that? It didn't sit right in my gut.

After checking the lock on my weapons closet, I settled onto the couch, tossing and turning for a good hour before I finally abandoned sleep. There was far too much on my mind.

And so after donning a shirt and downing a pint of water to clear my head, I stole out the front door toward the square where I knew I'd find my quarry.

"Rivelin, fancy seeing you here," Haldor said with a slight smile as I settled down beside him. The square was subdued this night, compared to the others. Those still celebrating the end of the Fildur Trial were out in the meadow, where most would remain until dawn. Not Haldor. Every night, he brought fresh flowers to lay at Freya's stone feet. The fire demons still worshipped the Old Gods. They'd never become part of the Grundstoff Empire, though Haldor had lost everyone dear to him in a battle against Isveig. He'd been a lonely, quiet man when he'd arrived in the Isles, until he'd met Lucien. They'd married each other a year later. Still, Haldor came here every night without fail to remember those he'd lost all those years ago. Many of us here in Wyndale had similar stories.

"How are the memories?" I asked him quietly.

He sighed. "Same as they always are. Fresh as the day they were made. It's both a blessing and a curse, a demon's mind. I can remember everything I've ever seen and heard and tasted. But the horrors of my past echo with an almost-crushing vibration."

"And yet you're one of the happiest folks I've ever met."

"Yes, well." His eyes crinkled in the corners when he smiled. "Love changes everything."

"Hmm. I think I've heard you say that one too many times, but I'm glad it works for you, Haldor. I really am," I said. "Want to take a walk?"

"Where to?"

"The Archives."

He stood and motioned for me to lead the way. "Now you've got me curious."

We moved out of the square and down the main thoroughfare of the village, where silent shops sat closed for the day. Only a few windows were lit up in the rooms above them, and the sound of our footsteps was loud amidst the rare moment of calm tranquility. During Midsummer, Wyndale was rarely quiet for long.

"What are you looking for?" Haldor asked after a few moments.

Shops signs creaked as we continued around the corner toward the Village Hall. "I need to know everything I can about Isveig the Conqueror and his power over ice."

He looked at me, surprised. "I thought you'd demand to know how Viggo made his fireworks. I saw the way you were looking at him earlier."

"Fireworks? That's what they're called?"

He nodded.

"And how did he make them?"

"Fire demon secret recipe." Haldor chuckled. Ah, so that explained it. "I thought you wanted to know about Isveig's conquering."

"Not his conquering. I know about that. I was there, unfortunately. I need to know about his magic."

We came to a stop outside the Village Hall. This time of night, the place was closed, and it was one of the rare instances where we used a deadbolt to lock the doors. Trust was an important component of our community, but we didn't want a tipsy visitor to wander in and accidentally ruin our Archives. I extracted the keychain from my belt and unlocked the door.

Once inside, Haldor lit a lantern that hung on an iron hook beside the door—one I'd crafted myself. The orange glow revealed the long, narrow building with timber beams arching high overhead. A hanging candelabra dangled over four expertly crafted dining tables set out in the center of the stone floor, all facing the desolate hearth. Ancient shields decorated the walls, along with the ivy that spilled in through a crack in the far left corner. In winter, life and laughter filled this place, but most preferred the outdoors during the summer months.

Haldor's melancholy seemingly forgotten, he sauntered across the empty dance floor and twirled. "Have you shown Daella this building yet? I bet she'd like it."

I gave him a dark look. "Don't you start."

He chuckled and continued to twirl until he reached a door along the rear wall. "You forget how well I know you, Riv. You actually look *happy* around the orc."

I scowled.

"Yes, that look right there. I'm seeing it less often these days."

"Can we please just go into the Archives and focus on what's important?"

"I'd argue this is important, but very well." Haldor pushed open the door and waited for me to follow. We descended a curving stone stairwell that saw little use. When I'd first arrived in Wyndale I'd spent hours combing through the stacks, but many of the books were written in the language of the humans, and I didn't have the patience to listen to one of our resident humans translate.

But I remembered there'd been a few books from Grundstoff, from before it had become an empire. I hoped there'd be answers about Isveig inside.

When we reached the bottom of the stairwell, Haldor lit a few more lanterns scattered throughout the small underground room. Seven rows of dusty shelves were packed with ancient tomes and scrolls and loose papers bound by twine. I moved to the section written in the language of the Old Gods and began to rifle through the nearest book.

Haldor folded his arms and leaned against the shelf, watching me. "What's this about, anyway?"

I had considered not telling Haldor about Daella's... affliction, but if anyone in this village could help me solve this thing, it was him.

"Isveig rammed an ice shard into her hip."

Haldor flinched, then let out a low whistle. "How is she even alive? Usually, that causes instant death."

I snapped the book shut, and a cloud of dust rose around us. "So you do know about his power."

"Not his power, per se, but I spent enough time around ice giants in my youth to know how they operate. They love to use their ice shards on the battlefield like deadly spears. If the shard embeds itself in someone's skin, it chokes their lungs and freezes them to death. Horrible way to die. It's how Isveig was so successful in his conquest. Hard to fight against that unless you've got some form of Galdur sand, like Fildur."

The leather-bound book creaked as I clenched it tighter. "That's what Daella has to look forward to unless I can find a way to reverse its magic. Isveig has control over the shard somehow, that's why it hasn't killed her yet. But he's threatened to unleash its power if she doesn't return to Fafnir less than two months from when he shipped her off. I'm not sure how long she has now, but it can't be more than a few weeks."

"I see. I'll admit, despite what I said earlier, I'm surprised," Haldor said quietly.

"Surprised by what?"

"You want to save the orc."

I pulled another book off the shelf, if only so I had something to look at other than his scrutinizing gaze. "It doesn't seem right sending her back there, and there must be a way to get that shard out of her body."

"I'll help you look. I just have one question."

I glanced up. The thoughtful, melancholy Haldor stood before me now rather than the boisterous life of the party he was most hours of the day. He tapped the edge of the book. "What are you going to do if there is no cure?"

"There has to be a cure."

"Some folks can't be saved, Rivelin. You can't protect everyone."

Ignoring him, I flipped through the book. It was a tome that told the story of the Kingdom of Grundstoff and their devotion to Ullr, the God of Ice. He'd once ruled their lands until he ascended to Valhalla with the others, though the giants had never recognized any of them as gods themselves. They worshipped the ice and everything that sustained it. To them, it was above and beyond the standard four elements. And so, everything else was inconsequential.

Everything else but fire, which they hated and feared. Isveig feared it so much he'd taken every opportunity to destroy it, and kept Daella away from it as much as he could.

"I'm a fate's damned idiot," I muttered.

"That's true, dear Riv. Mind telling me what brought on such an astute observation?"

I snapped the book shut and placed it on the shelf. "Fire."

"Water."

I frowned.

"Earth. Air. There, we've named them all."

"You are an obnoxious man sometimes, Haldor."

"*Demon*, and thank you. Now why are we talking about fire? I'm quite fond of it myself."

"Daella has an ice shard in her hip. What's the opposite of ice?"

"Ah." He absentmindedly scratched his left horn. "I see where you're going with this. It's a good idea, but don't you think she would have tried that by now?"

"I'm not sure," I said. "She told me Isveig has tried to keep her away from fire all these years. I bet that's why."

"Won't that burn her?" he asked.

I thought back to all the days she'd spent working

with me in the forge. On more than one occasion, she'd touched a hot surface without gloves, and she hadn't even flinched. So much knowledge of orcish history had been lost over the years, but there was one fact that had never been forgotten. Orcs ran hot.

"I don't think it will burn her at all."

I said goodnight to Haldor and returned home to a silent house that didn't feel so empty anymore. Even though she was in the bedroom asleep, I could feel Daella's presence all around me. It was in the angle of the armchair she'd shifted to face the hearth, where wood still gently smouldered. It was in the plate of scraps she'd left beside Skoll's bundle of blankets for when he returned from his nightly patrol through the Ashborn Forest. And it was in the empty mug she'd washed and left sitting upside down to dry beside the sink.

With a slight smile, I looked back at the bedroom door. I didn't want to wake her, but I hated to wait until morning to tell her my idea. If we could melt that shard, I knew she'd want to do it as soon as possible. She could be free of Isveig. She wouldn't have to return to Fafnir. She could stay here and drink her tea every night beside the fire, petting Skoll whenever she wanted...and be happy.

As I debated whether to wake her or wait until the morning, another peculiarity caught my attention. Several of my desk drawers hung open, where I stored parchment, ink, and wax seals. Moving closer, I examined the disturbance. A couple sheets of parchment were missing, and the tip of my quill was wet with ink.

I frowned. To whom could Daella be sending letters?

She'd made it clear she had no one back in Fafnir. No one but Isveig, and she hated and feared him. So why—

Footsteps reverberated down the hallway. I turned, expecting to find Daella walking toward me, unable to sleep, just like me. But something heavy and hard slammed into my skull.

My knees buckled as darkness took me.

25

DAELLA

A wet nose nudged my arm, but it was the stab of pain that woke me. I opened my eyes just as Skoll bounded onto the bed. My skin still burned from where he'd shoved his snout on me, but a quick rub of the blanket and it was fine. I closed my eyes and started to drift back to sleep. Until he started whining.

He paced across the quilt, bits of his dark gray fur floating through the air. The volume of his whine increased as he suddenly went still and stared at me with those luminous eyes.

"Skoll, what's wrong?" I asked, before throwing my legs over the side of the bed.

My worst fears rushed through my mind. Somehow, Isveig had arrived in Wyndale, and he was locking every single person here in chains. He would drag them back to Fafnir and throw them into the hot, humid dungeons beneath the castle. They'd never again see daylight.

But no, that couldn't be right. I knew his scent as well as I did the Draugr, and I would smell him the second he stepped foot on this island. I took a sniff of the air and only found smoke.

"Fire." I ran to the door, barefoot, and followed the scent into the hallway. Around the corner, orange flames danced. Skoll's paws pounded the floor behind me as I raced into the living space. Flames engulfed the parchment on the desk, and Rivelin was lying face down with a trail of blood snaking across the floor.

"Fuck." I fell to my knees and placed the back of my trembling hand against his cheek. Steam hissed from the contact, and a groan rumbled from his chest.

I blew out a breath of relief and sat back on my heels, trying to understand what had happened, but the crackle of flames drew my attention once more. The fire had spread to the wall. Soon, it might engulf the entire room.

I ran into the kitchen for some water. By the time I'd returned, Rivelin had rolled onto his back and was staring up at the ceiling with a very familiar, very distinct scowl. Skoll was licking his cheek, still whining.

After I carefully doused the flames, I returned to Rivelin's side and got a look at the wound on his forehead. A purple bruise had formed, swelling up like a stone. There was only a small gash in the center of it, and the blood had already started to slow. I heaved out a very long sigh.

"You look like you're about to cry," Rivelin muttered.

"Why would I cry? This is a perfectly normal way to be woken in the middle of the night. A fire, a little blood, an unconscious blacksmith. What's the problem?"

Rivelin coughed out a laugh, then groaned. "I can't believe you're making a joke at my expense."

"I can't believe you set fire to some parchment and then...what, exactly, did you do? Run into the wall?"

Rivelin winced and started to sit up, but I was there by his side before he made himself pass out again from expending too much effort too soon. I slid under his shoulder and hooked my arms around his back. Slowly, he climbed to his feet, his formidable weight bearing down on me. He teetered for a moment, clearly struggling more than he wanted to admit. Before he could object, I helped him over to the sofa and gently tried to sit him down. The way he landed on the cushions was anything but light, however.

For a moment, he just sat there blinking. Skoll had abandoned whining for frantic sniffing around the spot where I'd found Rivelin.

"Your vacant stare is beginning to worry me. Is there a healer in the village?" I finally asked.

"There's an apothecary down the road, but she won't have anything to help this. I'm just stunned and dizzy."

"From what, Rivelin? You still haven't told me what happened."

"I got hit on the fucking head."

I frowned and joined him on the sofa, folding my bare legs beneath me. "What are you talking about? Someone was here? In the house?"

"I was looking at my desk, and then I heard footsteps. Thought it was you, of course. Turns out some bastard came into my home and took a hammer to my head."

I sucked in a sharp breath. "Did you get a look at their face?"

"No." He blinked again, and I frowned.

"You need to lie back and close your eyes. I'll get you some water and a cold compress for your head."

"That will hurt your skin," he said roughly.

"I can manage."

As I stood to go, he reached out and grabbed my hand. "Daella, were you using my parchment and ink to write a letter to someone?"

I bit the insides of my cheeks. So that was why he'd been looking around his desk when the intruder had attacked him. He'd noticed, though I could have sworn I'd put everything back into its rightful place.

Rivelin cracked open his eyes when I didn't immediately reply. His gaze scanned my face, and then he sighed. "You did. Are you going to tell me to whom you were writing? Because from everything you've told me, I didn't think you had a friend back in that shit city you've been trapped in all your life."

A familiar set of walls rose around me, protection from him and everyone else I'd ever faced. What would he do if I told him the truth? Would he even believe me?

I sighed. "I wrote a coded letter to Thuri, Isveig's sister."

"I thought you said she was on that ship with you."

"She was, but she's a strong swimmer. If I could make

it out of the Elding alive, maybe she could, too. I sent her a note to find out if she somehow made it back to Fafnir." And I could discover if Gregor had been telling the truth. "Don't worry. Even if Isveig intercepts it, he'd never understand what it means."

Rivelin looked at me for a good long while. The dying embers from the hearth warmed my back, but there was a chill in the air that made strands of steam curl from my skin. Even in the dead of summer, the night's cool kiss awakened the fire in me.

He finally said, "I want to trust you, I really do."

"And I want to trust you. Where were you tonight? When I got up to write my letter, you were gone."

"I was in the Archives, searching for a way to melt that damn ice shard stuck in your hip. Turns out, we need fire. That's what you've needed all this time. And to think it never occurred to me until tonight."

Hastily, I stood. "What?"

There was a roaring in my head as unadulterated hope rushed through my bloodstream like flaming oil. Rivelin, despite his wound, looked so certain, so *confident*. I'd accepted my fate a long time ago. Hoping for a different future had hurt more than the quiet acceptance of the truth: I would never rid myself of the shard, and one day it would take my life. The only way out was Isveig's offered freedom, and deep down I'd doubted I would truly gain that.

To even consider there might be a different path ahead made me feel as if I'd been running across a battlefield for miles.

"It's fire, Daella," he said. "I think we use it to melt the ice."

"But the ice is inside me. To burn it away, you'd have to burn me, too," I said, barely louder than a whisper.

"You're immune to fire, I'm certain of it."

I shook my head and backed away, heading toward the kitchen. I needed a moment to think. Tonight's series of events felt as peculiar as a dream. Could there truly be a way out of this? Was this why Isveig had kept me away from flames? I'd always assumed it was because he was fearful of them—and he likely was—but this was so much more.

How could I have been such a *fool*?

After filling a glass with water, I returned to the living space. Rivelin had abandoned all attempts at recovery and was now poking at the embers in the hearth. Then he took a bellow to the sparks. Brilliant orange light flashed across his stern face as the flames roared to life. I pressed a hand to my heart, hating the deep-seated fear that slashed at my hope. What if Rivelin was wrong? How could we be certain this wouldn't boil my skin? My parents had faced the flames once. And they had not survived.

But that had been the flames of dragon magic.

Rivelin caught the look on my face, crossed the room, and gently took my hands in his. "It won't burn you. Can you trust me on that?"

Could I trust him? I wanted to. Deep down, I knew his idea was a good one. I'd touched some hot tongs in his forge, and they hadn't burned me. And yet, I could feel the weight of my fear in my bones. My palms were sweaty, my chest tightened, and my head felt as if I were the one who'd been hit by a hammer.

But I knew what my mother would say if she were here: *Ris upp fyrir ofan, Daella.*

Rise above, Daella.

A tremor went through my heart, but I lifted the bottom hem of my nightdress and exposed my scar. Rivelin's eyes sharpened on the puckered skin and the faint blue glow. The skin around his jaw tightened. "Every time I see what he did, I want to forsake my quiet island life and feed the emperor my sharpest blade."

"What kind of wine would you pair it with?" I asked.

A vicious glint lit his sun-gold eyes. "Whatever the dreck is that comes from his veins."

"Are you just talking like this to distract me from the fact you're about to put a torch against my bare skin?"

"Only partially," he said with a smile that was far closer to an orc warrior's feral grin than an expression I would have expected from a village blacksmith. "Did it work?"

"Only partially."

Rivelin turned back to the flames and stuck the end of a torch in the hearth. Sparks scattered into the air above our heads, and the roar intensified. Skoll chose that moment to exit the building. I didn't much blame the wolf for that.

When Rivelin pulled the torch out of the hearth, the end blazed like an inferno. Fire licked the air, the dancing forks bleeding into a deep, terrifying red. I swallowed around the painful lump in my throat.

"Trust me." He inched closer, his brow raised in question.

I nodded and reached for something to steady me. He passed the torch to one hand and held out the other for me to take. When I slid my fingers into his palm, he squeezed tight, as if he truly understood how difficult this was for me to face.

And then, without warning, he pressed the edge of the torch against my skin.

I braced myself for pain, but instead, a soothing heat curled through me. The fire lapped at my skin, its greedy tongues searching for purchase. But my body seemed to reflect the fire on itself, as if my hip was coated in a protective material. Similar to oilcloth, but for flames. Rivelin had been right all those days ago. Fire didn't burn me.

All it did was make me feel warm.

With an awestruck laugh, Rivelin pulled the torch away from my skin. His eyes darted across my hip, and his expression dimmed. "Ah."

I glanced down. The scar looked the same as it had for years—a healed yet rough patch of bumpy pink skin covering a faint blue glow. The torch hadn't burned me. But it hadn't melted the ice shard, either.

There would be no escaping Isveig. He'd made certain of that.

26

DAELLA

"It didn't work." I sighed and moved over to the sofa, where I promptly dropped onto the cushions like a puppet whose strings had been snipped. The ice shard had started throbbing, like it knew I was trying to rid my body of its cruel magic.

Rivelin tossed the torch back into the hearth to let it burn down with the other logs, then joined me. His left shoulder and thigh pressed into mine. He felt so warm and powerful, and I suddenly realized just how small the sofa was. There was no way to put space between us. Not that I wanted to—I just found it difficult to concentrate with him so close.

"I'm sorry I gave you hope. I really thought it would work," said Rivelin.

"Deep down, so did I." I looked up at him and caught his stare. A quiver went through me. "You really should rest. That wound on your head…"

"I feel fine now. I'm an elf, remember? We heal fast."

"What kind of bastard would attack you in your own home?" I scowled, and in unison, we said, "Gregor." I shook my head. "I just don't understand why. Attacking you accomplishes nothing, even if he does want revenge. If anyone would understand how fast you heal from a wound like that, it's him."

Rivelin shifted sideways and took my chin between his fingers, gently guiding my eyes to meet his. "I don't want to talk about Gregor."

I swore my heart skipped a beat, an expression I'd always rolled my eyes at before. But I'd felt it—a pulsing tremor that stole my breath away. "I assume we need to start on the next trial in the morning. Should I leave you to get some rest?"

"Absolutely fucking not."

"Oh?" A smile curved my lips. "Is there something else you have in mind?"

His hand glided from my chin to my ear as he slowly slid his fingers through the strands of my hair, then gripped them in his fist. My breath caught as he tugged me closer and brushed his lips against my ear.

His breath caressed my skin, sending a shiver through me, and he said, "Someone broke into my house and attacked me. There's only one thing that can make me feel better. I want your perfect lips wrapped around my cock."

A shiver stole down my spine. "I thought you said you feel fine now."

"Did I say fine? I meant I can't stop thinking about

dripping wet and hot you were when I fucked you in my forge."

I shuddered, reaching for his belt, my knees digging into the cushions. "Well, in that case, I should heal your affliction."

Rivelin watched me with hooded eyes as I undid his belt and tugged his trousers down his legs. Wetting my lips, I gazed down at his cock, wondering how I would fit the entire length in my mouth. Something in me heated, my core tightening.

Slowly, I gripped his shaft and lowered my mouth to the tip. I brushed my lips across it. A hiss escaped him, his hand tensing where he still gripped my hair. My core ached even more at the delicious thrill that went through me, just from getting a reaction out of him so easily.

I spread my lips and slid them down the length of him, moving my hand at the same time. A low guttural sound escaped his throat. "Fuck, Daella."

"Mmm." My voice rumbled against his skin as I took him in further, deeper and deeper until his tip hit the back of my throat. And then I moved back up and brought my hand with me. His hold on my hair tightened.

"So fucking perfect," he groaned.

I took him faster and deeper, my hand and mouth working in unison. As I tasted and sucked and licked every inch of him, I felt his tension mount and his cock stretch larger. I squeezed his balls with my free hand, and that was all it took. His climax crashed through him, rocking into me. A groan spilled from his lips, and his seed coated my tongue. It tasted of salt and of him, somehow. With a smile, I swallowed it down.

As I sat up, he gazed at me with such an intoxicating mixture of desire and affection that my heart nearly stopped working right then and there. His hand grazed my cheek, then he started to lift his tunic over his head. And I knew without a doubt, he wasn't done with me yet. Good. I didn't want him to be.

But when he was partway through undressing, he frowned and looked down. He patted his bare chest, his face paling. And then he leapt to his feet. "The fucking key is gone."

"What?" Confused, I watched as he hastily dressed and stormed toward the door leading down into his forge. By the time I'd stood from the sofa, he was back, angry lines bracketing his mouth.

"What's going on, Rivelin?"

His hands clenched. "The lock on the weapons closet is unlatched. Gregor stole my swords."

I followed Rivelin outside. Behind a hazy fog of clouds, only the bottom half of a crescent moon was visible, cutting through the night sky like a scythe. I tried not to take it as an omen as I walked down the road by Rivelin's side and the night's chill bit into my skin. My breath puffed from my lungs as I endeavored to keep up with him, his elven speed powering his strides.

It didn't take long for us to reach the eastern side of

the village. Gregor's windows were dark, and unlike the last time we'd paid him a visit—albeit more furtively than now—the chimney expelled no smoke. Rivelin pounded on the door but didn't wait for an answer. He slammed his boot into the wood and stormed inside.

I followed just behind him, casting a quick glance over my shoulder at the homes across the street. With this kind of noise, I wouldn't be surprised if someone came to investigate.

"Gregor," Rivelin called out as he moved through the messy room. "You can come out. There's no use in hiding."

But there was no answer or any sign of movement.

"I don't think he's here, Rivelin," I said.

Frowning, he took one last look around and returned to the road outside. I followed, quietly closing the door behind us, though I needn't have bothered. Several faces were already peering out their windows at us.

"We need to find him and the swords," Rivelin said, dropping his voice to a near whisper. "If he's angry and retaliates against the folk of this village, I'll never forgive myself for making those weapons. I broke the law, and I might have doomed us all."

"He's only one man. Even if he rushes into the village with a sword, there's far more of us than him."

"Us?"

"I...yes. Isveig was cruel to me, but he did have his sister train me to fight, and she's one of the best out there."

"I know that, Daella. But you spoke like you consider yourself one of *us*."

"Oh." My heart pounded. "I suppose I do, in a way. At least when it comes to Gregor."

Rivelin smiled slightly, but then he ran his hands through his hair, his expression now pained. "This is supposed to be a peaceful island, where nothing terrible happens, and yet here we are conversing about swords and making stands against the enemy. I thought, if we tried hard enough, this place could be immune from that kind of darkness. And yet it follows me no matter hard I try."

I moved to stand before him and pressed up onto my toes to palm his cheek. "Don't lose hope just yet. There may be no need for a fight. All we have to do is find Gregor before he makes his move."

"Any idea on how we can do that?" he asked.

I thought back to the last time I saw Gregor. He'd been lurking in the trees. "I think he's hiding out in the Ashborn Forest."

We waited until dawn before setting off to the forest. It would be more difficult to find him—and a hidden stash of swords—in the dark, and if he'd been awake all night for his thieving activities, he might find himself drifting off to sleep during the day, despite his best intentions.

After tugging the pack over my shoulders, I jogged

270

down the steps and breathed in the scents of the village morning. Milka was already baking bread, judging by the earthy aroma drifting out of her open window from down the road. The old dwarf across the way sat on his toadstool with his pipe. He lifted his hand, waving. Dew clung to the vines crawling up the side of Rivelin's house, and birdsong filled the air. I breathed it all in and smiled.

"Morning, my dear," a soft voice called out to me.

I turned to see Mabel shuffling down the road, her smile as bright as the morning sun. Today she wore a dark green tunic, the edges embroidered with ancient words only I would recognize. *Ris upp ur oskunni.* The belt cinching her waist was a set of twisting chains, and the clasp had been forged into the shape of a dragon spreading its wings. Only Draugr wore clothes etched in dragon symbols.

The world beneath me seemed to tip sideways.

"Where did you get that belt?" I asked, hating the accusatory tone in my voice. But she'd been there in that village with the Draugr that day. I'd believed her to be innocent when I found her hiding in the cupboard. Had I been wrong?

She hobbled closer, leaning on her cane. "My husband gave it to me. It was his mother's, and her mother's before that. It was passed down in his family for centuries. I would have passed it on to our daughter, had we ever had one."

"It's an orcish belt?" I asked, furtively scenting the air. No hint of Draugr.

"That's right. Just like this tunic."

"Oh. All right." I suppose it might make sense. Still, something about it unnerved me. It felt as though I were looking in a mirror, but a warped version of myself was looking right back and grinning like a fiend.

"Here." She held up a linen sack. "I made you two some pasties for your journey."

I relaxed and smiled. "How did you know we were going on a journey?"

"I live over by Gregor." She chuckled. "You two made quite the ruckus last night. I heard every word you said, including the bits you probably didn't want me to hear. Nevertheless, it makes no difference to me what our dear blacksmith crafts. Just so long as he gets them back and puts them someplace safe."

I nodded. "We'll do our best. And thank you for the food."

"I just want my home protected, you hear? We all do. Why do you think so few of us stepped forward for the Games? It's Rivelin's turn, and we know he'll find the right words to keep us safe from that monster across the Boundless Sea. And you will, too."

27

DAELLA

Mabel's words followed me all the way into the forest. I'd wondered why so few had put themselves forward for the Midsummer Games, when such a prize was within reach. None of them knew what Rivelin would ask of the island. He could never tell them, but they trusted he'd make the right choice. They believed he would find the perfect words to protect them from the empire.

And they were right to put their faith in him. He would do it.

If I had my way, I'd steal it all away from them. Or I would have, when I'd first arrived here. I didn't think I could do it anymore, even if it meant I would never taste freedom again. Perhaps there was another option, but I didn't see a way out of this.

"You're quiet," Rivelin said as we walked along the trail that wound east through the Ashborn Forest. A marvelous collection of trees stood like silent sentinels all around us. Redwoods with their brilliant rusty bark were interspersed with oaks and big leaf maples, forming a lush canopy overhead. Rabbits scampered by, along with red-bellied newts. Everywhere I looked, there was life.

Isveig *hated* life, and magic, and the elements themselves—except for the kind that thrived in the frosty wilds.

"I'm just thinking. It won't be long before I must return to Fafnir."

Rivelin glanced at me sharply. "You have a couple weeks yet, and we'll find a way to free you before then."

"If the fire didn't work, nothing will."

"I haven't looked through all the tomes in the Archive," he tried.

But I knew time was running out.

We continued to search for any sign of Gregor, venturing deeper into the forest. The day passed quickly, and soon, the haze of dusk began to creep through the dense trees. After taking a break to feast on one of Mabel's mouthwatering pasties, I broached the idea that we should turn back.

"I don't think we're going to find him out here, at least not today," I said quietly from my perch on a fallen log. I brushed the crumbs from my trousers and stood. "By the time we get back, it'll be dark."

Rivelin braced his forearms on his knees and frowned. "He can't have just vanished."

"Perhaps he stole the swords and went north to one of the other villages. He could do what you thought I would and pawn them off for a bit of coin. That could be all this is, instead of some plot for revenge."

"That seems unlikely," he said.

"Well, he's not out here, so we should get back. We can't protect the village if we spend the night in the forest."

For a moment, I thought he might argue. Rivelin was a very stubborn elf, I'd discovered. It made sense with everything else I'd learned about him. He had decided on his role in life and he refused to waver from it. In his mind, if he bent he might break. If I wanted to reach him, I had to do so in terms he would understand.

"We need to get started on the next trial for the Midsummer Games," I said. "If we don't win this one, Viggo's lead will be impossible to erase. And Isveig is far more of a threat than Gregor."

He looked up. "You're right."

Just as he stood to go, a screech echoed through the skies above. A thunderous boom soon followed, like the heavy beating of a war drum. The trees quaked in response, their rustling branches raining leaves all around us.

My heart jolted in my chest. "What *is* that, Rivelin?"

"A dragon," he murmured with a hint of confusion in his voice. "But I don't know why they'd be here. They only leave their cave to hunt at night, and they rarely venture far from the mountains."

Still, the dragons—or at least one of them—were very much here. The trees above seemed to spread wide, like the pages of a book fanning open. A red-scaled dragon swooped low and landed on the ground just before me. Hot air blasted into my face.

Sulphur and spice and saltwater. Hints of leather and dust.

The scent of the dragon consumed me, choking the breath from my lungs. I stumbled forward and fell to one knee before the creature. Its leathery snout inched toward me and sniffed. Even though it was bound, my hair whipped my face and neck, stinging my skin.

"Aska," Rivelin murmured from somewhere nearby. "Stay back. This is Daella. She will not harm you."

I glanced up sharply. The dragon was so close now I could see the varying shades of red on its scales and the reflection of my own face in its bulbous orange eyes, along with the sharp points of every tusk along its wings and the wicked teeth that were larger than my head. I could smell the smoke and fire and the overwhelming power that seemed to pulse from its skin. A tremor went through me.

I swallowed and managed to find my voice to say, "Aska? That's its name?"

"Her name, yes," Rivelin said, though he sounded more tense than I'd ever heard him, almost as if he wasn't convinced these dragons were as harmless as he'd told me. "The others are Eldi, Reykur, and Hita."

How odd. Those were orcish names.

"And why is she here?" I whispered.

A pause. "I do not know."

That was not particularly reassuring, nor did I breathe even when the dragon relaxed onto her haunches and neatly folded her leathery wings against her back. She blinked at me, then sniffed again, cocking her head.

The dragon clearly smelled something. Was it me and my orcish blood, or…I glanced down at my pack. It still sat open on the forest floor, where I'd tossed the almost empty sack of Mabel's mushroom pasties. Even all these hours later, the savory scent of them hung around us like a cloud.

I cocked my head and extracted the final one. "Is this why you're here? You'd like some of Mabel's treats?"

Aska eagerly thumped her tail, spraying dust and fallen leaves into my face.

"Well, fates be damned," Rivelin said.

I started to place the food on the ground in front of the dragon, but Aska shoved her snout into my hand before I could manage. I tensed and slowly opened my palm. Tail still thumping, Aska gently took the pastie from my hand and swallowed it in a single gulp. I could only watch, dumbfounded. All these years, *this* was what I'd been afraid of? She was no more terrifying than Skoll.

Aska nudged my hand again, a deep rumble coming from her throat.

"I'm sorry," I said. "That was our last one."

She closed her eyes and sighed as she leaned her muzzle against my palm. I stroked her snout, a strange sensation kindling in my heart. It was that tug—that impossible-to-resist urge to bond myself to this dragon, to use her magic as mine. I'd felt this urge all my life, but it had been so easy to force it down when Isveig had eradicated all the dragons.

All but four, it turned out.

And if I was not careful, I knew I'd give in to this desire. I couldn't ignore it forever. No one ever did.

Slowly, I pulled back.

"Daella," Rivelin said, snapping my attention away from Aska and those flaming eyes that seemed to see through me, right into my soul. "Is your hand all right?"

"What? Of course it is. She wanted my food, not my fingers."

"I meant your skin," he said so intently, a chill caressed my bare arms. "No one can make contact with dragons. It burns. That's why I can't get close."

I blinked. "Oh. I'm fine. I suppose that's not much of a surprise since I seem to be immune to fire in general."

"Yes, but I do wonder…" He stared at the dragon for a good long while, then blinked and shook his head when Aska suddenly pushed off the ground and returned to the skies, leaving behind a whirlwind of leaves and dirt. "Your mother was an orc, and she died in a Draugr fire, you said?"

I frowned. "Yes, that's right."

"That's what I thought. I'd hoped, perhaps, Aska's fire might melt your ice shard, but it's too much of a risk to try." He sighed. "We best return to Wyndale. After the past few days, I think we could both use a good night's sleep."

The next week passed quickly. Gregor never showed himself, and we focused our attention on the trial when we weren't working on commissions in the forge and Rivelin wasn't digging around the Archives for a way to melt my ice shard.

For the Jordur Trial, we were to use the elements of the earth to create something truly remarkable. Unfortunately, this task didn't line up with Rivelin's strengths the way the last two had. Every morning, I'd catch him at the dining table, surrounded by piles of sticks, rocks, and flowers, looking completely helpless. Truth be told, I wasn't much help.

"Perhaps we could make a rock formation." I poked around at the pile of stones. It was one day before we were to present our creation to the spectators. So far, we had little to offer.

"We could. And then we would lose," Rivelin answered dryly.

I dropped into the chair across from him and tried not to stare at the way his freshly washed hair curled across his ears. The past few days had been fraught with tension between us. I hadn't mentioned our intimate moments, and neither had he. Every now and then, I'd catch him staring at me from across the forge, sparks and heat dancing between us. But he never took it further than that, and neither did I. As far as I could see, whatever this was between us was doomed. Soon, I would be forced to leave this place, and I'd never find the freedom to return.

All I could do was ensure Wyndale was protected before I went.

"Right." I flattened my hands on the table. "From what I can tell, the Games tend to follow the same pattern each year, yes? You always do something with a boat for the first task, and then you have to create something using fire for the second one. And now we need to present something earthen for the third. Is that the same every year?"

He nodded. "That's right"

"So what have others done in the past?"

Rivelin drummed his fingers on the table. "Nature wreaths, bug hotels, flower arrangements, art using stones. Some have crafted bowls or plates. The truth is, all of these work just fine, but none of them are spectacular enough to guarantee a win. After that fireworks display, Viggo will have something up his sleeve, I guarantee it."

A thought occurred to me, and I leaned forward. "Has anyone ever baked something?"

Rivelin went still. "I don't know the first thing about baking."

"Oh, but I do." I smiled.

R ivelin headed to the market to collect a list of ingredients from the grocer—flour, eggs, butter, milk, and sugar—along with some sweet spices from the apothecary. He returned just as I finished clearing the dining table of earthen debris and scrubbing it with a saltwater dishrag.

He dumped his cargo by the sink and eyed me warily. "Are you certain you know what you're doing?"

"I grew up making these." I motioned at the satchel. "Did you get the muffin tray from Mabel?"

"Yes, she had one, just like you thought."

"Good. Get me a bowl, then fire up the hearth. I'm going to need some gloves, too."

His lips twitched as he moved to the cupboard. "Someone is feeling bossy."

"You best believe it. We have a lot of cupcakes to make."

The morning passed in a delicious haze of baking. At first, Rivelin watched me mix the batter and frosting, only jumping in to hold the tin over the fire. Soon, his house filled with the sweet scent of sugary perfection. After the first batch cooled, he sampled my concoction and gave me a wide-eyed nod of approval. Two more batches in, he jumped in to help mix.

When he poured the bag of flour into the bowl, a cloud of white sprayed his face and clothes. He blinked, coughing, and I couldn't help but laugh.

"You're supposed to pour it into the bowl, not on your face," I said.

He waved at the fog of flour and slowly approached, like a wolf stalking his prey. "Oh, is that so?"

"Now Rivelin. Wait—"

He took his flour-dusted hand and smeared it across my face. My mouth dropped open, and as I reached for the bowl of frosting, Rivelin wrapped his hands around my waist and lifted me onto the dining table. Leaning close, he pressed his forehead against mine. Steam and flour and heat whorled between us.

"You look impossibly appetizing today, baking cupcakes in my kitchen with the scent of my house and my forge—and *me*—all over you."

Shuddering, I breathed him in and tasted his scent, realizing that yes, at some point, ours had mingled, despite sleeping in different rooms and scarcely touching each other for days.

"They say the way to a man's heart is through his stomach," I said.

A man's *heart*.

As soon as I'd said it, I wanted to take it back. How foolish and embarrassing could I be? Now Rivelin would get the wrong idea. He'd believe I expected more from him, that I'd read too much into a brief moment of passion. It had been meaningless and nothing more.

And I didn't think I could face him every day, let alone work beside him, if he thought I was falling for him.

"My heart, eh?" He brushed his nose against mine, and a quiver went through me. And that was when I realized my fear of leaving Wyndale was not entirely about Isveig. I had met someone who understood me and had devoted his life to protecting his people—the people he'd chosen as his. He tried to hide how much he cared behind a gruff voice and scowl, but I could see the truth in him. Inside, he was just as soft as one of these cupcakes.

I smiled at him—*really* smiled. And I couldn't remember the last time I'd tried to fake one. It had been days. Maybe even weeks.

He gripped the back of my head and kissed me fiercely, like he'd yearned for this moment just as much as I had. My toes curled as he explored my mouth with his tongue, tasting me as if he'd never get his fill. My heart throbbed painfully in my chest, a delicious, intoxicating thrill going through me. His touch set me on fire, but even more than that, everything about the way our bodies fit together felt achingly *right*.

When he pulled back, he ran his fingers through his hair and sighed. "I'm sorry. I can't fucking control myself when I'm with you."

"What is there to be sorry for?" I wound my arm around his waist and tugged him closer. I wanted him here, like this. No more dancing around it or avoiding the tension that burned between us every moment of every day. Unless we could find a miraculous solution, I didn't have much longer in Wyndale. Time was flying by. It was a waste to pretend like there wasn't something powerful between us and not to relish this unexpected bond. Every moment was far too precious not to take it by the horns and *live*.

"I am not the kind of man you need in your life," he said roughly. "I'm an insufferable, grumpy bastard. Those are your own words. As much as I'd like to spend every night in bed with you, you'll be far better off if we don't. In fact, I've started asking around about a house here for you. One that you can call *yours*. There are a couple vacant ones over near the—"

I pressed my finger to his lips. "You're an insufferable bastard, but you're also protective and courageous and *kind*. No one has ever treated me the way you do. *No one*, Rivelin."

"You mean, like when I tossed your beloved mother's dagger into the sea and then threatened you with bodily harm?"

"Eh, I would have done the same to you," I said with a slight smile. "A murk washed up on your shore. What else were you to do?"

He searched my eyes. "I don't deserve anything with you."

I hopped off the table and pulled my tunic over my head. "You deserve it all."

We couldn't remove the rest of our clothes fast enough. When our garments were tossed across the floor, covered in flour, Rivelin hungrily lifted me back onto the table and took my breast in his mouth, teasing my peaked nipple with his tongue. I dropped back my head and moaned, tangling my fingers in his hair. Fates be damned, I had wanted this for days.

His free hand gently squeezed my other breast, then he slid his palm across my nipple. A delicious ache tightened my core.

Rivelin lifted his head and captured my mouth in his. His soft lips consumed me, his kiss so intent it was as if he thought he might never have the chance to touch me again. Our bodies crashed together as a hunger unlike any I'd ever known clutched me in its grip and held me there. My breasts pushed against his sculpted chest, and I hooked my leg around his thigh, tugging him closer.

I needed him, now more than I ever had. We'd given in to this before, but there was something different about it now. It was as if all the walls around my heart had finally crashed to the ground, becoming chunks of rubble. Rivelin had breached my defenses, and what was more, I was glad for it. For the first time in my life, I did not need to hide the truth of who I was and how I felt. I was free to just be me.

A deep groan rumbled from the very depths of his soul as he pressed his swollen tip against my core. Chills swept through my entire body at the feel of him there. His cock brushed against my clit. *Oh fate.* I spread my legs wider and arched toward him, my body begging him to take me here on this table with flour painting our cheeks and arms.

He inched inside me, slowly at first, before he thrust so hard and deep I cried out.

"Rivelin," I gasped, clenching around him.

"That's a good girl," he murmured as he palmed the table on either side of my hips. He slid out, then pounded into me once more. Sparks of pleasure spotted my vision. Already, everything within me coiled so tightly I could barely breathe.

"Lean back," he commanded. "I want to see you squirm while I bury my cock inside you."

Another wave of pleasure washed over me at the

dirtiness of his words. Heart pounding, I lowered myself to the table, feeling the scrape of wood against my back. I stared up at him and put both feet on the table, spreading my thighs even wider. I'd never been so bold in front of anyone, but something about the way he looked at me made me want to show him every inch of my body, show him exactly how much I craved his touch.

I could give him every part of me, and he would not use my emotions against me or wield them as a weapon. He would merely give himself over to me as readily as I did to him. I trusted him, I suddenly realized, my heartbeat loud in my ears.

I trusted this elven blacksmith with every single ounce of my heart and soul.

He gazed down at my soaking wetness with feral need pouring across face. Gripping my hips, he thrust inside me so hard the table rocked beneath me. The bowl of flour tumbled over the side and dusted the floor. I moaned, holding the table as it shook. At the sound of my pleasure, a wicked glint lit Rivelin's eyes, and he thrust faster and harder until I was nothing but a panting mess, desperate for more.

Suddenly, he lifted me from the table and carried me to the wall, keeping our bodies locked tightly together. Steam hissed between us, the heat of it matching the fiery need in my core. More gently than I expected, Rivelin trapped me between the hard planes of his chest and the timber beams of the house, but it was his eyes that captured me. They were a bright, burning gold.

"You're beautiful," he murmured, dropping his forehead to mine. "Everything about you is perfection."

He rocked his hips against me, gently this time, as if he were savoring every second he could spend inside me. I wrapped my arms around his neck and met his intense gaze with one of my own, one I hoped he understood. I wanted him. No, I *needed* him, here and now and every night to come. A slight smile tipped up the corners of my lips, conjuring a deep groan from Rivelin.

"Stay with me, Daella." My name rolled across his tongue like a prayer as he continued to thrust inside me. "We'll find a way to keep you in Wyndale. I want you here, in my forge and in my bed."

My heart throbbed, my fingers tightening around the silken strands of his hair. "For how long?"

"I can't imagine I'd ever want this to end."

Desperate desire pounded in my head. Truth was, I felt every single word as if I'd spoken them myself. Being here with him like this was the best thing I'd ever known.

"I don't want this to end, either," I whispered back.

His thrusts grew deeper, and I slid my hands across his broad shoulders, relishing every inch of his powerful body, every flex of muscle as he savored how I felt wrapped around his cock. Our heavy breaths mingled between us, steam fogging the air.

Heat burning through me, my core tightened. As if sensing my building orgasm, Rivelin groaned and plunged inside me, again and again until—

White hot spots stormed through my eyes, and a

powerful rush of fire swept through me. I cried out, shuddering between his chest and the rough wall, the powerful quakes of my climax pounding through every inch of my body. Rivelin released a primal groan as he came only seconds after, his throbbing cock emptying inside me.

I sagged against him, my heart pounding so fast I swore it might shake out of my chest. And with my head against his shoulder, I could hear the same frantic heartbeat from him.

He pressed his lips against my forehead.

"I want to be yours, at least until day breaks," he murmured against my hot skin. "I don't want to stop kissing you and touching you and tasting you."

I met his eyes, smiled, and whispered, "Then don't."

That night, Rivelin finally joined me in the bed.

28

DAELLA

I had a bounce in my step as I wandered through the maze of stalls set up along the perimeter of the festival, absentmindedly twisting the handmade bracelet on my wrist. Rivelin and I had not gotten much sleep, but I'd never felt more awake. No, that wasn't quite right. I'd never felt more *alive*. Humming cheerfully —I went with the tune about Isveig I'd heard from the bard that first week—I stopped by Elma's booth, where she had a platter of various cheeses set out for the occasion.

"Morning, Elma," I said with a smile. "Thought you'd be at the Inn."

She eyed me carefully as the shadows whispered across her skin, and for a moment, I worried she'd decided she didn't like me very much after all. "Pointless being there with the trial ceremony looming. No one will be in town right now."

"Well, lucky me, I guess. I'd love some of that cheese."

She grinned. "You know the drill. No coin, no cheese."

I dropped a pile of gold onto the counter that Rivelin had given me and exchanged it for a block of crumbly cheese. As I popped the delicacy into my mouth, Elma smiled and wished me luck. Right now, I didn't really feel we needed much of that. I'd already spotted the other contestants, and while our cupcakes wouldn't quite be the runaway hit like fireworks were, I had a good hunch we'd still win.

It felt like everything was starting to fall into place, even though we hadn't yet found my cure. So as I headed to the stage, I should have expected what happened next. Gregor appeared from nowhere, grabbed me by the waist, and hauled me into the bushes again.

I elbowed him in the gut and twisted away from him.

"What in fate's name do you think you're doing?" I hissed.

He looked even worse than the last time I'd seen him, and that was saying something. His golden hair hung in tangled clumps around his gaunt, dirt-stained face. Had he been eating?

"I need to talk to you," he said wearily. "About Rivelin. Again."

I heaved out a sigh. "I see what this is. You're holding his swords hostage. What do you want in exchange for them? Something to do with the Games?"

"What?" Confusion rippled across his face. "Rivelin has swords?"

"Don't play the fool. What do you want for them?"

He held up his hands in surrender. "I don't have them. I didn't even know he *had* swords. Do Odel and Haldor know? It's against the laws of this island."

I eyed him, taking in his puffy eyes and—shockingly —his bare feet. His shirt was in tatters, and he hunched over, like he was in pain. "Someone broke into Rivelin's house, knocked him out, and stole some swords. Are you really saying it wasn't you?"

"That kind of thing doesn't happen in Wyndale."

"Except it did happen, and you're the most likely culprit."

He frowned. "And you saw this yourself?"

"Yes. I mean, I saw the aftermath. I found Rivelin unconscious, wounded, and bleeding on the floor. Then we realized the swords were missing."

"That's clever of him." Gregor paced, his bare feet thumping against the ground. "Where was this wound? On the front of his head or on the back?"

I narrowed my eyes. "His front. What are you trying to suggest?"

"Rivelin is the mastermind. Think about it, Daella. He wants to win this thing more than anyone, and he's willing to do whatever it takes. I was his biggest competition, and he got me kicked out by framing me."

"Stop being so delusional. You weren't his biggest competition. Viggo is. And besides, we all know—"

"You're right. Viggo's winning." Gregor's eyes widened. "And I bet you'll find those 'stolen' swords in his house. Rivelin will have put them there. If he gets all his competition kicked out of the Games, he wins by default. It's ingenious, really. I should have thought of it myself." He eyed me. "But I bet you wouldn't be too happy about him cheating like this. Orcs are infamous for their principles."

I flinched. "Don't speak about orcs like you know anything about us."

I needed to find Rivelin and tell him Gregor was wandering around acting irrationally. The elf looked like he'd been to Hel and back, but he had to be hiding the stolen swords somewhere nearby. And judging by his confusion, I didn't doubt he'd try to use them.

"Has he charmed you yet?" Gregor called out as I turned to go.

I paused, glancing over my shoulder. "What are you on about now?"

"He had a meeting with Odel and Haldor when you first arrived here. They agreed Rivelin would invite you to stay at his home so he could charm you and make you fall in love with him. They thought it would be the best way to convince you not to tell Isveig about this place. Because the three of them want to hide things from you. About dragons."

I scowled at him, but something in my heart twanged at the words. *So he could charm you and make you fall in love with him.* "You're lying."

He spread his arms out on either side of his body, a

move that revealed his scruffy dirt-stained tunic. "Do I look like I'm lying?"

"*Yes.*" I started toward him, hands fisting. No need to fetch Rivelin when I could take care of the bastard myself. I knew a move that could flatten him on the ground, then I would put him in a chokehold and drag him before the Village Council. They could deal with him and his crimes as they saw fit.

A bell chimed in the distance, signalling the start of the presentation. Gregor's eyes widened. Without another word, he spun on his bare feet and took off through the trees in a blur of motion. As an elf, he was fast. Too fast, and I had no hope of catching up with him.

I stared after him for a moment, listening to the chimes fade and the roar of the crowd fill the silence it left behind. But I barely heard any of it, too focused on Gregor's words. Surely it all had to be a lie. I'd asked Rivelin if he dealt in dragon magic—if anyone in this village did—and he'd looked straight in my eyes and told me no. I'd only met him a handful of weeks ago, but still. He wouldn't lie to me about something that big... would he? He wouldn't pretend to have feelings for me just to keep me from finding out the truth? Would he?

Gregor had done nothing but try to ruin everything since the Games began. He was a saboteur. That was all he was trying to do now. If he turned me against Rivelin...well, I didn't understand what he hoped to accomplish, but he seemed desperate enough to try anything.

Nodding to myself, I returned to the celebration and

joined Rivelin at the stage, where the rest of the competitors had already gathered. Hofsa shot me a sharp look, noting I was late. I wondered how she'd feel about her son's continued attempts at sabotage.

Rivelin leaned in and whispered, "Where were you?"

"I'll tell you later," I murmured back. "After we win."

He frowned but didn't argue. There were hundreds of spectators watching us, and many had enhanced hearing. I didn't want to risk anyone overhearing me talk about his swords. Contrary to what Gregor believed, I didn't think Odel or Haldor would be angry about the weapons. I couldn't say the same for everyone else, though. Half the folks here weren't from Wyndale. They might not *know* Rivelin the way the residents did.

The way *I* did...or thought I did.

I glanced at the other contestants. Hege, the dwarf, had brought a brilliant flower arrangement of lilies, wisteria, and white roses. It was a strange combination, but it somehow worked, and the sweet scent of them filled the air around the stage. Nearby, her wife, Nina, encouraged her with a smile.

The quiet human named Godfrey held a sculpture made entirely of leaves. Formed in the shape of a fenrir, it was an impressive sight. If he wasn't already so behind, he'd gain a lot of important votes in this task.

Then there was Viggo, the fire demon. Much to my surprise, his submission wasn't as impressive as the others. All he had was a small pouch that sat on the stage. I took a sniff. Jordur sand. Interesting. Did he plan to use it for some kind of demonstration?

Movement in the corner of my eye caught my attention. I turned to see Odel and Haldor huddled together off to the side, away from everyone else. They were whispering furiously, muscles tight around their eyes. Haldor shot a glance my way, and then averted his gaze just as quickly. I frowned. What was that about?

Rivelin placed a strong hand against my back, and the roar of the crowd washed over me. I'd been so focused on Haldor and Odel that I'd missed everything. The presentation was over, and the spectators were approaching the stage to taste the hundreds of cupcakes I'd spent hours baking with Rivelin. I stumbled aside, almost numb.

"Look at them," Rivelin said, smiling, as the crowd descended upon the food. "They love the cupcakes. *You* did this, Daella."

But I couldn't find it in myself to truly appreciate the delighted moans and frost-covered smiles. Gregor's words still echoed in my ears, even more now that I'd seen the strange meeting between Odel and Haldor. But no, it was ridiculous. Rivelin had only sought me out because he didn't want me poking around. He'd initially agreed to keep an eye on me, not romance me.

He wasn't using me...was he?

"Yes, it's wonderful," I said as brightly as I could, trying my best to smile. "It looks like we're getting some votes."

He searched my face, his brow pinched. "Are you sure you're all right?"

"I'm just tired. We barely got any sleep last night."

"Daella, I know when you—"

"I saw Gregor," I blurted out.

He tensed. "Where?"

"He was in the woods behind the merchant stalls again. But the *things* he stole, he didn't have them. He didn't even know what I was talking about when I tried to make him tell me where they were."

Rivelin scowled and started to head to the stalls, but I grabbed his arm to stop him. "He already got away. With the speed he has, it will be impossible to catch up with him now. You're fast, too, but he's already long gone. We don't even know which direction he went."

"What did he want?" he snapped.

I swallowed and decided to tell him everything. It would be the only way to rid myself of all these doubts. I needed to look into his eyes while he told me that every word Gregor had told me was a lie. I needed to hear he hadn't seduced me only to divert my attention away from dragon magic.

I needed to know that whatever was between us was real.

But before I could say a word, Hofsa rang the bell atop the stage. Holding aloft a half-eaten cupcake, she called out for all the crowd to hear, "It seems we have a winner!"

Indeed, she was right. Our glass jar of pebbles now sat even with Viggo's, who had done nothing with his sand, while the other two only had a handful more pebbles in them. The crowd roared their approval.

Any hope I had of speaking to Rivelin about Gregor's accusations whispered away on the wind as hundreds of cheering spectators surrounded me, sat me on a vine-covered chair, and lifted me in the air.

29

RIVELIN

The folk of Wyndale embraced Daella as if she were one of our own. Everyone knew she was the one behind the cupcakes, even if I'd proudly stood beside them as we presented her concoction to the crowd. I was hopeless in the kitchen, and it was not a well-kept secret.

I watched my neighbors raise her on a chair made entirely of branches and vines, purple flowers sprouting along each leg. It was a part of the celebration reserved for someone the village deemed remarkable, used only once every year. For Daella to have won it meant something, something that stirred my heart in a way I wanted to ignore.

Especially with Gregor on the hunt. With a frown, I started toward the merchant stalls. It didn't matter if he'd fled. I would do whatever it took to track him down, and I could tell by the smile Daella had given me

—the fake smile—he'd said something that had troubled her.

But before I made it halfway across the meadow, Odel blocked my path and latched her hands on my arm. She dragged me behind a tent without a word, to where Haldor was pacing and scratching at his horns. That wasn't a good sign.

I looked from one tense face to the next. "What's wrong? Is it Gregor? Has he done something else?"

"Riv, my friend," Haldor said with a wince. "There's a rumor going around, you see, that you had a stash of weapons in your forge."

My stomach dropped, and I tried to school my expression into something neutral, something smooth like stone. "Where did you hear that?"

"An anonymous note was left in the Village Hall. I don't know how long it's been there, but I found it this morning," Haldor said quietly, flicking a tense gaze at the nearby crowd. But with the cheers and the laughter, our conversation would be hidden well enough, even from prying elven ears.

I frowned. "An anonymous note?"

"Yes, on a piece of parchment stamped with your wax seal in fact, which is why I thought it might be some kind of prank. Though, since you have never been a jester, that makes little sense."

I looked at Daella. She clutched the arms of the chair, but a ridiculous smile lit her face. My stomach twisted as I tried to shove down the first thought that rose to the

300

surface of my mind. She had been digging around in my drawer the night of the attack. She'd confessed to taking a sheet of parchment to send a letter to Isveig's sister. At the time, I'd thought it was strange. Thuri was likely dead.

"She wouldn't," I murmured.

"Who wouldn't what?" Odel asked, her wings twitching behind her. They only did that when she was feeling extraordinarily distressed.

"Someone came into my house the other night, attacked me, and burned the lot of my parchment," I said grimly, pointing to the faint scar on my forehead. I healed fast, but there was still a small mark left. "They gave me this."

Odel's wings twitched faster. "You were attacked? Why didn't you say anything?"

I looked from her wide-eyed face to Haldor's. My old friend knew me too well. His expression hardened.

He said, "Because of the damn swords. It's true, isn't it? You've been forging them all this time."

I ran my fingers through my hair. "I never intended to use them."

Haldor looked pained. "You broke the laws, Riv."

"I've been carrying a sword or dagger with me everywhere I go. For fourteen long years. No one has ever said anything, or tried to stop me. I don't see how this is any different." I patted the dagger I currently had strapped around my waist, to emphasize my point.

"This is true." Odel glanced from me to Haldor, her lips a flat pink line. "We named him Defender of

Wyndale. Perhaps we can say he was merely doing his duty."

Haldor paced beside the tent, his fiery skin and hair a stark contrast to the emerald green linen. He was my oldest friend here, and he understood me in a way very few did. And he understood the violence in my past, something I'd fought hard to leave behind.

To him, it might seem as if I planned to return to those ways.

"Where are the swords now?" he finally asked.

"Gregor has hidden them away somewhere. I searched for him in the Ashborn Forest but came up empty. He showed up just before the ceremony, though, and said something that upset Daella. He can't be far."

"You think it was Gregor?" Odel frowned.

"It doesn't make much sense, Riv. Why would he steal your swords? Especially if he left that note," said Haldor.

"I..."

I had no answer for that. Because Haldor was right. It wasn't logical. And while Gregor wasn't the brightest elf I'd ever met, he wasn't that much of a fool, was he? Once again, my gaze drifted toward Daella, but the tent blocked my view of the celebration. The cheers had yet to die down, however, which meant she was still on that chair.

Daella clearly didn't steal the swords that night, but had she stolen my parchment so she could leave Odel and Haldor that note? No, I couldn't think that way.

Perhaps this was Gregor's true game. He wanted to turn us against each other.

"He's clearly not thinking straight, or he's playing a game he's not smart enough to win," I argued. "No one else in this village has a grudge against me the way he does. I got him kicked out of the Midsummer Games, remember?"

Haldor nodded, but he didn't look convinced.

"Riv, you know we love you, but you aren't the friendliest chap around," Odel said gently. "Can you think of anyone else who might want to sabotage you?"

I wanted to say no, of course there wasn't. Viggo's fireworks had made me suspicious at first, but Haldor had made it clear they were a fire demon thing. Besides, he'd easily won two trials back to back. Why would he bother trying to sabotage me? Until today, I hadn't been much of a threat.

And why would anyone else in Wyndale be against me? It was a peaceful island village where nothing terrible happened. I'd spent so many years ensuring that was true, by doing whatever it took to keep the danger *out*. None of Isveig's murks or warriors had ever found us.

Until a few weeks ago.

Daella knew about the swords. She was the only person on this island who had ever laid eyes on them. She'd been rifling around in my desk drawers. I'd trusted her enough to show her the dragons, and I'd told her what I planned to ask the island if I won. Had she been pretending to soften toward me this entire time? Was this her move?

If she wanted to set me up to fail, she'd make it look like I was trying to take out my competition. And my biggest competition right now was...Viggo.

I closed my eyes, hating the words I couldn't hold back. "I think I know where the swords are. We should check Viggo's house."

30

DAELLA

I'd lost sight of Rivelin in the chaos. The rough bark of the chair scraped my skin every time the villagers of Wyndale hoisted me higher in the air. A part of me wanted to relax and enjoy this unexpected celebration—were they that impressed by my mother's cupcake recipe? But my focus was on Rivelin and our interrupted conversation.

Where was he? Had he gone after Gregor? And why did I have a sick feeling in the back of my throat?

The chair jolted as the procession finally returned to the stage, and the villagers lowered me to the ground. I smiled my best fake smile at all of them and thanked them for the honor. Elma was there, and so was Tilda in a bright sunny dress that matched her beaming smile, and Milka the dwarf baker, too. I still didn't see Rivelin, or Odel, or Haldor anywhere.

I wandered through the crowd, searching for his

silver hair. When I walked down the row of merchant stalls, I found Lilia leaning across her bar top and waving me over, her kind smile as bright as ever. But when she got a look at my face, the brightness dimmed.

"Everything all right, Daella?" She dragged a rag across the bar top, keeping an eye on me.

"I can't find your brother anywhere. Have you seen him?"

"Sure have. He left with Odel and Haldor a few moments ago. Looked like they were heading toward the east side of the village." Her hand slowed. "Has something happened?"

"No," I said, then shook my head. "I don't know."

As I turned to go, she reached out and gently touched my arm. "Don't let him push you away. He's been better these days, with you around."

"Better?"

"You know, with how closed off he is. He really struggles with the past—what the emperor's mercenaries did, what he did in response. I think he's been punishing himself for it all these years by hiding away from the world. But you've gotten him out of that damn house." She smiled gently. "If he's somehow messed things up between you two, just try and give him a chance to fix it, eh? I like you a lot. It'd be nice if you stayed."

I smiled, but it felt strained. "Thanks, Lilia. I mean that. I just need to talk to him, that's all."

I accepted one of her offered tankards of sweet ale and then wound through the crowd to the other side of the meadow. It was quieter on the dirt path that cut into the village, and it would likely stay that way for a good long while. Today's celebration seemed like it was only getting started.

Lilia had seen Rivelin and the others heading east, so I took the fork in the path that led to the cluster of homes on that side of the village. From up ahead came familiar voices. Rivelin was speaking urgently, though I couldn't make out his words from this distance. I picked up my pace and turned to the corner to find him standing in the middle of the road with his missing swords scattered on the ground all around him.

I slowed to a stop. Odel caught sight of my movement and looked up with a fierce scowl, her pink wings twitching wildly. I'd never seen her look so angry. Haldor stood on Rivelin's other side. He rubbed his chin, sighing with closed eyes.

"You." Odel pointed a shaky finger at me. "You did this to Rivelin, didn't you?"

All the blood drained from my face. "What?"

"That's right." Viggo emerged from the open door of a small timber home, where boxes of red roses decorated the two ground-floor windows. He glared in my direction. "I didn't even know Rivelin had swords. There's no logical reason to suspect me of stealing from him. It was *her*."

For a moment, all I could do was stare at the four of them, trying to piece this together. The house must be Viggo's. Odel and Haldor had found Rivelin's swords inside. But instead of suspecting *he'd* stolen them, they blamed...me?

"You think I stole Rivelin's swords and planted them in Viggo's house? But why would I do that? I'm on Rivelin's side. I'm his assistant in the Games," I told them, furrowing my brow. "I didn't even know where Viggo lived until just now."

Haldor nodded, absentmindedly scratching the base of his red horns. The demon usually wore an expression of delight, but he just looked tired now. "Yes, that does seem to be the case, but there are, unfortunately, other things we must take into consideration. Such as where you've come from and how you arrived with a murk sigil on your Grundstoff Empire armor."

I flinched. "I thought we'd gotten past that. I have no true loyalty to Isveig."

"Well, see, that's what you've told us, love," Odel said with an apologetic smile. "But we only have your word for it and nothing more. And then all this happens..." She gestured vaguely at the swords. "Ever since you've arrived, someone has had it out for Rivelin."

I tried to catch Rivelin's eyes, to search for confirmation he felt the same, but he wouldn't look at me. A sharp stab of pain went through my heart. "And so you believe I'm behind it all."

"If you have a better explanation, I'm all ears," said Haldor.

I motioned at Viggo, who stood on his steps watching the exchange. "The swords were in *his* house. Or perhaps it was Gregor. Have you suddenly forgotten about him?"

Odel sighed. "He maintains he had nothing to do

with the destruction at the forge and that he was set up
to take the fall for that."

"And you *believe* him?" I asked, my heart pounding.
"He's sabotaged other Games in the past. You *watched*
him goad Kari into attacking him."

"He has always played within the confines of the
rules, which is why it's been so difficult to do anything
about him." Haldor sighed and started to elaborate, but
he was interrupted by a thunderous boom from the sky
above.

Inwardly, I groaned. This was just what I needed—a
rainstorm. I had no salt or tent with me to protect my
skin, which meant I needed to get inside. I needed to
go...*home*. But I did not think my home here was mine
any longer. It never had been.

My heart ached as I tried, once more, to catch
Rivelin's gaze. His hands were on his hips, and he stared
at the ground, at the swords that surrounded him. Everything about his posture and crumpled expression
screamed resignation.

He truly believed I was behind this.

Unshed tears burned my eyes. I had not cried in so
very long—I never gave Isveig the satisfaction, even
when I was alone and knew no one would see. There'd
always been a chance he was listening at the door,
waiting for me to break. So I had always held it in. I'd
never cracked. And yet I could not stop the tears that
now streaked down my face.

Blinking them away, I turned toward the road that

would lead to the western side of the village, and eventually, out of this place.

And then a shadow passed overhead.

Wind gusted against me as thunder boomed once more. I looked up, and my heart nearly stopped. That hadn't been thunder. Heavy wings beat the air as a dragon landed on the road just in front of me, his monstrous claws slamming into the ground, his leathery tail whipping back and forth. Dirt sprayed behind him like a cloud of mist. He flared his nostrils, sniffing, his luminous eyes bearing down on me like the weight of an anvil. Bright light flared beneath his emerald scales.

This was not Aska, the dragon I'd met in the forest.

As he settled on the ground, I lifted a trembling hand toward his snout. He stared at me, and I stared right back, my heart pounding my ribs.

And then he roared.

The force of his bellow knocked me off my feet, and my backside slammed into the dirt. Shouts erupted from behind me, but I didn't dare take my eyes off the beast. His eyes were narrowed slits as he stalked toward me. But then he whipped his head around, like something else had caught his attention.

The dragon sniffed the air again.

His attention landed on a house only a few feet away.

"Reykur!" Rivelin's shout cut through my terror. "Back away. Daella means you no harm."

But Reykur was no longer focused on me. He stalked toward the house, his claws punching deep holes into the dirt. The dragon took one last scent of the air, opened his maw, and unleashed his brutal flames upon the building.

I cried out and flattened myself on the ground, wincing at the intoxicating heat that washed over me. I'd never felt anything like it before. It was a heat so all-encompassing that it consumed every inch of me with brutal, unrelenting pain.

Rivelin suddenly appeared, grabbed my arms, and hauled me away. Then he turned to the dragon, as if to call him back. But it was too late. A conflagration consumed the building. Tongues of deadly flames licked the skies. It would only take moments for the building to become nothing more than a pile of ash.

As the fire danced, Reykur swivelled his head our way. A low grumble spilled from his throat as the dragon took a step toward Viggo. He reared back on his hind legs and roared. My heart pounded. The dragon had burned down Godfrey's house. Would he burn down Viggo's, too? With Viggo still on the front steps?

"No, Reykur," I whispered. "Stop."

A long moment stretched by in silence.

The dragon blinked, closed its maw, then spread his wings to fly. He was gone in the blink of an eye, vanishing into the sky so quickly it almost felt like he'd never even been there, if not for the destruction he'd left behind.

Rivelin knelt beside me, the muscles tight around his eyes. Soot stained his tunic and cheek. "Daella. Are you hurt?"

"She's fine, Riv," Haldor said tiredly as he and Odel

slowly approached. Odel's wings were twitching so fast, I thought she might faint from the effort. "But I can't say the same for Godfrey's house."

"That was Godfrey's house?" I managed to choke out.

Viggo finally emerged from the safety of his steps to join us before the blaze. "Interesting, isn't it? Godfrey got some votes in today's trial and now he's been targeted. It looked like I was about to be targeted, too. By Rivelin's dragon. Who *obeyed* Daella when she told him to stop. One might wonder why."

Every single head turned my way.

31

DAELLA

I stood and faced the gathered enemies. Then I summoned my best smile despite my inward turmoil. It felt like donning an old, familiar set of fighting leathers I thought I'd packed away in a trunk, never to be worn again. For once, it did little to bring me comfort. It just felt *wrong*.

"That's quite the theory you've come up with. It's a shame it's not founded in reality. Now, I don't know about you, but I'd love to finish my ale." I collected the forgotten mug from the ground. Some of the ale had spilled during the dragon attack, but there was enough left for a few sips. And they were sorely needed. "Someone should probably do something about this fire. We don't want it to spread."

Haldor turned to Viggo and nodded gravely. "Have some of your sand?"

Viggo inched closer to the fire and pulled some

Vatnor sand from a pouch he wore by his side. He tossed a few grains toward the inferno, whispering beneath his breath. Water gushed forward in magnificent, stormy wave, wild and far greater than anything I'd seen before. Interesting. I never would have expected a fire demon to have a stash of Vatnor sand.

I narrowed my eyes. He'd been quick to accuse me, too.

"You made an error in judgement, love," Odel said, stepping up beside me as the flames died down. "Riv would never order one of the dragons to attack this place. You should have stuck with Gregor's crimes. Might have gotten away with it then."

I closed my eyes, forcing myself to remain calm. "I didn't do any of this. I know nothing of dragons, and I certainly don't know how to use one in an attack."

"You're an orc," Viggo said with a sneer. "Orcs were *created* in dragonfire, and then your kind bonded with them. The original Draugr. If anyone was going to order them to target one of us, it's you."

I took a step back. "What?"

"Don't pretend to be so surprised. Mabel told us everything about you," said Viggo. Odel and Haldor nodded in agreement.

For a moment, I couldn't speak, too astonished by what he'd said. By the time I'd been born, orcs had mostly died out from a disease that had swept through the world several hundred years earlier. Records of our past were hard to come by. Over time, knowledge of orcish history had been lost. My mother had told me many tales, but I'd never known how much was true and how much was myth.

Isveig had refused to speak with me about it. I'd often wondered if there were things he didn't want me to know.

But dragons and orcs...it was too wild a story to accept.

Unless it wasn't.

Rivelin came closer, but his hooded eyes still refused to meet mine. "What's this about orcs and dragons?"

"It's not true," I insisted.

"Mabel has never lied about anything," Viggo countered. "Orcs were forged in dragonfire, and they know how to control the beasts by bonding with them. Daella is behind all of this."

Rivelin finally looked at me. His yellow eyes blazed with inner fire, boring through me with enough heat to scald my bones. I lifted my chin and refused to back down. I wouldn't let them turn this on me. In fact, I had questions of my own.

"Funny, Gregor seems to think Rivelin is the one behind it all," I said, hating every word of it. "He's approached me twice now, trying to warn me. Now I see why."

A muscle worked in Rivelin's jaw. "And yet you told me you didn't believe a thing that bastard said."

"I didn't." I folded my arms. "But now that you're trying to blame this on me, I'm starting to think he might have been telling the truth."

Rivelin laughed bitterly, a sound so achingly different

from these past few days. "Really, Daella? This is your move?"

"Almost all of your competition has been targeted with *your things*. Your forge got destroyed, your hammers got stolen, then your swords did, too. That was your dragon who attacked, not mine. And now you're trying to pin the blame on me. Of course this is my move."

His nostrils flared as he stared at me. "Prove it."

"Prove what? My innocence?"

"That's right."

I scoffed and took a step back, and he tracked my movement like the eagle-eyed elf he was. "How am I supposed to do that?"

He glanced at Haldor, who stood just beside him. The fire demon nodded.

Haldor said, "We'll take you as our prisoner, which is what we should have done the moment you arrived on this island. You can stay in the Archives beneath the Village Hall. It's a comfortable room, and your needs will be fully met there. After the Midsummer Games have concluded, we'll consider releasing you."

"Prisoner," I said in a whisper, my eyes locked on Rivelin's stony face. "You want to lock me up after I've told you *everything* I've been through. You'd really do that to me?"

"I wouldn't do that to the Daella I thought I knew," he said in a rough voice, "but after what's happened today, I don't see how that Daella wasn't a lie."

"A lie." I fisted my hands and looked between him

and Haldor. Odel stood off to the side, her face in her hands, while Viggo looked on almost eagerly. He was loving this. "Tell me, Rivelin. Did you have a council meeting that night I arrived in Wyndale? Did you agree to take me in because you're a handsome elf with no attachments? Because you're a charmer? Because you thought you could seduce me and get me on your side?"

Shock rolled across Rivelin's face. He tried to cover it up with his mask of disinterest, but he failed. I'd seen it. And from his lack of a response, I knew Gregor had not been lying. Not about this. Perhaps he hadn't been lying about any of it.

I shook my head and took several more steps back. "So it's true. Everything you said to me, everything you did." My voice nearly broke, but I forged ahead. "You were trying to placate me so you could twist everything around and make them hate me, just so you could win your ridiculous competition. Well, good job. You succeeded."

"I—" Rivelin tried.

"I've heard enough." I took a step back. "I'm leaving."

"I'm afraid we can't let you do that," Haldor said, but I shut him up with a scowl I felt in the very depths of my soul. The time for niceties was over.

"I *am* leaving." I looked at Rivelin, who merely stood there with a hard, unyielding gaze. "Don't try to come after me. I want nothing to do with your Games, and I will use this Vindur sand against you if you try to lock me up." I patted the pouch of sand by my side, the gift from Kari. "I don't know how, but I'll figure it out. Stay away from me."

And with that, I pulled off the handmade bracelet, tossed it at Rivelin's feet, then took off down the road, running as fast as I could.

32

DAELLA

As soon as I reached the edge of Wyndale, despair choked me. I'd fought hard to keep it together when facing Rivelin and his fellow villagers, but now that I'd put some space between us, I couldn't hold back the tears.

Salted lines streaked down my face as I left the merry village behind for the dark, lonely woods of the Ashborn Forest. I had no idea where I was going, or how long it would take to get there, but I knew I had to keep moving for as long as I could. If the villagers truly believed I'd caused so much damage to their peaceful world, they would hunt me down no matter what I'd said to keep them away. I had a small bag of Vindur sand, but I didn't know the first thing about magic.

A numbness crept over me as I continued pushing forward down the overgrown path. Thorny branches scraped my bare arms, but I didn't stop to tend to the cuts. Eventually, I slowed to a walk when my lungs began to ache, and I glanced over my shoulder to search for any sign of pursuers.

The forest looked still and silent. For now.

I tried to think as I continued to press forward. How had it come to this? Why hadn't I seen the warning signs? But the truth was, I *had* seen them, and I'd dismissed them. When Rivelin's tools had appeared on Gregor's floor, I'd thought it strange. It had seemed so *blatant*. I'd been foolish to ignore that gut feeling.

Rivelin had planned all of this to win the Midsummer Games, and now he would get away with it because he had the perfect scapegoat: a hated murk from the Grundstoff Empire. And if he was willing to do all that, if he was willing to burn down someone's house using dragonfire, what else was he capable of?

Heart pounding, I slowed to a stop. The thought hadn't occurred to me before, but the words lit up in my mind now, impossible to ignore. What if he'd been lying about what he planned to ask of the island? He had a dark, violent past. He said he'd moved on from that, that he'd left it behind. What if he hadn't?

What if he truly was a Draugr?

My hands clenched. Perhaps I shouldn't have run.

But what was I to do against a village full of angry elves, demons, dwarves, and humans who believed I was the enemy? They would refuse to listen to me. They would lock me up. Still...there had to be something I could do, and at least I had some time to figure out what. There were seven days before the final ceremony of the Midsummer Games, where Rivelin would no doubt be crowned the winner.

The trees rustled overhead as I continued my dash down the forest path. There was a bite in the air, a chill that hadn't been there a moment before. Frowning, I picked up my pace. I needed to find shelter for the night, then move north to the village of Milford. I had some coin now, along with the Vindur sand. Perhaps I could buy a weapon before returning to Wyndale to take my stand.

My stand against Rivelin.

That thought hurt more than I wanted to admit. I'd opened up to him in a way I hadn't with anyone in years, and I'd truly believed he'd done the same with me. There had been something there between us, something I'd yearned for all my life, despite believing I'd never have it.

Despite believing I would never be free, let alone learn to trust someone.

He'd broken down my walls just to stab me in the heart. Rivelin was worse than Isveig had ever been. At least the ice giant did not hide his monstrous nature.

I wandered the forest for six full days before I admitted to myself I was lost. I'd tried to follow the path Rivelin and I had taken north toward the mountains, but I'd chosen the wrong fork somewhere in the dark. I was hungry, tired, and soaked in layers of dirt. The ground had been my bed for the crisp, lonely nights.

As I tried to retrace my steps, the wind whipped my hair, bringing with it the scent of storms. Grimacing, I glanced up at the dense canopy just as a steady drizzle cut through the leaves. A few splatters hit my arms, and pain lanced through me. With a silent sob, I pressed my back against the trunk of the nearest tree and searched for something I could use as shelter.

But everywhere I looked, there was nothing but bushes and trees and leaves gusting in the wind. The rain was growing heavier now, slashing against my body like knives. Shuddering, I ran for a fallen log and dove beneath it, but it did little to block the storm.

I crawled as far beneath the log as I could manage and folded myself into a ball. Big droplets of rain slammed on my exposed shoulder and the left side of my back. I shivered and squeezed my eyes tight, praying to Freya. The Goddess of the Elements had never looked kindly on me or my people, and yet I whispered her name as my skin came alive with burning welts.

If I had any hope of survival, I needed the storm to stop soon. It would be raining back in Wyndale, too, and Rivelin would know I'd take shelter. I had no idea how close I was to the village or if he and the others were still looking for me, but they might be. And if they found me now, I would be too weak to fight back.

With those thoughts rolling around in my head, I

hissed and started crawling out from beneath the protective log. I needed to keep moving.

The air suddenly warmed, a soothing heat caressing my aching skin. Trembling, I lifted my head to spy a red-scaled dragon bursting through the canopy, her leathery wings beating at the rain-soaked air. My breath caught. It was Aska, come to find me once more. But this time, I had none of Mabel's treats, and I was on the run from Rivelin. Had he sent her after me?

Aska landed heavily on the soaked forest floor and stalked toward me, her claws churning the dirt. I braced myself for the impact.

The dragon swept a wing over my head. An excruciating moment passed, where I could not bring myself to breathe. And then the wing merely stayed there.

Swallowing, I looked up. The dragon's wing was blocking the downpour, and the sharp stabs of pain faded slightly, though I was still soaked to the bone. Every single inch of my body hurt, but....the dragon was holding off the worst of it now.

I turned toward her long snout and searched those ember eyes. Slowly, she blinked, as if to confirm my unspoken question. Aska had not swooped into the forest to harm me or take me to Rivelin. She was... protecting me.

"Why?" I whispered.

She blinked again, then settled on her haunches. The wing remained right where it was, and the rain transformed the forest into a haze of mist and soggy leaves. I leaned back against the fallen log, still shaking. The pain was not getting worse, but it was still unrelenting. My hair was a wet clump against my back, and my clothes were waterlogged. I would struggle to improve unless I got dry.

I dropped my head against the log and sighed. Aska remained still, only occasionally shifting her wing, the warmth of her body soothing my pain, just a bit. And as I sat there like that, with my deepest fear protecting me, I couldn't help but wonder if Mabel had been right in what she'd told Viggo and the others. No one knew where orcs had come from. Or, if they did, they'd never told me.

Could it be because we had a link with dragons somewhere in our past?

As the moments crept on, the rain eventually slowed and then stopped. Aska stood and stretched, and beads of water rolled off the leathery, veined wings edged in tusk-like claws. Patches of her skin were raw and pink, where familiar welts were beginning to form.

I pushed to my feet and carefully approached her. "You're hurt. The rain gave you welts, like me." I shook my head. "I don't understand why you helped me."

She gazed at me for a long moment with those ember eyes, then flattened her body to the ground. She shifted sideways, as if to expose her back to me. Built into her body was a small seat made from glistening scales. This was nothing folk-made. It was a part of her.

Without another word, I grabbed the small tusk growing from her neck and hauled myself onto her back. Intoxicating heat flooded my senses, the sensation charging through me like a thunderstorm. Suddenly, I felt wild and vicious and free. This was raw magic unlike anything I'd ever felt before. Body trembling, I tried to steady my breathing, but my lungs were as on fire as the rest of me.

The dragon lifted her head and roared.

33

RIVELIN

A knock sounded on my door, barely audible over the heavy drumming of rain and crashing thunder—the last storm of the summer. I frowned and continued to stare at my cold hearth rather than get up and be forced to interact with someone. It would likely be Haldor, Odel, or Lilia, trying to convince me to leave my house. That would not be happening.

Skoll whined and nudged my leg. He'd remained by my side for six days, even when Viggo had tried to encourage him to track down Daella. The fenrir would be able to do it, too. With his heightened sense of smell and speed, he'd have found her within a day.

And yet, I'd told Viggo to back off and leave Skoll be. They only wanted to find her so they could lock her up.

I should want that, too, after everything she'd done. But I didn't, not after seeing the look on her face when Haldor had mentioned their plan to take her as our prisoner. That flash of fear wasn't something anyone could fake, not even her.

"Rivelin, dearest, please open up." Mabel's frail voice infiltrated my determined avoidance. I sighed and stood. If it were anyone else, I would continue my lonely solitude, but I couldn't ignore the kindest woman in the village.

Skoll panted happily and rushed into the hallway, where he wagged his tail in anticipation.

"You're supposed to be on my side," I grumbled to him.

When I opened the door, Mabel gave me a frank look from head to toe, then she pushed inside like she owned the place. She inspected the living quarters, her lips a flat line. There was a stack of dirty dishes on my desk, and my rumpled blanket and pillows were still on the sofa. I hadn't been able to bring myself to return to my bed.

"Rivelin, you need to snap out of it," she said, thumping her cane against the floor.

Skoll padded to her side and gently nuzzled her leg in encouragement.

I sighed. "Why?"

"Well, for one, you still have one trial left, and you need to win the Midsummer Games for the sake of us all. But more importantly, you need to sort things out with Daella and bring her back home."

Home. My chest ached. If only this truly had become Daella's home. Instead, she belonged to Isveig more than I'd ever realized.

"Mabel, I appreciate what you're trying to do here, but haven't you heard what happened?"

It had been all anyone could talk about for days. Poor Godfrey was beside himself after losing his home, and so he'd dropped out of the Games for fear Daella would attack him again. Hege had also withdrawn, certain Daella would come for her and her wife next. But it was Viggo, the smug bastard, who had truly come out on top. Since he hadn't stolen my swords, there was nothing stopping him from finishing the competition. And winning.

Then there was me, the Defender of Wyndale, who had failed miserably.

The Defender who had not joined the group that had taken off into the Ashborn Forest to track down our new enemy. It was a miracle they'd never found her, and eventually, they'd given up, choosing to return to their nightly feasts and celebrations rather than hold on to their fear and anger.

But they had not stopped talking about her.

"Oh, yes," Mabel said. "It's all gotten a bit out of control, hasn't it?"

"What did you expect? One of Isveig's murks came after us and then got away."

She leveled her intense gaze at me. "You don't truly believe that, do you?"

I frowned. "Don't you?"

"Hmm." Mabel hobbled over to my desk, collected the dirty dishes, and headed into the kitchen.

I followed. "That's hardly necessary, Mabel."

329

"Oh, I'm not cleaning them." She dropped the dishes into the sink. "You are."

My frown deepened, but I moved to the sink regardless. "All right. But only because it's you."

She leaned against the countertop as I filled the sink with water. As I worked through each dish, she nodded and offered a towel to dry them off. By the time I was done, my hands were covered in suds and wrinkled skin.

"That right there is water, one of the four elements," she said as I placed the final dish back in the cupboard. "Now, did you know there are two creatures in this world who suffer from that element's kiss, so long as there's no salt to dull it?"

"Isn't there just one? Orcs."

"No. Orcs and…?"

I searched my mind for an answer, but there was only one thing it could be.

"And dragons?" I asked, my heart sinking. "So what you told the others is true, then. Orcs and dragons are somehow related."

"Orcs were first forged in dragon flames. That's how they came to be. My late husband, who was an orc himself, had an ancient tome that chronicled the entire history of his people, and all that was in it. Unfortunately, it went missing when Isveig attacked our town."

I paced from the sofa to the armchair. "If that's true, then why don't you believe Daella was involved in the dragon attack on Godfrey's home? Having a connection to the dragons means she's the only one who could have done it."

Deep down, my hope had lingered this past week. A desperate part of me wanted to believe this whole thing had been a colossal, horrible mistake. I'd spent the past six days trying to patch together a way Daella could be innocent, but I always came up empty. Nothing else made sense. All signs pointed her way, and she had run.

"This was in the book, too. No one can order a dragon to attack unless they've formed a Draugr bond with them," she said. "Unlike other folk, orcs don't need Fildur sand to do that. That said, if Daella had, you would know."

"All right. How?"

She stared at me intently for a moment, then said, "That ice shard would no longer be a problem. The magic of the bond would counteract it to keep her safe. Dragonfire can be a wondrous thing."

I searched her gaze, taken aback. "How in fate's name do you know about Isveig's ice shard?"

"Haldor told me. I'm fairly certain he told a few others, too."

"Of course he did. You can't say anything in this village without it turning into gossip." I sighed and ran my hand down my face, thinking. "Let's consider all this true. If Daella didn't order the dragon to attack Godfrey's house, who did?"

"Now, see, here's where I might need your help. I had a poke around the remains of Godfrey's house after the embers died. There was an awful lot of Vatnor sand scattered around everywhere. It no longer has any magic to it now, of course, 'cause of the dragonfire. I reckon

Reykur caught scent of it and came to destroy it out of fear. Dragons don't much like Vatnor sand. It's one of the few things in this world that can kill them."

I sat hard on the arm of the sofa. Viggo had used some sand to stop the fire, but it had only been a few grains. "You're saying someone scattered Vatnor sand all over Godfrey's house to tempt a dragon to destroy it?"

"That's the long and short of it, yes."

Shaking my head, I dropped my head into my hands. I wanted to believe her, but I didn't see how I could. "Daella still could have done all that with the right motivation. She's ignored her allergic reaction to water before."

"You mean when she leapt into the lake to save someone's life?" Mabel said with a snap to her tone. "You are dear to me, Rivelin, but I need you to pull your head out of your ass."

I sat up a little straighter, caught off guard by her bluntness.

She continued, "You two have been joined at the hip for weeks. When would she have gone hunting for Vatnor sand? Where would she have even found it? It's not as if it's scattered around everywhere like dirt. Think about what you're saying."

The blood drained from my face as her words sank in. In the days preceding the attack, Daella and I had spent almost every waking moment together. We'd worked the forge during the day and passed the evenings on the rooftop, sharing stories and watching the sun ease behind Mount Forge. Then when darkness came, we'd sat by the hearth with our mugs of tea just enjoying each other's company. We'd barely spent a moment apart. She could have tried sneaking out the front door after we'd both gone to bed, but I had never been a heavy sleeper. The sound of the creaking floor beneath her feet would have woken me.

But what was more, where would she have gotten all that Vatnor sand, even if she had tried to find it? There was only one person on this island I'd ever seen carrying a pouch of it around. And the dragon had taken a brief interest in him.

Viggo.

"Daella didn't do it," I murmured.

"Ah, that's a good lad." Mabel hobbled over and patted me on the back. "Took a while, but you got you there."

I closed my eyes. "I've failed her."

"Pull yourself together," she chided. "And go get your woman."

34

DAELLA

The dragon took off through the trees. Her extraordinary body shoved through the canopy and exploded out the other side in a whirlwind of sticks and leaves. The dark, thunderous sky enveloped us.

I held on, gritting my teeth against the ferocity of the wind. Aska spun to the left while keeping low above the forest. When her claws skimmed the canopy, she swooped higher, closer to the pregnant clouds. I realized the break in rain and been just that—a break—and she was taking me away from danger before the torrent began anew.

True fear rattled inside me when I risked a glance below. I caught glimpses of the ground through the trees. It was so very far away. One wrong move, and I'd be dead from the fall. Still, the exhilarating magic rushed through me and burned my fear away. I lifted my eyes and gazed forward at the sky opening up before me.

I could see for miles. The verdant forest rolled toward the gentle foothills clustered at the base of the jagged mountain range, backlit by the setting sun. Shades of gold and orange drenched the lands like strands of fire. There were no dark clouds near the mountains, no storm. Just three small dragons soaring through the humid skies.

A little quiver of unease went through me at the sight of them. Aska was clearly the gentler of the two I'd met so far, and she had sought me out likely because she remembered the time I'd offered her some treats. The others would not have that same connection to me, and after Reykur's attack on Wyndale, I couldn't be certain what I'd face.

Still, Aska carried on, soaring close to the others. The dragons bellowed and fell into formation behind her. I cast a glance over my shoulder, the wind biting my cheeks. Up close, they were as majestic as I'd remembered. Beautiful and fierce and strong, their scales glinting with unleashed fire.

When we neared the base of Mount Forge, Aska landed gently on a rocky ledge and strode inside the cave where Rivelin had first shown them to me. It was dimly lit inside, and the stench of dragons invaded all my senses and weighed on my exhausted, hungry body. Before I could make sense of it, my eyes grew heavy, and I sagged forward. I desperately tried to cling to consciousness, but the magic of this place pulled me under.

I awoke with a warm, leathery body enveloping mine. Jolting upright, I blinked at where the dragon's sleeping form curled around me, like a cat protecting its young. Her breathing was slow and even, though her nostrils flared, as if scenting me. I noticed her skin, like mine, was covered in red welts. Guilt flashed through me. She was only hurt because of me.

I looked around the cave. Daylight splashed in from the world outside and revealed the three other dragons sleeping soundly all around me, their scaly bellies pointed up at the stone ceiling. Yesterday—or however long it had been—they'd seemed so impossibly large. But now, in the still quiet, it was clear they were nothing but youngsters. Something in my heart warmed at the sight of them, and magic crackled in my blood.

"Thank you," I whispered to Aska. She cracked one eye, let out a little huff, and went back to sleep.

I slowly extracted myself from my makeshift bed and walked to the cave entrance. A flock of starlings spun through the air in an elaborate dance, twisting this way and that. The sun beamed down on the rolling hills, and the heady warmth of summer settled into me. My clothes were dry now, but a few painful welts were left behind by the downpour. I'd survived, though.

And now I had to decide what to do next.

"Daella!" a familiar voice called out from somewhere nearby.

Rivelin.

I sucked in a breath and darted inside the cave. *Shit.* I should have known he'd search here. Had he spotted me? Where could I hide? I cast my glance toward the slumbering dragons. He'd mentioned before he couldn't get near them. Quickly, I rushed across the cave floor to duck out of sight behind Aska.

But he was too fast. He was there at the entrance of the cave less than a heartbeat later.

"Daella," he said.

I froze, only inches from Aska. She hadn't moved, but I could tell by her shallow breathing that she was fully awake now. Would she step in if he tried to drag me away? And did I even want her to? If she tried to protect me, she might burn him alive.

And even after everything, the thought of that felt like a knife through my heart.

Slowly, I turned to face him. His breathing was ragged and his hair was mussed, but he'd never looked more handsome. His rugged form was backlit by the brilliant morning sun, and the sleeves of his black tunic were rolled up to his elbows to reveal his well-built forearms. Those glowing yellow eyes pierced through me, and for a moment, I almost forgot to breathe.

"Daella," he murmured again. "You're all right."

I blinked and reality rushed in around me once more. Shaking my head, I took a step closer to the dragon. "Sorry to disappoint."

Pain flashed across his stoic face. "This isn't what you think it is. I'm here because I made a mistake."

I paused with my boot half a step further. "What do you mean?"

"I was wrong. We were both wrong." He entered the cave, his hands spread wide on either side of him. "It was Viggo. He set us both up, trying to knock me out of the Midsummer Games. Trying to turn us against each other. And it worked, because I am a fool who can't see the truth even when it's staring me right in the face."

My heart rattled. "This could be some kind of trick, another lie. You can't come any closer because of the dragons, which means you need me to walk out of here willingly. It's the only way you can truly take me as your prisoner." *Like Isveig.*

"No," he said roughly, moving a step closer. "I would never do that to you, even if I thought you were behind the attack. I didn't even search for you in the woods with the others. I let you go. The only reason I'm here now is because I realized I was wrong. I know you can never forgive me. I don't expect you to. But I wanted to come and tell you it's safe now for you to leave. As of today, the Elding has moved west. A ship will be in the harbor now. You can return to the mainland." He took a step further. "With this. I dove into the sea and got it back."

Rivelin extracted something from his belt, and my breath caught in my throat. My mother's dagger. The orcish words seemed to glow beneath the light of the sun slanting into the cave.

Ris upp ur oskunni.

Rise from the Ashes.

I searched his face, scarcely daring to believe my own eyes. "I don't understand. Wasn't this all some kind of game? You sabotaged the other contestants and then put the blame on me in front of everyone."

"I did not, Daella. I truly believed..." He closed his eyes. "I truly believed you'd done it all."

"But," I whispered, "who else could control a dragon? You're the only one with any sort of relationship with them."

"It's a long story, and I can explain on the way. But we don't have much time if you want to reach the ship before it departs."

I swallowed thickly. "I want to believe you, Rivelin. I can't explain how much. But how can I be certain you don't—"

He crossed the cave in two quick strides, pressed the dagger into my hands, and took my face in his strong, calloused palms. He winced as the dragons' heat seared him, but he leaned in and brushed my lips with his. Steam hissed and swirled, engulfing us both. I gripped his shirt, desperate to give in to the feel of him, but his skin was so hot—too hot.

With a gasp, I shoved him across the cave. He stumbled away from me, back toward the open air. A fresh burn sizzled on his cheek from where he'd come too close to the dragons.

"What in fate's name do you think you're doing!" I shouted at him. "You could have gotten yourself killed."

"I would do anything to prove myself to you, Daella.

I'll heal from this, I'll survive. But you...if I had not come here instead of going to Midsummer, you might not. You must trust me and leave this place while you still have time."

"You fool," I whispered as an unrelenting wave of emotion burned through me. "You wonderful, ridiculous fool. You—wait. What are you talking about? Aren't you still competing in the Games?"

"No, I came here instead. For you." He scanned my face. "Despite what you believe, everything between was real, and now I'm here to prove it to you."

I strode toward him, my heart clenching. "You have to go back to Wyndale. You have to win the Games and ask the island to protect the folk of the Isles from Isveig."

"It's too late. The ceremony is happening now. I wouldn't make it back in time, and I have nothing to offer up even if I did. No one does. Everyone has either quit or been ousted, including Viggo, for what he did. Now let's get you going. You have so little time."

I searched his face. "There's more to this than you're saying."

For a moment, he didn't speak. And then he sighed, running his fingers through his long, silver strands. "If you want to be free of Isveig, you need to return to Fafnir and find a book he stole from the orcs. It has instructions in there that can bind you to a dragon with magic that will destroy the ice shard in your body. It's the only way you'll be free of him."

All the blood drained from my face, and I took a slow,

stumbling step away from him. "You mean become a Draugr."

He held up a hand. "Before you argue, let me explain. Being a Draugr is not the terrible fate we've always believed, as long as the bond between a dragon and its rider is done right. Mabel came to see me and told me everything she remembers from her time with the orcs. *You* can make that bond. You, Daella, as long as the dragon chooses you willingly. It's only when others— elves, dwarves, humans—*force* dragons to bond with them that the magic turns volatile. And when you do this, the magic will free you from Isveig."

My heart pounded. "Rivelin, I—"

"I know it's hard to imagine becoming the thing you've hated and hunted all these years, but you won't be like them, Daella. When I look into your eyes, I know there's no chance you could turn into that kind of crea- ture. Go to Fafnir. Find the book. And then come back to me, if you still want me the same way I want you."

I couldn't believe I was even considering this, but...I glanced at Aska and my chest warmed. Doing this would mean becoming the thing I'd hated for as long as I could remember. It would mean embracing the darkness I'd fought so hard against. But what I'd hated and feared, it hadn't been the whole truth. The full portrait had been smudged.

Somehow, deep down, I knew there was truth in Rivelin's words. But that did not mean his wild plan was the answer to all our issues. How could I possibly find this hidden book? And then how could I ever get away from Isveig again? He would never let me leave.

"What if I fail?" I whispered.

"You won't."

I inhaled, trying to memorize the scent of his leather, his smoke, his steel. My heart ached at the idea of leaving him, especially now when we'd only just found our way back to each other. The six weeks had felt like years, like I'd known him all my life. It was not nearly long enough.

Forever wouldn't even be long enough.

And now I would return to Isveig empty-handed. It was only a matter of time before he sent someone else to investigate the Isles, no matter what I told him. He would tear this land to shreds.

I couldn't leave these people to that fate.

I pressed my lips together, then asked, "Did you withdraw from the Midsummer Games?"

"What?"

"You're not there competing now, but did you formally withdraw?"

"No, but it doesn't matter." He tugged me closer, our hips locking together. "I may be fast, but I'm not fast enough for that. Besides, I need to take you to the harbor. You don't know where it is."

"I have an idea." I smiled. "And you're not going to like it."

35

DAELLA

R ivelin stared in astonishment when I hauled myself onto Aska's back. I gave her neck a quick rub as she slowly climbed to her feet, rolling off the last remnants of sleep. The warmth of her body enveloped me like an old hug, like one I'd known all my life, almost as familiar as my mother's had once been.

"This isn't the first time you've done this," Rivelin murmured, noting how easily I settled in to the seat carved into her scales. "How?"

"Aska found me lost in the woods when it was raining last night, and she brought me back here." Smiling, I rubbed her neck again. "Turns out, dragons like it when you feed them."

"I think it's far more than that."

"It seems Mabel was right. Orcs and dragons have a special connection." It was still so wild to consider, the origin of the orcs. But it made sense. We had fire within

345

our veins. We thrived in the summer sun. And Isveig hated us. He'd never told me more because he didn't want me to know the truth.

"Run as fast as you can," I told Rivelin. "I'll meet you back in Wyndale."

"Wait. What is it you plan to do, Daella? We need to get you on that ship."

I smiled. "You asked me to trust you, and now I'm asking you to trust me. I'm going to win the fates-damned Games for you, but I'm going to need you to step back. And don't try to argue with me about the ship. I'll get there after I finish this."

The muscles around his eyes tightened, but then he nodded and shifted away from the mouth of the cave. I smiled, leaned forward, and whispered into Aska's ear, "Fly, my friend."

She didn't need any more encouragement than that. The dragon took off at a run and hurtled into the sky, soaring up toward the clouds. Her heavy wings pounded against the wind, and I clung to the tusk as she raced toward Wyndale. Below, the world was nothing more than a blur of brilliant greens and muddy browns, pock-marked by the violets and pinks and golden yellows of the flowers scattered across this beautiful island.

Only moments passed before the village came into view before us. Clusters of timber homes were nestled in the small hills that rolled toward the shoreline in the distance. A snakelike river cut through the forest and fed into the lake near the cove, the water sparkling beneath the sun. I smiled as we dipped closer and the sight of the

Midsummer celebration arrived in all its splendor. There were streamers and paper lanterns everywhere, and children danced through the tall grass with flowers in their hair.

Screams peppered the air as we drew closer, and I spotted several faces turned up at us in horror.

I leaned forward and whispered, "Gently now. Let's show them they have nothing to fear. And that you are the grandest beast of the air."

Air, the final element and the final trial of the Midsummer Games. And I did not need even a speck of my Vindur sand when I had something as majestic as a dragon.

Aska slowed as she glided above the crowd that was slowly clustering around the empty stage. We swept by once, then turned and sailed past one final time before angling back toward the shoreline in the distance. I had to hope it had been enough, that they understood why I was here. There was little else I could do other than land and explain, but I worried some might take that as another attack. Was Mabel down there? Could she possibly explain to them that I—

A strange flash of red from the Boundless Sea snagged my attention. I lifted my eyes from the celebration to scan the choppy waves. In the distance, dozens of crimson boats from Emperor Isveig's armada sailed across the stretch of blue—and they were headed straight toward Hearthaven. I sucked in a sharp breath, my blood freezing.

Isveig had found us.

Aska slowed as if she felt my sudden uncertainty, but I barely noticed, too focused on the approaching ships. My heart pounded painfully against my ribs. Weeks ago, Rivelin had warned this might happen, that Isveig might come after me. Yet I'd dismissed those fears.

But even seeing it now, it felt impossible. So horribly, heart-wrenchingly impossible. The Elding had shifted to another island, leaving Hearthaven exposed.

I scanned the ships. There were so many—too many —but it would only take one to conquer this island. These folk were not fighters. They would not stand a chance against the army that was coming for them.

Tears burned my eyes at the thought of the battles and the blood, the wreckage left behind by Isveig's army. He had already destroyed so much.

I tightened my grip on Aska's tusk. I could not let him destroy this island, too.

Throwing all caution to the wind, I leaned forward and said, "We're going to land now, Aska. Aim for the stage. If any of them react poorly to you, don't fight back. Just drop me off and fly away. All right? I don't want you to get hurt."

Aska rumbled in clear displeasure.

"If you do this, I'll make sure you get an entire sack of Mabel's treats."

The dragon practically shimmied beneath me and emitted a sound that was an awful lot like a purr. Instantly, she twisted and dove toward the stage. I ground my teeth and clutched the tusk, regretting my decision to metaphorically dangle the treats in front of her face.

More screams rent the air as Aska thundered onto the stage, the wood creaking beneath her. Dirt and leaves sprayed into the air, a whirlwind of earthen debris. I gingerly slid off Aska's back and landed in a crouch on the shattered stage, then collected Rivelin's jar—the only one remaining—from where it had toppled to the side. Quickly, I shoved the pebbles back inside.

I stood, clearing my throat, but kept my eyes locked on the glass jar at my feet. "As Rivelin has not formally withdrawn from the Midsummer Games, this is his entry for the Vindur Trial. He sent his assistant here on the back of his dragon as a beautiful demonstration of the power of air. You do not need to be afraid. She will not harm you."

And then I lifted my eyes to the meadow. Hundreds of shocked faces stared back at me.

Mabel stood right in the front, one hand on her cane and the other clutching her heart. She beamed at me and waved. Just beside her, Hege, the dwarf candidate who had withdrawn, walked forward, her steps purposeful. When she reached the stage, she shot me a wink and dropped two pebbles into the jar.

"Viggo should have known better than to go up against an orc. Glad you're back, Daella." Then she moved back to the crowd, where her wife, Nina, was waiting for her. The pixie gave me an encouraging smile.

Confused, I scanned the crowd. Some of the specta- tors looked surprised, yes, but no one was screaming or crying or fleeing from the meadow—from *me*. In fact, more were moving toward the stage now with their final pebble in their hands. I'd expected them to hate and fear me after everything that had happened, and yet they were acting as if nothing out of the ordinary was happening.

As elves and dwarves and humans edged forward to add their vote to the jar, Haldor wandered over from the merchant stalls. His hands were slung into his pockets, and he wore an easy smile. All the tension he'd held in his body the last time I'd seen him was gone. And he didn't seem at all bothered that a fire-breathing dragon now squatted on the stage.

"Daella," he said, his tone friendly. "I see Rivelin must have found you."

"You knew he was searching for me?"

"Of course I did. As soon as Mabel helped him figure out what Viggo was up to, he came straight to me and Odel. We're a team, you know. Or at least, that's how I've always wanted it to be. Riv hasn't always been keen to share things with us. Seems he's changed a bit, for the better."

Something in my chest warmed, but the heat died just as quickly. "We have a problem, Haldor. I need you to declare that Rivelin has won the Games."

He frowned. "I assume he's on his way back, isn't he? Don't you want to wait for him?"

"There's no time," I insisted, dropping my voice to a soft whisper so that no one else could hear. "I just spotted Isveig's ships heading this way. I need to say the words that will protect this island. *Now.*"

The fire demon's face went pale, even his horns. "That would mean trusting you with the island's gift."

"I know. But I am not the enemy. He is."

Haldor swallowed, then nodded, joining me on the stage. He clapped his hands to interrupt the crowd's murmured conversation, and an eerie silence swept through the festival. Every face turned our way, and those near the base of the stage quickly added their votes to the jar and fell still.

"I think it's safe to say that Rivelin and his assistant Daella, being the only contestants left and providing us all with *quite* the spectacle today—" The crowd cheered, interrupting Haldor's speech. He held up his hands to hush them. "—are therefore the winners of this year's Midsummer Games!"

If I'd thought the crowd was jubilant before, they were practically feral now. They cheered and danced and leapt through the air, spinning with wild abandon. A bard appeared from seemingly nowhere and jumped to the stage beside us, breaking out into an upbeat tune.

Hofsa pushed through the chaos and joined us. She lifted a wreath of wildflowers over my head and draped it around my neck before placing another like a crown on top of my hair. Then she handed me, almost reverently, a very small leather pouch.

I opened it up and looked inside, scenting it. At the bottom of the pouch were four grains of sand, each a different color. My heartbeat quickened. This was Galdur sand.

"What's this for?" I asked her. "I thought you couldn't find any sand on the Isles."

"We seem to find four grains every year, one for each element. Go drop them in the well and ask the island for what you wish."

Nodding, I clutched the pouch to my chest and mounted Aska's back once more. Flying would be the quickest way to reach the well with the crowd as wild as it was. Moments later, we were airborne, and the exuberant shouts of the crowd followed us all the way there.

I risked a glimpse of the sea just before we landed. The ships had grown closer. They would have no doubt sighted Hearthaven now. The Isles would no longer be a fabled tale, but at least I would be able to stop Isveig from reaching their shores.

I only wished Rivelin were here with me to do it. All this had been his idea.

Still, there was no time to wait for his return, and he might very well try to stop me now, if he knew what I planned. He wanted me to return to Fafnir to find that book, but the island might refuse to let me leave once I made the wish.

So when Aska landed a few feet from the wishing well, I slid off her back and hurried toward it. I gripped the side, careful not to squash the flowers and vines, and dropped the four grains of sand into the depths. They vanished in the blink of an eye.

I breathed deeply, then said, "As the assistant of this year's winner of the Midsummer Games, I've come to you with my request." I spoke quickly, not needing to consider my words. I'd thought about Rivelin's wish so many times in the past few weeks, it was engraved into my mind. And I had a way to improve it, just a bit. "No one can come to the Isles of Fable who will cause this place or anyone within it harm, and if anyone is already here who will cause harm, the island will find an appropriate solution."

There. I stepped back. I'd done it.

36

DAELLA

I took a moment to breathe before returning to the celebration, exhaustion and hunger sapping the last dregs of my energy now that my quest was ended. Aska sat near the well, swishing her spiked tail back and forth across the dirt road, reminding me a lot of Skoll. As I settled onto one of the crates that were nestled in the vines and flowers, I gave her a grateful smile.

"Thank you for all of this," I said. "I promise it will be worth it when I get those treats from Mabel. Plus, you'll be safe from Isveig a little while longer. You're going to have to figure out how to protect yourself when you're older, though. Never fly near Fafnir, all right? No matter what."

She merely blinked at me.

Hurried footsteps pounded the dirt, and I braced myself to get swept up into the rollicking crowd. They'd want to know what I'd asked for, and then they'd likely drag me back to the meadow to join the celebration. As this was Midsummer itself, I imagined the party would endure far into the night, likely until dawn. At least I would finally get to eat, so long as the island did not find a way to rid itself of me first.

But it was Rivelin who rushed around the corner, his tunic rumpled, his hair disheveled, and sweat beading on his brow. When he saw me, he slowed to a stop and sucked in a great lungful of air. He took in the flowers around my neck and on my head, and the dragon perched nearby. His face crumpled as he strode toward me.

"What have you done? Where is the sand?"

I stood. "I spotted Isveig's ships heading this way when Aska and I were in the skies. There was no time to wait for you. I took the sand and I made the wish. *Your* wish. To protect this island from anyone who would cause it harm. The folk of Wyndale will be safe now, Rivelin."

"You shouldn't have done that," he said roughly, grasping my chin in his hand when he reached me. "You should have left first. What if the island tries to stop you? What if you can't leave and take care of that fucking shard?"

"I didn't ask it to stop people from leaving."

He searched my face. "What?"

"I changed the wording. I asked it to take care of that issue however the island saw fit." A risk, I knew. The island often translated the wishes in unexpected ways.

He released a heavy sigh. "All right. Perhaps that will work." A pause. "Thank you, Daella."

I pushed up onto my toes and kissed him. He wrapped his arms around me, tugging me close, his kiss full of hunger. Our bodies locking together, his tongue explored my mouth, and a deep, guttural noise rumbled from his chest.

A heady warmth flowed through me, but it was marred by the knowledge of what was to come. I couldn't stay here if I wanted to survive. I had to leave Wyndale.

I had to leave him.

I only hoped one day I could find my way back.

Slowly, he pulled away. I could tell by the look in his eyes that he knew the direction of my thoughts. Dropping his forehead against mine, he sighed. "We need to get you on that ship before they depart. I don't think we have long."

I nodded and swallowed. "This book about orcs and dragons, you're certain Isveig has it?"

"Mabel said he took it when his army attacked her village. He must have known what it was, and he'll have hidden it someplace safe. If I were to guess, he'll have it in his quarters somewhere."

The idea of finding my way into Isveig's quarters made me shudder. It was the last place in the world I ever wanted to step foot in, and that was even if I could find a way. I'd return to Fafnir empty-handed, refusing to utter a word about where I'd been and what I'd seen.

He could never know four dragons had survived, despite his efforts to destroy them all.

And so he would lock me in that tower again.

"This seems impossible," I whispered.

"I know, Daella," he murmured. "But you are strong. And you are fierce. You will find a way to get that book, and then you will come back to me. Do you understand?"

Sighing, I nodded. "All right. I suppose it's time for us to say our goodbyes."

"Say our goodbyes," he repeated. His face slowly transformed, all the affection hardening into fierce determination. "No, what am I saying? I'm coming with you. You're not facing that monster alone. I'll get you back out of that castle even if I have to kill the emperor myself."

My eyes widened. He couldn't do that. If he tried to go up against Isveig, the emperor would have him arrested or killed almost instantly. As an elf with silver hair, he would stand out amongst all the humans and giants on the streets of Fafnir. He wouldn't even make it off the ship.

"You can't. Isveig will know you're against him the moment he sees you," I said.

"I can, and I will." He cupped my cheek. "Where you go, I go. I am with you until the end."

My heart ached with affection for this grumpy bastard of an elf, who would stride into the den of his greatest enemy. All so I would not have to face this on my own. For him, leaving the Isles was no easy feat. This was his homeland now; these were his people. And yet he would walk away from it all. For me. I couldn't let him do that.

"No, you—"

My objection was interrupted by a dragon snout nudging my back.

"What is it, Aska?" I unwound myself from Rivelin's arms and turned to her. He took several steps away to avoid her unyielding heat.

She blinked, then nudged my hip. The hip with the ice shard.

"Oh." I gave her a sad smile. "Yes, that's why I need to leave. The emperor put it there, and he'll use it to kill me if I don't return to Fafnir soon. But I'm going to try to find a way back here. And maybe, if you'd like, we could create a bond with each other then."

Suddenly I felt very shy, as if I were asking the dragon to become my best friend. And in a sense, I supposed I was. But she did not seem to like that very much. She huffed in my face, sending a cloud of sulphuric steam at me, and nudged my hip again.

"I'm sorry," I said, searching her ember eyes. "I don't know what you want."

"She's trying to tell you something." Rivelin stepped closer as the dragon edged back, and he started to lift up my tunic.

Heart pounding, I caught his arm. "*Now?* We're out in the open in the middle of the day, and there is a dragon standing right there."

"Daella, my love," he said in a low, velvety caress. "Let me see your hip."

Rivelin lifted the tunic and gently pushed down the waistband of my trousers, exposing my scar. It was still there, of course, puckered and pink. The ice shard was embedded just beneath the skin, but—I gasped. It no longer glowed with the pale blue light of Isveig's power.

"I knew it. No wonder Aska was so eager to obey you. At some point, she must have bonded with you," Rivelin said, smiling wider than I'd ever seen before. "Her magic, it's counteracted the shard. You don't have to worry about the emperor anymore. You're free, Daella. You're fucking free."

Free.

Emotion swelled in my chest. Swallowing hard, I gazed at Aska, almost afraid to believe it could be true. But the dragon bowed her head, purring. And that was when I remembered. There had been a moment in the forest when I'd first climbed onto her back. Unrelenting magic had rushed through me, potent and all-consuming. The heat had been exhilerating. We must have bonded then.

I shuddered at the thought, unable to hold back the intoxicating relief that flooded through my veins like strands of fire.

Unbidden tears streaked down my cheeks as I turned to face Rivelin. He was staring at me with such open adoration that every last remaining defense inside me shattered like glass.

I leapt into his arms, sobbing.

That was when the screaming began.

37

DAELLA

Rivelin and I broke apart and took off down the winding road. The screams were coming from the festival on the outskirts of the village, and it would take us at least a few minutes to get there. I didn't want to think about what those screams might mean.

Had something gone wrong with my wish? Had I asked the wrong thing of the island? Or worse, had it rejected me because I was only Rivelin's assistant and not Rivelin himself?

We finally reached the edge of the meadow and started down the hill when a line of ice giant warriors shifted into view. They were all armed with deadly spears and protected by thick leathers, the shoulders engraved with the wolf sigil of the Grundstoff Empire.

Isveig's sigil.

I choked out a cry and stumbled to a stop, taking in

the sheer number of them. There were at least a hundred warriors...though I would have expected more from all those ships. Still, a hundred was more than enough to conquer this island. My plan had failed. Instead of protecting Wyndale, I had doomed them.

"Daella!" a voice called out from somewhere near the merchant stalls. A familiar voice. A friendly voice.

With my heart in my throat, I turned toward the sound. Thuri was bounding toward me, her pale blue braid thumping against her back. She wore a smile and carried a tankard of Lilia's famous ale. In her hands, it looked quite small.

For a moment, all I could do was stare at her, as if she were an apparition come to haunt me. How was she here? And where was Isveig?

"Daella," she said again when she reached me. "What's wrong? I thought you'd be happy to see me."

The world seemed to shudder back to life around me, sights and smells and sounds all at once. It was then I noticed the screaming had stopped and the babble of conversation trickled through the festival like a pleasant stream. The merchants were cooking up some food for the evening, and the crowd was milling about as if nothing unusual was happening at all, let alone the arrival of a hostile empire. Even the ice giants looked relaxed, standing around and watching the festival with blatant curiosity.

I blinked. "I am, Thuri. Thank fate you're alive, but... what's happening? Aren't those Isveig's warriors?"

"Ah. No." She grinned. "They're mine!"

I clutched her arm. "Do you mean to tell me you took them from him?"

"I took everything from him," she said with a conspiratorial wink. "After I got your letter, I decided it was time to do something about my brother's monstrous rule, and there was far more support for me than I'd ever dreamed. It did not take much convincing for me to gather enough fighters to stage a revolt. They thought the Old Gods were making a statement by saving me. And so, here I am. Meet the new Empress of the Grundstoff Empire."

I laughed, delight chasing away the tension in my body. "I knew you could do it, Thuri. The empire will be far better off with you in charge."

"Apparently so. Even the elements are in agreement. Do you know that endless cloud finally dispersed? It drifted off as soon as I locked Isveig in the dungeons."

"In the dungeons? It's boiling hot down there." I shook my head, still laughing. "Isveig will hate that."

"Yes." She looked me up and down, then glanced at Rivelin, who stood within an arm's reach. "Which brings me to you. I thought you might need rescuing, now that it's safe for you to return home. In *my* empire, orcs and half-orcs have as much freedom as the rest of us. But it looks like you don't need saving after all."

I motioned Rivelin closer and wound my arm around his back. The scent of leather, smoke, and steel flooded my senses. "I think I'm fairly happy with the idea of visiting Fafnir now and again, but I have a new home here. I'd like to stay, as long as they'll have me."

Rivelin smiled and tugged me into his arms.

A s Thuri and I caught each other up on everything we'd been through since that life-altering storm, Rivelin made the rounds to explain the situation to the villagers. Everyone seemed to accept the presence of the warriors, but he wanted to let Odel and Haldor in on the details.

Thuri told me most had survived our shipwreck. They'd still been close enough to shore for rescue boats to reach them quickly and return everyone to Fafnir. Isveig had been beside himself when he'd heard I'd vanished, ordering his people to search the waves day after day until he'd finally decided I must be dead.

At a lull in the conversation, Thuri motioned for one of her guards to come closer. He carried a weathered, leather-bound book in his hands. He passed it to me. It was buttery soft under my fingers, smoothed by the passing of time. The words *Ris upp ur oskunni* were embossed on the cover.

"Rise from the ashes," I whispered.

"I found that in Isveig's quarters when I took over. Recognized those words as the same ones from your dagger and realized it was an orc book. I thought you might want it."

My heart swelled and I hugged it to my chest. Even though I no longer needed the book to learn how to bond with a dragon, just having this piece of my history meant the world to me. There was so much I didn't know about who the orcs used to be, and I could not wait to spend an evening on Rivelin's roof flipping through these pages.

"Thuri, I can't tell you how much I appreciate this."

A hush suddenly went through the crowd, and a string of colorful curses soon followed. Thuri and I turned in unison toward a pack of dwarves leading two chained prisoners across the meadow. Viggo was in the front, jerking and growling at his bonds, but the dwarves held him strong. Gregor stumbled just behind him, his head hung low. Still, he wore no shoes.

"What's happening?" I asked as Haldor and Odel approached, along with Rivelin.

Haldor scratched the base of his horns. "It's the strangest thing. There was a dwarf ship in the nearest harbor, over from the Glass Peaks. They were meant to leave an hour ago, but the captain ended up coming into Wyndale asking about two prisoners he was told to put to work in their mines. I asked him who told him such a thing, and he said it was a voice on the wind."

"And we just so happened to have two prisoners and nowhere to truly hold them." Odel cut her bright eyes my way, her delicate wings flared wide. "Something tells me this is your doing, Daella."

"Not me," I said, understanding at once. "It was the island."

And perhaps the Old Gods.

As we watched the dwarves haul the prisoners down the hill, pink lines dashed across the sky to signal the setting of the sun. It almost felt like a message from the island itself, as if it were trying to tell us this was the end of any threat against this peaceful land.

"What did they want, anyway?" Rivelin asked. "Did you ever manage to get it out of either of them?"

"From the Games?" Odel asked. "Gregor truly believed Rivelin was behind everything, but he was only looking out for himself. He hoped Rivelin would take the fall, and he could swoop in as the island's savior. Everyone would love him, then."

I scowled. "And Viggo?"

"Funnily enough, Viggo was the one who helped Gregor cheat to get chosen for the Games again. Viggo realized he would be the perfect decoy until he could turn suspicion toward you two."

"To what end?" Rivelin asked.

"Viggo wanted to bond with a dragon. He thought asking the island would prevent him from becoming poisoned by the magic," Haldor said. "When I asked him why, he said he thought it was the best way to defeat Isveig. He'd take the dragon, fly to Fafnir, and burn it all down."

My stomach churned. A part of me yearned to do something similar. After all, Isveig had destroyed so much, and the temptation to meet destruction with destruction was intoxicating in a way that only few could understand. But Rivelin could, I realized, as I met his knowing gaze.

But there was a much greater part of me that tempered that desire. In an attack like that, it would be inevitable for innocents to get caught in the crossfire. The castle would burn and so would everyone in it. Besides, his sister had taken care of him now, and he would suffer far more stuck in those humid dungeon cells.

"Here's one thing I still don't understand. Why in fate's name did Viggo burn all my parchment?" asked Rivelin.

"Ah." Haldor glanced my way. "He saw Daella send that letter to Thuri, and he thought it was meant for Isveig. He was trying to stop her from sending any more letters to the enemy."

I shook my head. "So everything he did, he did for the good of the island."

"He *thought* it was for the good of the island," Odel countered. "But he has done too much damage. And if he'd had his way, thousands of innocents in Fafnir would have died."

For a moment, no one spoke. We stood there in our huddle and let Odel's words sink in, understanding how easy it could be to lose sight of things. Emperor Isveig had gone to war, believing himself to be the world's savior. And Viggo would have done the same thing. It could have become a vicious cycle of rage and blood until it was the only thing left, until everything good was gone from this world.

"Luckily, all that's over." I turned to Thuri. "Now let me introduce you to Mabel. She makes a mean mush-room pie."

The entire village was out for Midsummer. The sky was lit with a million stars, and a soft breeze rustled the grass at my feet. I popped another cube of Elma's cheese in my mouth, leaning against the side of Lilia's wagon, where lanterns cast their light on the dancing crowd. Haldor had taken it upon himself to loose some fireworks between each song, dazzling everyone in attendance with their *oohs* and *ahhs* that rippled across the meadow in waves.

It was a beautiful, mystical night, and for the first time in my life, I no longer feared what tomorrow might bring. I had no idea what would happen next, but I was safe here, and I was free. That was enough.

"There you are." Rivelin stepped from the shadows to join me in the quiet calm, away from the merriment of the crowd. "Why are you hiding all the way over here? Some of this celebration is for you, you know. You won the Games."

"I believe that was *you*, Rivelin."

"I'm not the one who baked hundreds of cupcakes and rode on the back of a dragon. The win is yours, and I know you like to dance. Shall I ask the bard to play that tune about Isveig?"

"The troll one?" I grinned. "Oh yes, please. I just… first, I want to take it all in."

"Take all what in?"

"My freedom," I breathed. "And all that comes with it. Look at Hege twirling her wife through a meadow beneath a blanket of stars. Have you ever seen any two people more in love? And over there is Elma, cheerily serving up her cheese and her olives, and Lilia beaming every time someone asks her for an ale. Even Godfrey seems happy here. He's been so quiet and reclusive these past few weeks, but now look at him. He's dancing with wild abandon."

I felt the weight of Rivelin's stare, and I wondered if I'd gone on for too long.

He reached out and brushed a strand of hair behind my ear. "You see the beauty in things. It's one of the first things I noticed about you." A pause. "One of the first things I loved about you."

I started and met his gaze, my heart pounding.

His smile matched the gold in his eyes. "Would you like to dance with me?"

"You, dance? I thought you hated parties."

"With you, I would dance until the world ends."

My heart rattled in my chest as a wave of emotion rushed through me. I slipped my hand into his, mesmerized by the steam that fogged between us.

Rivelin pulled me against him, and I draped my arms around his neck. As I dropped my head against his chest, we swayed in the grass beside Lilia's wagon, the scent of summer weaving around us. I closed my eyes and memorized the feel of him and the sound of his pounding heartbeat against my ear. The rhythm of it was so familiar to me now, so *right*.

For so much of my life, I'd never had a home. Somehow, despite everything, I'd found one. With him.

And then, from the stage, the bard began to play my new favorite tune.

Once there was a northern troll
Whose face looked like a big blue mole!
He pranced around as if to rule
But he was nothing but an icy fool!

I grinned and unwound myself from Rivelin, then grabbed his hand and tugged him closer to the meadow where the revelling crowd went wild. "You said you wanted to dance with me. Well, come on, then. Let's *really* dance."

I thought he might bow out of this one. After all, he was the grumpy blacksmith who enjoyed his quiet solitude up on his roof, and this was quite the opposite of that. But when he saw my beaming smile, he matched it with one of his own and followed me into the meadow.

We reveled until dawn while dragons danced in the sky.

EPILOGUE
DAELLA

THREE MONTHS LATER

The full moon illuminated our path along the beach. Side by side, Rivelin and I strode along the coarse sand as the salty waves lapped at our bare feet. Skoll trotted along beside us, occasionally darting into the woods to investigate a new scent. A breeze from the open sea brought a brief respite from the humid summer heat. Life was better than ever.

Not long after Midsummer, Thuri left with her warriors back to Fafnir, and village life returned to normal. Everyone agreed to excuse Rivelin's sword-crafting. He was the Defender of Wyndale, after all, and he could have blades, just in case. A tranquility had settled over the quiet roads, and I awoke each day to the sound of birdsong and the warmth of the morning sun on my face—and Rivelin's strong arms wrapped around me.

He'd insisted I move in as a permanent resident of the house, and I hadn't argued. There was nowhere else I'd rather be.

By day, we worked in the forge. In the evenings, we often hosted guests, like Haldor and his husband or Kari and Godfrey, who had started seeing each other not long after Midsummer. Mabel came by most days to say hello, drop off treats for Aska, or read through my orcish history book with me. Lilia had packed up her wagon and headed north to Riverwold. I'd sent her off with the Vindur sand—I thought she might need it more than I did. I knew Rivelin missed her, but his sister was a wanderer, and he'd never try to keep her from following her heart.

A thunderous boom rent the quiet night. Smiling, I looked up to see Aska's red-scaled belly passing low overhead. She swooped by on her glorious wings and loosed a bellow that I'd come to understand.

"Hello to you, too, Aska," I whispered up at her, already looking forward to the next time we soared through the sky. We usually went flying together a few times a week. It might just be my favorite thing to do now—after spending time with Rivelin, of course.

"Have you noticed she comes out here every time we do?" Rivelin asked.

I patted the dagger at my side, where it hung next to my bag of salt. It felt right for it to be there again, even if I hoped to never use it. "It's because she knows we're on patrol. She wants to help."

"Well, she would spot a ship before we would."

Rivelin slung an arm around my shoulder as we continued down the silent stretch of beach, searching for any waterlogged folk crawling out of the surf. We came out here every few nights when there was a bite in the air, like tonight. The Elding had shifted its attention to the northern side of the island just after Midsummer, but it would head back this way soon, now that summer was fading fast.

When we reached the end of our patrol, I took one last look at the sea before putting on my boots and following Rivelin down the path to Wyndale. Skoll bounded off for his nightly hunt. We'd see him in the morning.

"Do you ever feel disappointed that we haven't found anyone yet?" I asked Rivelin as we fell into step beside each other.

He looked at me, surprised. "Do you?"

"I was lost and desperate when the Elding attacked my ship," I said. "But we were miles from Hearthaven. Thuri and everyone else ended up back in Fafnir, but I washed up here on this beach. Sometimes, I think the magic of the island somehow brought me here on purpose. It heard my desperation and it saved me." I sighed and continued. "There will be other lost souls out there who are just as desperate as I was. I hope the magic sweeps them up in the tide so they can have a chance at a different kind of life, like I do now."

Rivelin slowed on the path and palmed my face. In a murmur, he said, "You, Daella the Blacksmith, are a lot softer than you want everyone to believe."

I smiled at the memory of all those weeks ago when I'd said the very same thing to him. "Blacksmith, eh?"

"Well, you're certainly not a murk."

"Hmm." I lifted my hand and ran my fingers through his silken strands. "Does that mean I'm your official partner? Perhaps we should add my name to the sign."

"You can add your name to anything of mine you'd like." He tugged me closer, then slid a familiar bracelet around my wrist—the one we'd made together all those months ago. "Because I want you, Daella Sigursdottir, to become my wife. I don't care that we've known each other for little more than four months. I know the heart of you, the fact you are kind and strong and fearless in the face of adversity. You see the good in things, even when life has gifted you with nothing but cruelty. My love for you is endless, so all-consuming I cannot truly breathe when you're not near. And all I want is to spend the rest of my life trying to make you smile."

"You're pretty poetic, for a blacksmith." Heart pounding, I whispered, "Are you asking me to marry you?"

"With every fiber of my being."

I gazed up at him, at this man who had changed my life in ways I never could have imagined. To be happy and free and in love, it had always been a dream. Someone else's fate, but never mine.

"Yes, Rivelin," I said with tears of joy filling my eyes. "I'm all yours."

My smile felt as bright as the stars.

GLOSSARY

DRAUGR - those who bond with dragons and channel their power

FENRIR - wolf-like creatures who can form powerful bonds with folk

FILDUR - the elemental magic of fire

FOLK - beings in tune with the Galdur; includes elves, orcs, pixies, trolls, fenrir, demons, giants, kraken, and dwarves

FREYA - the ancient goddess of the elements

GALDUR - the elemental magic that runs through the bones of the earth; can be controlled by rare sand

GLOSSARY

JORDUR - the elemental magic of earth

MIDSUMMER GAMES - a yearly celebration that takes place in Wyndale, complete with a tournament; the winner may ask for one gift from the island

THE OLD GODS - ancient beings who crafted the world and gifted the folk with Galdur

VATNOR - the elemental magic of water

VINDUR - the elemental magic of air

ACKNOWLEDGMENTS

First, and foremost, to my husband for encouraging me to write this book, for listening to me ramble, and for making dinner when I spent long days at the keyboard.

To the incredible group of artists I commissioned for this book. First, to my amazing illustrator, Deandra, for bringing Daella and Rivelin to life for this cover. To Sylvia at The Book Brander for the perfect typography and branding. To Zayeos for the beautiful forge and hammer illustrations. To Lily for the perfect dragon logo. And to Cartography Bird for the gorgeous map of the Isles.

To my editor, Noah, for catching my errors and making sure all the details of the world make sense!

To Rachel at NerdFam, for helping me get the word out about this book and helping me reach readers who might like this odd little story.

Finally, to every single one of you who took a chance on this book. Thank you for reading!

ALSO BY JENNA WOLFHART

The Mist King

Of Mist and Shadow

Of Ash and Embers

Of Night and Chaos

Of Dust and Stars

The Fallen Fae

Court of Ruins

Kingdom in Exile

Keeper of Storms

Tower of Thorns

Realm of Ashes

Prince of Shadows (A Novella)

Demons After Dark: Covenant

Devilish Deal

Infernal Games

Wicked Oath

ABOUT THE AUTHOR

Jenna Wolfhart spends her days dreaming up stories about swoony fae kings and stabby heroines. When she's not writing, she loves to deadlift, rewatch Game of Thrones, and drink far too much coffee.

Born and raised in America, Jenna now lives in England with her husband and her two dogs.

www.jennawolfhart.com
jenna@jennawolfhart.com
tiktok.com/@jennawolfhart